HOW *NOT* TO SURVIVE A VACATION

Also available from DS Publishing

Sisters in Crime Desert Sleuths Sisters in Crime
Chapter Anthologies:

SoWest: So Deadly
SoWest: Crime Time
SoWest: Desert Justice
SoWest: So Wild
How NOT to Survive the Holidays

HOW *NOT* TO SURVIVE A VACATION

Eighteen Original Southwestern Tales
from authors of the
Sisters in Crime Desert Sleuths Chapter

DS Publishing
Scottsdale, Arizona

DS Publishing
How NOT to Survive a Vacation

This is a work of fiction. All the characters, places,
and events portrayed in these short stories are either
fictitious or are used fictitiously.

Cover Artist: © Brian Azevedo
Cover Layout: Kästle Olson
Interior Design and Formatting: Deborah J Ledford

ISBN: 978-0-9828774-0-1

DEDICATION

This book is dedicated to the authors who guide our
hands, the independent bookstores who support our craft,
the Sisters in Crime organization for giving us a forum for
our voices,
and, of course, to all readers who love a good mystery.
You give us the strength to put our words on the page.
Thank you.

ACKNOWLEDGEMENTS

The Sisters in Crime Desert Sleuths Chapter would like to
acknowledge and thank our editors who worked tirelessly and
devoted many hours to create a finished product in which all
Sisters can take pride. Thank you editors, Chantelle Aimée
Osman, Deborah J Ledford, Suzanne Flaig and Merle
McCann for a job well done. We send additional thanks to
Deborah J Ledford for the exceptional book design, and Jean
Steffens for the administrative assistance. Juliet Blackwell,
Rebecca Cantrell, Sophie Littlefield, Kelli Stanley and Simon
Wood, thank you for taking time to provide great blurbs.
Much appreciation to Brian Azevedo for the stunning cover
art he created for this revised edition. And to Kästle Olson
for the captivating cover layout. Most of all, thanks to the
contributing authors who helped make this book a reality.

TABLE OF CONTENTS

PART I: *MARINE GETAWAYS*

DEATH ON THE INTERGALACTIC SEAS   1
JoAnne Zeterberg

A REAL HULA-DUNIT   17
R K Olson

THE BRIDE WORE BLACK   25
Merle McCann

CHECKMATE   41
Diana Manley

SINS OF THE FATHER   53
Susan Budavari

NIGHTFALL ON BLACK BEACH   69
Martin Roselius

WISH YOU WEREN'T HERE   83
Chantelle Aimée Osman

PART II: *MOUNTAIN GETAWAYS*

THE TRIP OF A LIFETIME   99
Kris Neri

HELL TO PAY   107
Barbara Goodson

TABLE OF CONTENTS

PART II: *MOUNTAIN GETAWAYS - continued*

COWGIRLS DON'T CRY　　　115
Judy Starbuck

MURDER AT THE TOADSTOOL CAFÉ　　　127
Connie Flynn

TRAGEDY IN THE PINES　　　143
Lori Hines

LOOSE END　　　155
Deborah J Ledford

PART III: *DESERT GETAWAYS*

THE PLACE I WAS BEFORE　　　165
Suzanne Flaig

THE OLD MINER　　　169
Howard B. Carron

THE ROUGH EDGE OF SPRING　　　179
Robin Merrill

THE HAUNTED HOGAN　　　193
Nancy Nielson Redd

SHE'S MAKING YOU CRAZY　　　209
Margaret Morse

MARINE GETAWAYS

DEATH ON THE INTERGALACTIC SEAS
JoAnne Zeterberg

THE Wookiee on the Lido Deck was my first clue that this wasn't a typical Alaskan cruise. Over six feet tall and covered in synthetic brown fur, he bellied up to the bar beside me and made a noise that fell somewhere between a squeak and a growl. The bartender nodded and started making a drink. I looked at the bottle of Alaskan Amber on the bar in front of me. Not even half empty. Until now, I'd hallucinated only once and that was nearly fifteen years ago after too many shots of tequila at a college frat party.

I squeezed my eyes shut, then slowly opened them. A bear-like face stared back at me.

"How you doin', sweetheart?" the Wookiee asked in a thick Jersey accent.

"Uh, fine. I guess." I drained what was left of my beer in one long draw.

"Here you go, Vinny." The bartender placed a frosty blue drink in front of the Wookiee. "Good to see you again."

Vinny the Wookiee took a sip through the drink's long orange straw. "Ahh, now that's what I'm talkin' about. See ya around, Mac. Take it easy, sweetheart," he said to me and headed toward a chaise by the pool.

"Who was that?" I asked Mac.

"Oh, that's Vinny De Franco. Comes on this cruise every year. He's always the first in line for a drink after we set sail from Seattle." Mac picked up my empty bottle and raised his eyebrows in question. I nodded and he cracked open another beer for me. "That's how we got our little routine down. He growls and I fix his drink like I know what he said. He only drinks one thing, so it's easy."

"He dresses like that for the whole cruise?"

1

Mac looked at me like I'd sprouted a third nostril. "Of course he does. What did you expect?"

A good question. Mac moved down the bar to greet a couple wearing sleek spandex unitards, complete with triangle-shaped badges. The exposed skin on their hands and faces was painted blue and the man had some sort of antennae that bounced over his head whenever he moved.

I turned my back to the bar and glanced around the Lido Deck, which was getting more crowded by the minute. There were people dressed in futuristic pseudo-uniforms, a few in robot costumes and a green woman wearing a long white wig and scales. I was the only person in normal clothes, save for Mac and the perky blonde woman striding toward me.

"Isn't this great?" asked Kristy, my best friend and soon-to-be-former vacation planner, as she climbed onto the barstool next to me.

"I'm not so sure." I looked at the odd assortment of beings before me. "What exactly is this?"

Kristy signaled Mac and ordered a piña colada. "Well, it looks like there was a little misunderstanding when I booked the trip. I thought it was a 'fantasy' cruise, you know, like 'all your vacation fantasies come true'."

"Yeah, and…" I circled my hand for her to continue.

"Well," she cleared her throat. "It turns out it's a science fiction fantasy cruise. Isn't it great?"

I could see the hope in her eyes, but I wasn't letting her off the hook that easy. "You mean we're stuck with a boatload of freaks the entire week?" My voice was louder than I intended and the blue couple at the end of the bar shot me dirty looks.

"Lower your voice," Kristy said, pulling me close enough to whisper. "First of all, it's a ship, not a boat. And, they're fans, not freaks. You know, Star Trek, Star Wars, The Matrix, that kind of thing." I just stared at her, so she hurried on. "Look, Echo, I know this probably isn't the post-break-up vacation you expected, but look on the bright side."

"Which is?"

Kristy took her drink from Mac and twirled its paper umbrella. "There's got to be some lonely guys in this group."

OUR staterooms were postage-stamp-sized boxes that held all the warmth and charm of a crime scene. Okay, that may be a bit of an exaggeration. But at least most of the indoor crime scenes I'd been to in my career as a detective for the Seattle Police Department had windows. The most my stateroom offered was a cheap watercolor of the Alaskan shoreline.

I wasn't sure what to wear to dinner since my options didn't include any "alien" fashions, so I decided to keep it simple. I'd just pulled on my favorite little black dress when there was a knock at the door. Conveniently, I didn't have to move to reach the doorknob—or the bed, or the dresser, for that matter. I opened the door and Kristy breezed in, looking stunning in a red silk cocktail dress.

"Wow, you look great," I said as she completed a look-at-me spin. "That dress should be illegal."

"I think it is in Utah, Idaho and on Vulcan," Kristy said with a laugh as she settled on the edge of the bed. She gave me a visual once-over. "Redheads always look great in black."

"Speaking of which, just let me put my hair up and I'll be ready." I headed for the bathroom vanity. "There's a black sweater in my bag. Would you grab it for me?"

I pulled my hair into a twist and was slicking on a coat of lip gloss when Kristy appeared in the bathroom doorway. She wielded a small picture frame as if it housed a shrine to the anti-Christ.

"What is this?" she demanded. "I can't believe you brought a picture of him with you."

"Gimme that." I snatched the frame from her hands and stuffed it into the bowels of my duffle bag. "If you must know, my plan is to have a few glasses of wine one night, feel sorry for myself one last time, and toss his cheating ass overboard. It's called closure."

Kristy smiled. "Now that's what I call a good breakup plan. Come on. Let's go find ourselves a couple of handsome space rangers."

WE ate dinner with two Captain Kirks, one Mr. Spock, a Princess Leia and a couple dressed in his-and-her Romulan attire. Based on the conversation, it seemed as if they all knew one another from previous sci-fi cruises and events. The Kirks carried on a lengthy trivia discussion, trying to outwit one another with quotes from the original Star Trek series, while Princess Leia and the Romulans talked animatedly about the finer points of wine tasting. Mr. Spock spent much of the meal observing the others and looking bored.

I noticed that Spock and Leia wore matching wedding bands, as did the Romulan couple. The diamond in Mrs. Romulan's engagement ring was a stunner. Brilliant-cut and huge, it sparkled like starlight every time she moved her hand. As the meal progressed, Mr. Spock and Princess Leia barely spoke to one another. Clearly, all was not well in their little corner of the universe.

After dinner, Kristy and I watched a musical "Galactic Review" in the ship's theatre then headed to the piano bar for a nightcap. It was there, amidst dozens of otherworldly characters, that I spotted another human. He stood at the bar, a bottle of beer in hand, and appeared to be watching a group of aliens swaying on the dance floor. He looked miserable. I liked him immediately.

"Grab us a table," I said to Kristy. "I'll get the drinks."

I sidled through the throng of aliens, deflecting a Keanu Reeves wannabe in a trench coat who wanted to dance, and made it to the bar.

"A glass of Merlot and an Alaskan Amber, please," I said to the bartender. Out of the corner of my eye, I saw the human glance in my direction.

"So," I said to him. "You visit this part of the galaxy often?"

The human smiled, showing off a matched set of dimples and eyes the color of jade.

"Can't say as I do. How about you?"

I smiled back. "Not much." I nodded toward Kristy, who'd snagged a table next to the piano. "My friend thought she was booking an Alaskan fantasy cruise. She missed the science fiction part of the title. What's your excuse?"

He tipped his beer bottle toward the dance floor. "My buddy's the third Klingon on the left. We like to bet on college football, my alma mater against his. My team lost, so here I am." He held out his hand. "Jake Stevens."

"Echo McClelland." Jake's hand was warm, with just enough calluses to tell me he wasn't a desk-job kind of guy. "So, Jake Stevens, what do you do when you're not playing wingman to a Klingon?"

"I'm a deputy with the Cascade County Sheriff's Department in Montana. I've also got a small horse ranch up there. You?"

I smiled. "I'm a detective with the Seattle PD."

"Wow. What are the odds?"

Cheers rose from the dance floor as the piano player kicked off an energetic tune. Princess Leia and Mr. Romulan from our dinner party slipped into the crowd and start gyrating to the music. Though the song had a lively ragtime beat, they danced close together, leaving barely a whisper of space between them. That left Mr. Spock and Mrs. Romulan alone at the table. With their pointed ears, close-cropped black hair and dour expressions, they looked like the perfect pair.

Before I could come up with a witty reply to Jake, the bartender returned with my wine and beer.

"Well, I better get back to my friend. It was nice to meet you, Jake."

"Same here. Maybe I'll see you around?"

"I sure hope so. We humans have to stick together."

TWO hours later, I left Kristy in the bar with a hunky Han Solo look-alike and headed back to my cabin. As the elevator lowered me to my deck, I debated whether to toss my ex's picture off the ship's bow or stern when the time came.

I'd just decided that the stern, with all its rough churning water, was a better fate for Rob's effigy, when the elevator dinged and the door opened to Mr. Spock and Princess Leia having a heated discussion in their cabin doorway. They stopped yelling and turned to glare at me as I stepped off the elevator. I moved quickly past them to my cabin across the hall, and went inside. As soon as my door closed, the argument started up again. I couldn't make out any words, but the venom in their tone was crystal clear. Moments later, a door slammed and all went quiet.

THE next morning I rose at sunrise, tossed on my sweats, pulled my hair into a ponytail and headed to the Promenade Deck for a jog. Through the light fog that swirled around the ship, I made out the rocky Canadian coastline off the starboard railing to the east. The sun hung low, a lemony orb peeking through the mist. I was on my second lap, warmed up and settling into an easy rhythm, when I heard footsteps approaching from behind.

"Mornin'," Jake said as he came up beside me and slowed his pace to match mine. He wore black jogging shorts and a gray sweatshirt that proclaimed him property of the Cascade County Sheriff's Department. His hair was tousled and curly from the humidity. This cruise was looking better and better by the minute.

"Hi, yourself," I said, smiling. "How'd you sleep?"

"Better than my buddy, Dave," he said with a laugh that seemed to hold just a bit of sympathy. "Too many Finagle's Follies last night with a beautiful Lieutenant Uhura. He's one hurtin' puppy this morning."

I was about to ask him what went into a Finagle's Folly when a woman's scream shattered the air from the deck above us. Jake was off like a shot for the nearest stairwell and I followed close on his heels. At the top of the steps, we found a plump, gray-haired woman in workout clothes leaning over a chaise lounge. She stepped back as we approached, revealing the prone figure of Princess Leia.

"I think she's dead," the woman shrieked. "Oh, my God, I think she's dead!"

Jake took the woman gently by the shoulders and guided her to a nearby chair. I went to check for a pulse along Princess Leia's neck, even though the dusky pallor of her skin told me I wouldn't find one. I took a quick look at the body, examining it as closely as I could without disturbing it further, then looked over at Jake and shook my head. The woman next to Jake buried her face in her hands and sobbed.

By this time, a few other early morning exercisers had

started gathering nearby, including the Kirks from dinner the night before. They looked distressed, clearly having recognized our table mate.

A college-age crewman dressed all in white hustled up to us. "What's going on?"

Jake's voice was quiet, but firm. "This woman is dead," he said, nodding toward Princess Leia. "We need you to call your captain, the ship's doctor and head of security. Then get some help to keep those people back."

The kid blanched when he looked at the body, but then moved quickly toward a phone on the bulkhead wall.

Jake knelt down beside the older woman and placed a hand on her shoulder. She looked up at him through tear-filled eyes the same color gray as her hair.

"Ma'am, I know this has been quite a shock, but do you think you could answer some questions for us?" he asked.

She looked at Jake's Sheriff's Department sweatshirt, took a deep breath and nodded.

Over the next few minutes, we learned that her name was Bea, she'd come on the cruise with her husband, and she'd been out for a morning walk when she found Princess Leia. At first she thought the woman was sleeping, but then noticed the unnatural color of her skin.

"I'd seen her yesterday afternoon at the cocktail party," Bea said. She pulled a tissue from her pocket and dabbed at her eyes and nose. "We were waiting at the bar for our Kenobi Coolers and got to talking. I told her how nice it was to see another Star Wars character. My husband and I dress as Jabba the Hut and Queen Jamillia and we're always outnumbered by those darn Trekkies. Anyway, I knew her skin wasn't made up that color. That's what made me think something was wrong when I saw her this morning. Then I...I touched her hand and she was so cold. I guess I screamed, I don't really remember, and you folks came running. I'm sorry, but that's all I know."

"That's all right," Jake said, patting Bea on the shoulder. "You did just fine."

As Jake stood, two uniformed men approached. Both appeared to be in their mid-fifties, but that's where any similarity stopped. One was tall and slender, with an aristocratic air and countenance. His uniform was impeccably pressed, his shoes polished to a mirror-like shine. The other was portly and short with the red-veined nose of a man who enjoyed his alcohol a bit too much. He carried a black satchel, and his uniform, though seemingly clean, had a slightly slept-in look. He moved quickly toward the chaise bearing Princess Leia.

"I'm Captain Van Horne," said the taller man in a rich baritone. "That is Dr. Geiger. Our security chief's been detained on another matter, but will be here shortly. What's happened?"

Jake introduced us and mentioned our law enforcement backgrounds, then recapped the details as we knew them. Dr. Geiger walked over and joined us, a somber expression on his face.

"She's dead," Geiger said, confirming the obvious.

Bea whimpered and covered her face again. I inclined my head to the side and the four of us moved several paces from the crime scene. Two uniformed crewmen herded away the Kirks and other onlookers, giving us privacy.

"Did she die naturally?" Captain Van Horne asked.

Geiger scratched his chin. "Difficult to tell at this point. Could be any number of things."

"I don't think so," I said. The three men looked at me. "There's some blood under the chaise. My guess is that if you turn her over, you'll find a head wound of some kind."

"People drink on theses cruises all the time," Geiger said with a shrug. "This wouldn't be the first time someone fell down and hit their head. As a police officer, you must know that even minor head wounds can be dangerous."

"That's true," I said. "But she wasn't alone after she hit her head. Look there, on the arm of the chaise. If I'm not mistaken, that's a bloody fingerprint. It's too smudged to be useful, but it's clearly a print."

Geiger harrumphed. "She could have easily done that herself, touched her head then tried to get up. Or, maybe she did it as she sat down."

"Take a closer look," I said. "Her hands are clearly visible and they're clean. No blood."

"Are you saying this woman was murdered?" demanded Captain Van Horne.

"I'm saying she wasn't alone after she hit her head. I also witnessed a pretty heated argument between her and her husband last night. I think we need to take a closer look before we rule anything out."

As I spoke, Jake walked to the chaise and appeared to be studying Princess Leia's head. The movement of the ship had caused her head to roll to one side and her mouth was opened slightly.

"Check this out," Jake said. "Looks like there's something in her mouth."

We approached the chaise, the doctor and Captain on one side, Jake and I on the other. Sure enough, there appeared to be some hairs inside Princess Leia's mouth.

"Do you have gloves and baggies?" I asked the doctor. He produced two pairs of rubber gloves from his case along with some small plastic bags. Geiger and I put on the gloves. Princess Leia's head was turned more toward me, giving me the better view.

"May I?" I asked the doctor. At his nod, I carefully opened Princess Leia's mouth wider. What had looked like bits of hair were actually small tufts of fur. After Jake snapped a picture with his cell phone, I removed them from the tip of her tongue and sealed them in a baggie. I could see more fur on the back of her tongue.

"I think there's something in her throat." I stepped back, addressing Geiger. "Take a look."

We switched places and he leaned in. After examining her mouth for a moment, he reached into his satchel and removed a pair of curved Kelly forceps. He straightened her head, inserted the forceps, and after a moment of maneuvering the instrument pulled out the obstruction—a ball of tan and brown fur slightly smaller than a tennis ball.

"What's that?" Captain Van Horne asked. I shook my head, as did Jake.

"It's a Tribble," Bea wailed from her chair. "Someone killed Princess Leia with a Tribble!"

"WHAT the heck is a Tribble?" Jake asked, looking at the bagged ball of fur sitting in the center of the table.

More than an hour had passed since Dr. Geiger removed the Tribble from Princess Leia's throat. We had moved to the interview room of ship's brig and been joined by Marvin Mallick, the ship's Deputy Chief of Security. The windowless room smelled of ammonia-based cleaner and offered little in the way of comfort. The table and six chairs, all made of unpainted metal, were bolted to the concrete floor.

A video camera was suspended from a ceiling mount opposite the room's only door which led to the main security office and two holding cells beyond. I could hear muffled conversations and the ringing of phones coming from the outer office.

The head of ship's security, Michael Wolfe, had arrived on the crime scene as Dr. Geiger was bagging up the furry murder weapon. A retired police officer on the high side of sixty with a slight build and quiet manner, Wolfe readily accepted Jake's and my offer to assist in documenting the crime scene. After photographs were taken and evidence collected, Princess Leia's body was moved to sickbay.

Now, below decks in the brig, we waited for Chief Wolfe and Captain Van Horne to return with Princess Leia's husband.

"It looks like something my cat would cough up," I said of the Tribble. "Only bigger."

Mallick, a doughy, forty-something man with a comb-over, cleared his throat. "They're very gentle little animals, really. They purr like cats when they're happy."

Jake and I exchanged a skeptical glance.

"I mean, in theory of course," Mallick added. "Season two of the original Star Trek series, 'The Trouble with Tribbles'. They breed real fast, you see, and they almost took over the Enterprise. Klingons hate them. But then, Klingons hate just about everything."

Our Star Trek 101 lesson was interrupted by the arrival of the Captain, Chief Wolfe and Mr. Spock, whose real name, we learned, was Dennis Frankle. His late wife, ironically enough, was Leia Frankle. As Frankle took a seat at the table, he glanced without visible reaction at the bagged Tribble then looked away.

By prior agreement, Chief Wolfe, Jake and I proceeded to question the husband alone, while Mallick and the Captain went to review video from the ship's surveillance cameras. As we settled in to start the interview, I noticed the blinking of the red light on the ceiling camera. Chief Wolfe made a formal statement of the date, time and parties present for the video, then addressed Frankle.

"We're very sorry for your loss, Mr. Frankle," Chief Wolfe began. "But given the unusual circumstances surrounding your wife's death, we need to ask you some questions. You can answer, decline to answer or request to have legal counsel present at any time during the process. Do you understand these options and are you willing to speak with us at this time?"

Frankle nodded without looking up. "Yeah, sure. I still can't believe she's dead."

"When did you last see your wife?" Wolfe asked.

Frankle rubbed a hand over his eyes. He wore none of his Vulcan makeup this morning, no green skin or pointy ears, but I noticed that his eyebrows had been plucked into Mr. Spock's distinctive upward angle.

"She left our cabin around two-thirty this morning and never came back."

Wolfe made a note. "Was it unusual for her to stay out all night?"

"Not on these cruises," Frankle said with a derisive snort. "She liked to party and I don't, so she'd go out on her own."

"How did you feel about that?"

Frankle glared at Wolfe. "How would you like it if your wife stayed out all night drinking and doing God-knows-what else?" He took a deep breath and exhaled sharply. "I hated it, okay? But that was Leia. We'd go on these cruises and she'd cut loose for a week, then we'd go home and things would go back to normal. I learned to live with it."

"Mr. Frankle, I overheard you and your wife arguing last night shortly before two-thirty," I said. "What was the argument about?"

Frankle stayed quiet and stared down at the table. The muscles of his jaw tensed and released, tensed and released.

"Mr. Frankle, your wife's been murdered. I need you to answer me," I pressed. "What did you and Leia argue about?"

Tears filled Frankle's eyes and he shook his head. I looked at Jake and raised my eyebrows, tossing the questioning to him.

"Mr. Frankle, did you kill your wife?" Jake asked.

The bluntness of the question seemed to shock Frankle out of his haze. "No! Are you crazy? I loved her. I would never hurt her."

"Then tell us," Jake insisted. "What were you and Leia arguing about last night?"

After another long moment, Frankle sobbed, "She said she was leaving me for that scum-sucking Romulan. She told me they'd been having an affair since the last cruise and wanted to come clean. Last night after dinner they agreed that she'd tell me and he'd tell his wife."

"Are you talking about the Romulan couple from our dinner table?" I asked.

Frankle nodded, tears continuing to flow. "I loved her so much. I can't believe she'd leave me for that piece of Romulan trash."

There was a knock and the door to the interview room opened.

"Chief," Mallick said. "We've got the video from the upper deck camera. You're gonna want to see this."

WE left Frankle secured in the interview room and gathered around Mallick's computer. The video from the previous night was of surprisingly good quality. Wolfe explained that the system was less than a year old and state-of-the-art.

"We archive the video from all the cameras for each cruise because we don't have the capability to monitor every camera live twenty-four-seven. Go ahead, Mallick. Let's see what you've got."

Mallick hit a key and the video started to roll. "As you can see from the timestamp, we're looking at two fifty-one a.m."

From the left side of the screen, two figures entered the frame. Princess Leia, a.k.a. Leia Frankle, and her Romulan lover. The couple appeared to be arguing and Leia Frankle was clearly distraught, throwing her hands into the air one minute and shoving the Romulan in the chest the next. The Romulan grabbed Leia by the arms and pushed her against the bulkhead, shaking her as if to quiet her down. With one shake, he went a bit too far. Leia's head hit the bulkhead and she went limp. The Romulan caught her before she fell and carried her to a chaise, where he lay her down. He touched her head, as if checking for injury, then leaned on the chaise with one hand while patting her face with the other. When she didn't respond, the Romulan hesitated for a moment then moved quickly out of camera range.

"Okay," Jake said. "That's the conk on the head, but it doesn't look like he did anything else."

"Keep watching," Mallick said. "It gets better."

Nothing much happened for several minutes. Princess Leia moved slightly as if regaining consciousness, but then went still again. Then, another figured entered the screen. This figure was also dressed as a Romulan, but was much smaller than the first. The Romulan approached Princess Leia, removed something from a pocket and bent over the now prone figure. We watched the murder of Princess Leia in silence. I've seen a lot in my career, but watching the actual killing of a woman made me feel sick.

"That was Mrs. Romulan," I said when Mallick stopped the tape.

"There are a lot of Romulans on this ship, Detective McClelland," Chief Wolfe commented. "And her face was never clearly shown. We're going to have a hard time proving who it was."

"I don't think we'll have too much trouble," I said. "Mr. Mallick, would you please roll the recording back to where the second Romulan comes into view. Good, now go forward slowly. There—stop!" I leaned toward the screen. "Can you zoom in on this area here?" I pointed to the smaller Romulan's hands. A very large diamond glittered on the ring finger of the left hand. "I saw Mrs. Romulan wearing that ring at dinner last night. Unless you've got a lot of wealthy Romulans on this ship, she's our killer."

"HERE'S to crime solving on the intergalactic seas!" Kristy raised her glass to toast Jake and me. We touched our glasses to hers then took a sip. "So, did Princess Leia's killer confess?"

Our cocktail table on the Lido Deck gave us a perfect view of the ripe orange sun as it sank below the horizon. Mac the bartender kept our glasses full—Captain's orders, he said—and I felt pleasantly buzzed and satisfied after a good day's work.

"Not at first," I said. "But after Chief Wolfe told them about the videotape, Mrs. Romulan caved."

"Turns out, Mr. Romulan was having second thoughts after telling his wife," Jake picked up the story. "And that's what he and Leia were arguing about. Mrs. Romulan followed them and when he knocked Leia out accidentally, she took the opportunity to take her out for good."

Kristy shuddered. "I never did like Romulans."

LIGHT from the full moon reflected gold on the churning water below and needles of icy sea spray stung my face. I pulled the frame from my coat pocket and, with a glance over my shoulder to make sure no one was watching, tossed Rob's picture into the roiling sea. As I watched it disappear into the froth, I felt a hand on my shoulder.

"Kristy told me I might find you here," Jake said. "You okay?"

"I'm better than okay," I smiled and turned to face him. "I was thinking I might head somewhere a little quieter on my next vacation. Like Montana, maybe."

"Funny you should mention that," Jake said as he pulled me close. "I was thinking I'd like to spend some time exploring Seattle. That is, if I could find the right tour guide to show me around."

I laughed and kissed his cheek. "I'd like that. In fact, it would be no Tribble at all."

† † †

JOANNE ZETERBERG is a professional writer and editor working in the Scottsdale, Arizona tourism industry. Her work is published regularly in *Experience Scottsdale*. Her short story "The Gift" appears in *How NOT to Survive the Holidays* (DS Publishing, 2009). She also has had articles featured in *Business Week* and *The Business Journal*. JoAnne has studied with internationally known psychic mediums James Van Praagh and John Holland, is an active member of Sisters in Crime, and is currently working on a romantic suspense novel set in Alaska.

A REAL HULA-DUNIT
R K Olson

THE first clue had come when Clare shattered her ceramic coconut, sending Singapore Sling-drenched shards flying. Intent on draining every last drop of my Maui Wowie, I hadn't noticed Ted walk into the cabana bar, but I had seen Clare's fist slam her drink to the table and followed her gaze. He looked good. Really good.

She stood and I tore my eyes away from Ted in time to see her send the remaining portion of her cup flying past his ear. Fiery red hair with a temper to match, she was picking up speed. I wanted to run for cover, but at the same time I knew I was the only one who stood between her and a charge of domestic violence. I tackled her. For once in my life I was glad I had thirty pounds on her.

"Get off me!" she said, flailing her arms and legs against the sandy bar floor.

"Take a breath, Clarey." I was sprawled on top of her, yelling into her ear. "This will not play well for you in divorce court."

"I don't care. I will kill him. Get off me now."

Funny how your mind works in times of stress. I found myself wishing I hadn't skipped Pilates for the last two months. Of course, that thought had also crossed my mind once or twice as I packed for this last minute trip to Maui, and again each time I pulled out a bathing suit for our daily treks to the beach. So perhaps I was overly distracted about how large my backside might appear to the afternoon crowd when she bit me.

"Ow!" I grabbed my wrist and rubbed the teeth marks. "You bit me!"

"Damn right," she said, scrambling out from under me

and making tracks for the door. It wasn't really a door, more like an open spot in the foliage through which Ted had appeared, and subsequently disappeared.

"Here, Miss," the massive bartender held out a shot glass. "Pour a little on the wound, drink the rest."

I obeyed, dropping back into my chair. "I'm sorry, Tiny." I gave the bartender my most innocent look. "Charge any damages to her bill." The crowd went back to their drinks as busboys scurried to clean up the mess.

"Why she so mad? Tiny asked.

"That was her husband…soon to be ex-husband. She was supposed to be here to get over him, not try to kill him."

I grabbed my phone and dialed my secretary. "Patti, get me a seat on the next flight off Maui. Text me the details." I hung up the phone and fanned myself with the menu. We hadn't ordered any food, no wonder the drink had gone to my head. "Tiny, will you make me a cheeseburger with the Maui onion barbeque sauce? I might as well enjoy one last meal."

It had been a good time until then, like when we were girls at camp or, years later, on spring break. My cousin Clare and I had grown apart after college, but when she asked me to make a last minute trip to the islands to get over her philandering husband it had sounded like fun, almost like old times.

We spent each day in a cabana on the beach, our every whim attended to by doting cabana boys. Most nights we sat on the lanai of our small suite and caught up on the last two decades of our lives.

"Here, Miss." Tiny set the burger in front of me. "How is the arm?" I stared down at the red teeth marks, rising into welts.

"Well, she didn't break the skin. I think I can forego the rabies shots."

He smiled. "She coming back?"

"I have no idea." The booze, combined with the physical exertion, hit me. I was exhausted. It was seven p.m. by my watch. "Okay if I take this to my room?"

"Sure. Just set the plate outside the door, we pick it up."

I left a hefty tip and made my way along the back of the hotel to our suite.

A very loud whisper woke me from a sound sleep. "Maggie." I heard a loud rap on the door. I opened my eyes and read her lips in the dim light. "I was here all night." She glanced toward the door. The knocking became insistent. "If anybody asks we were together all night—"

"You bit me!"

"Shh. Sorry. I'm very sorry. I got a little crazy." The banging continued. She lowered her face to mine. "I was here all evening. Remember?"

I nodded, then shook my head "No, I don't..." I looked toward the door. "Stop that pounding!" I slipped my dressing gown over my undies, and went to open it.

The chain pulled taut as I attempted to throw the door open. "What?" I stared with indignation, hand on my hip, until I realized this left my entire front exposed to one very fine specimen of masculinity. I gathered my robe together with my free hand, salvaging a little dignity. "What...what can I do for you?"

"I need to speak to Clare Fontaine." He stuck a badge in my face.

"Clarey, it's for you."

"AHH, it feels good to lie down." Twelve hours had passed since the interrogation. Exhausted, we had finally made our morning trek down to our cabana on the beach. I propped my feet up and admired my vivid fuchsia toes. "I cannot believe I lied to the police..."

"Hush." Clare put a finger to her lips and peeked through the flaps that surrounded our cabana. Stepping out, her shadow tiptoed past the canvas sidewall and around the back. Seconds later she slipped back in between the front flaps.

"There's no one in earshot. Still, it could be bugged."

"Are you delusional? It's a canvas cabana not the frickin' Watergate, Clarey."

"You don't know Ted. He has—"

"He had," I corrected her, thinking back to last night's

encounter. I had let the very fine Detective Markum into our room and then rushed to slip into my most flattering sundress. I checked my reflection in the bedroom mirror, straining to hear their conversation from the living area.

"Clare Fontaine?" he had asked. "Wife of Theodore Fontaine?"

"Soon to be ex-wife." Clarey had said. "Look, I don't know what he told you but I never touched him."

"When was the last time you saw him, Mrs. Fontaine?"

"Call me Ms. Parker. I'm taking my maiden name back as soon as the divorce is final."

"Again, Ms. Parker, when was the last time you saw Mr. Fontaine?"

"We spoke outside the cabana bar earlier this evening. He went his way, I went mine." Clare tidied the stack of magazines on the coffee table.

"Where did you go then?"

"I…I walked. I…went for a walk on the beach. Then I came back here." She snagged my dirty wine glass from the table and moved toward the kitchenette, then dumped the dregs into the sink. "Why? What did he tell you? If that son of a—"

"Your husband is dead, Mrs. Fontaine." The glass shattered as it fell from her hand into the porcelain sink.

"Dead? Ted?" She began to laugh. "It rhymes, how funny." She choked back a sob. "No, no, he was fine. He never looked better. He was the picture of health."

"He was. Until someone shot him," Detective Markum said. He was not laughing.

"SO where were you last night, if you weren't in our room?" I asked her now, watching her smooth lotion onto her legs.

"I really did go for a walk on the beach."

"And?"

She looked up at me as she massaged her calves. "What makes you think there's more?"

"Well you knew you needed an alibi, so…either you must have killed him or something else happened."

"I caught up with him after he left the bar and I told him

I was here first and he would have to leave. He said 'Don't be a ridiculous, Clare. I'm not going anywhere.' I stood there for a minute, then I followed him and watched him go into one of the villas. I didn't know what to say, I felt like a fool. I really did walk on the beach. I was so angry I could have killed him." Her hand flew to her mouth. "But I didn't. I swear it, Mags. I didn't kill him. I still love the pig."

She adjusted the chaise so that it was flat, like a long narrow bed. Lying back, she looked up through the small opening where the tent pole exited the canvas roof. "I went for a long walk and I calmed down. Then I headed back to the villa to see if we could work it out." She sighed. "I saw their silhouettes through the window. He was with another woman."

"Any idea who she was?" I asked.

"I couldn't tell. She was in his arms." She wiped the corner of her eye. "It's not like I didn't know. It's just...seeing them with my own eyes just made it so...so real."

"I'm sorry, Clarey." And I was, I really was, even though I knew her tears weren't genuine. The marriage had been over for years and everyone knew it. "Listen, at least you don't have to go through the whole messy divorce now."

"No. Now I can go through a messy murder trial." She wailed. "If it wasn't for you, I would be the prime suspect. The wife always is, you know." She lowered her voice. "Oh Maggie, you have to believe me. I didn't kill him. Thank God I have you to be my alibi."

I poured us each a glass of guava juice. "Cheers," I offered, as she took hers. "Here's to freedom." Our glasses clinked. "In every sense of the word."

She drained hers and settled back. "I wonder who did kill him. He was a lousy husband, but he wasn't a bad guy."

"They may never know." I pulled my cover-up over my head and folded it. "I guess, unless they find the gun, or someone with a motive and no alibi. Maybe it was a robbery. He carried a lot of cash, always wore a Rolex, right?" I stood and grabbed a kickboard. "I'm taking a quick dip. You rest. And don't think too much."

I drifted just beyond the surf, my body submerged in the cool water. I gripped the board, resting my chin on the edge and stared back at the shoreline. Beyond the sand stood three terraced rows of what the brochure termed villas, essentially a series of one-bedroom duplexes. Behind were the adult and family pools, the manicured grounds and the open-air bar where Clare had caused such a scene. Overlooking it all was the large hotel which housed the suite Clare and I shared.

Ted's villa was in the first row, it would have been simple for Clare to arrive unseen once the sun went down. Just a short walk up from the beach, to a secluded spot where she could peek across the patio at a sight she was never intended to see. I wondered where she had gone after the melee. I knew she wasn't back in the room before nine o'clock when I had quickly packed the essentials into my largest bag, then fallen into a surprisingly deep sleep. Who says there's no rest for the wicked? An hour later I had been awakened by Clare and the banging Detective Markum.

I floated for some time, lulled by sun and the sea, when I thought I heard his voice. "Mrs. Fontaine?" I opened my eyes and squinted toward our cabana. "Mrs. Fontaine, you are being charged with the murder of your husband." Detective Markum, out of place in his well-cut suit, handcuffed a bikini-clad Clare. He removed his jacket and placed it over her shoulders. She turned and surveyed the water. I let my head slip below the surface.

TED was a cheater. A serial cheater. And he was preparing to do it again. With me. I had run into Ted one night when I stayed on in the lobby bar, listening to the band, after Clare headed back to our room with a headache.

Was I interested? Let's just say he wasn't the first jerk to turn my head. But I was torn between lust and loyalty, a concept Ted could not grasp. "Maggie, there's only a token amount left in any bank account she can find. After the divorce is final, and she settles for her pittance, I'm off to a little place I have in the Caribbean. Even if she figures out where the money is, it will be too late. No reason we can't be together then, right? Picture us making love on the beach," he had breathed into my hair the night before.

I almost fell for it. He was that kind of guy. Irresistible. Nearly irresistible.

Ted had far more enemies than a fuming wife. For that reason I knew, no matter where he went, he kept a gun nearby. I grabbed it from behind the Gideon Bible and held it under the pillow I clutched to my body.

"Finally," Ted said, emerging naked from the bathroom. "I've wanted this for so long." He came toward me and I stood, raising the pillow, as if ashamed of my nakedness. I was ashamed of my foolishness.

I thought now of how well things had gone. Nothing had been planned in advance. Really, it all simply fell into place. If the busboy from the bar hadn't come to retrieve my dishes at the exact moment Clare, flaming hair flying, had returned to our room, it would have been perfect. Still, they had no evidence against her.

I had begun toweling off when the cabana boy handed me the phone. Patti spoke. "Good news, be at the airport in one hour. I have you confirmed on the next flight to Grand Cayman."

RONI OLSON, having spent most of the last four decades raising her four children, has recently altered her lifestyle to focus on her lifelong desire to write. Transplanted from the Pacific Northwest, Roni enjoys living in Scottsdale, AZ with her dog, Jemima. Her story "Relativity" appears in *How NOT to Survive the Holidays* (DS Publishing, 2009). Now working on a traditional mystery series, she is the current president of the Desert Sleuths chapter of Sisters in Crime.

THE BRIDE WORE BLACK
Merle McCann

Seattle
August, 1909

LATE on Friday evening, Seattle Police Captain Patrick Finn completed his paperwork in preparation for his coming vacation. Just past ten, he was startled by the ring of the newest telephone recently installed on the wall behind his desk. "Finn," he barked into the mouthpiece.

He listened intently to the panicky voice, and after assuring the man he would leave immediately, hung up the receiver and donned his cap. *So much for the family vacation.* His wife and three kids had been packed for two weeks, anticipating their trip to the fancy Moran Estate on Orcas Island, one of the San Juans in northern Puget Sound.

Finn checked his watch, made an entry in his official log, and hurried to the squad room. "Let's go, boys! Murder at Governor St. Martin's place. Bring the prisoners' wagon to the front of the courthouse. I'll meet you there in my car."

Heading for the station's door, Finn stopped to tell his Desk Sergeant of the killing. "I'm goin' there now." Finn hesitated. "Say, Andy, don't you know a fellow who works there?"

"Nigel Pendergast. He's been the governor's butler ever since St. Martin was elected and went to Olympia."

"Seems a Daniel Whiting was shot to death in the old gov's carriage house."

"No! Whiting and Julia St. Martin were getting married tomorrow morning."

Finn glanced at the clock. His men would be waiting. "Tomorrow?"

"Yep—read it in the paper."

"What do you know about Whiting?"

Andy rubbed his chin. "He's big money. Nobody knows how he made it." He smirked. "The governor and Whiting make quite a pair—birds of a feather, if you get my drift." He raised a warning finger. "Watch your step, Cap. Mercury's retrograding. Bad stuff happens when Mercury retrogrades."

"Don't talk to me about astrology. Talk about the St. Martins, and make it fast."

Andy grinned. "Jefferson St. Martin ain't near the scoundrel he once was, but he's still cuttin' deals. His wife's well liked, though. She's a big fish in Seattle's high society pond. Has her picture in the paper regular-like."

"I hear they've a five acre spread on Lake Washington. How big's their staff?"

"Nigel once said there's a long-time cook and two maids—the barn man's been with 'em longer than Nigel."

"Employee loyalty. Won't get much out of them."

AT the St. Martin estate, Finn and the four officers parked their rigs in the circular drive behind two horse-drawn carriages and a new Model T. Several couples, in formal attire, climbed into their vehicles as Finn stepped from his car. In a loud voice, he introduced himself and told them to return to the house until his men interviewed them.

Finn and his officers approached the large, carved door and knocked. They were met by a plump, flat-faced man dressed in a butler's uniform.

Finn gestured to the people outside. "Was the governor entertaining?"

"Yes, sir, a party to honor out of town guests."

"You're Nigel?" Finn asked as they walked into the house.

"Yes, sir."

See that no more people leave the premises."

"Of course. Please follow me. The governor is in the main salon."

They crossed the foyer and stepped down into a large, high-ceilinged room. St. Martin and his wife, clearly shaken, sat together on an oversized sofa in front of a cut-stone fireplace.

Above the mantel, two Tiffany gas sconces, matching the room's three chandeliers, cast a warm glow. In spite of the warm night air drifting through the opened French doors, the atmosphere felt frigid. Near the grand piano, opposite the fireplace, four string musicians packed up their instruments.

Governor St. Martin stood when he saw Finn. The captain introduced himself and his men and shook the governor's hand. He nodded politely to Mrs. St. Martin who held a hankie to her reddened nose.

"Governor, I'd like to see the victim," Finn said.

"Certainly," St. Martin replied. "He's in the carriage house."

Angling across the broad expanse of grass, Finn noticed a gazebo near the lakeshore decorated with ribbons and floral garlands. Rows of folding chairs circled the site.

At the carriage house, a dozen men clustered in the wide doorway, talking quietly. Finn eased between them with the governor close behind. He slowly circled the body lying on the brick floor several feet inside the doorway. A sizable puddle of blood had oozed from beneath the victim. A bullet hole was visible in the side of his formal coat.

Finn, scribbling notes, finished his preliminary examination as the coroner arrived. Finn nodded to him then crossed the room to where a fellow slouched forward in a chair, holding his drooping head in his hands. Two tuxedoed guests stood in front of him.

"Who are you and who's this guy?" Finn said to the taller of the two men.

"I'm Thomas O'Hearn, and this is Bill Stevens." He gestured to the man seated. "We've been holding Count Leonardo Di Franceschi, the killer, until you got here."

"Count what?" O'Hearn repeated the name. "What makes you think he's the killer? Anybody find the gun?"

"Didn't see a gun," O'Hearn said, "but I caught him kneeling over the body with blood on his hands and clothes. He must have hidden the gun before I got here."

Finn turned and scanned the area, noticing a Ford touring

car parked between the door and an older, but glistening horse-drawn landau. Beside the carriage was a sporty, red 1908 Ford Model S. Finn, like so many men, was a great admirer of Henry Ford's automobiles. He made a mental note to take a closer look at the *S* when he got the chance. "How soon after hearing the shot did you arrive?"

"Less than ten minutes. I was headed this way when I heard the gun fire."

Finn beckoned his officers over. "Two of you lock the suspect in the wagon and wait with the prisoner, and the rest of you start taking people's statements." Stepping around the governor, he approached the men in the doorway. "You heard O'Hearn's story. Anybody disagree?" They all shook their heads.

"Thanks, gentlemen. You can go back to the house but don't leave until you've spoken with my detectives. When the coroner's finished, we'll lock up the crime scene." Finn turned to the governor. "I'll examine the area more closely tomorrow in daylight. Keep people outta here."

As the crowd dispersed, he gave the governor a stern look. "Were you happy your daughter was marrying Whiting?"

St. Martin scowled. "Of course. Why do you ask?"

"Not every father would be. I hear he's of questionable character." Finn glanced about, "Is there another door into this building?"

"Yes, I'll show you." They crossed the room and turned into a small vestibule where, opposite the stairs that went to the second floor, an outer door existed. Finn pointed above. "What's up there?

"Storage."

Finn tried the knob on the exit door. It was locked.

"We rarely use that door," the governor explained. "The big sliding doors in front work easily and are accessible without having to cross the wet grass."

"Who has the keys?"

"I don't know. Wilma—Mrs. St. Martin—oversees such matters. Our barn man probably has a key. He'll be here in the morning."

IN the den, off the salon, Wilma St. Martin sat next to her daughter, Julia, the bride who would be dressed in black tomorrow instead of a wedding gown. Mrs. St. Martin, her arms wrapped around her daughter, rocked the young woman while imploring her to calm down.

"Begging your pardon, ma'am," Finn said. "I've a few questions for you and Miss St. Martin."

The women moved apart. Mrs. St. Martin dabbed her eyes with her handkerchief and looked up at Finn. Julia, whose hair was in disarray and her face red and swollen, seemed quite shy. She quickly turned from him, trying to control her tears.

"Mrs. St. Martin, where were you at the time of the murder?" Finn asked.

She took a deep breath. "In the main salon. We were about to toast our guests. I was standing with my husband, the governor, by the piano, waiting for Julia and Dan to appear."

"Then what happened?"

"Our friend from Boise, dashed into the room shouting that Dan had been killed."

Finn said to Julia. "Where were you, Miss, when the shooting occurred?"

Julia swallowed hard. "In the carriage house," she said softly.

"You saw the shooter?"

"No." She took a shaky breath. "The shot came from the shadows. It barely missed me."

"Had Mr. Whiting accompanied you there?"

"No, I went alone. He arrived a little later."

Finn frowned. "Oh? Explain that."

She took a deep breath. "During the evening, I mentioned Mother's new auto, and Count Di Franceschi asked me to show it to him. I told him I'd meet him at the carriage house in a few minutes."

"Did you know the count well?"

Julia clenched her jaw. "He's an old friend—my equitation instructor. He came each summer to visit his uncle, our barn man, and give me riding lessons."

"What's the uncle's name?"

Mrs. St. Martin answered, "Dominic Di Franceschi. He's been with us since before Jefferson was elected governor. He drives our coaches, cares for the horses and carriages, and tends our barn. He's a valued employee."

Finn rubbed his jaw. "Seems odd that his nephew, a noble-man, would be teaching equitation."

"Not if he needed the income," Julia snapped. "We didn't know he was a count. He was just *Dodo*—Leonardo."

Finn considered the silly nick name and dismissed it. "He came only in summer? If he needed money, what did he do the rest of the year?"

Julia blew her nose lightly. "He was a student musician, aspiring to the concert stage. His uncle helped with expenses."

Finn studied the girl. Speaking to him seemed painful for her. "Why would he murder your fiancé?"

Julia gasped. "He didn't! He could never."

"But, you can't say absolutely that Count Di Franceschi didn't fire the fatal shot." Julia shook her head and looked down. Her shoulders slumped. "Other than Di Franceschi, who might've wanted Whiting dead?" Finn prodded.

Julia blotted her eyes. "I don't know."

"Were you romantically involved with Di Franceschi?"

"Of course not. Tomorrow was to be my wedding day."

Julia's frosty words didn't deter Finn. "When did Di Franceschi arrive?"

Julia raised a palm. "This afternoon. Dom met him at the King Street Train Station."

Finn scratched his scalp. "I spoke to several guests who said they saw Di Franceschi leave the house and walk toward the carriage house. They never saw him again. Are you sure he left before Mr. Whiting arrived?"

"Yes."

Were you expecting Mr. Whiting to meet you there?"

"No."

Finn frowned. "Hmm. So, he just showed up. Was he spying on you?"

"I don't know."

"Did Whiting know Di Franceschi?"

"They just met at the party."

Finn turned back to Julia's mother. "Does your barn man live on the premises?"

She cleared her throat. "He has an office in the barn but his home is on Lake Union, near the university."

Finn made a note to check out the barn in the morning. "Was he here tonight?"

"Dominic is quite ill and can't tolerate the night air. I wouldn't allow him to work. We hired a service to handle the guests' motorcars and carriages.

"When can I speak with him and your household staff?"

"Tomorrow after nine."

"I'd like your guest list, Mrs. St. Martin, with their addresses, if possible."

She stood. "I'll get it for you now."

AT the police station, the captain studied Leonardo as two officers brought him into the office. Taller than either deputy, Leonardo's rumpled tuxedo couldn't diminish his elegance. His face had an open quality, wide cheekbones and a strong chin. His disheveled black hair, parted in the middle, looked as if he'd run his fingers through it many times in the last two hours. Finn saw knowledge in the man's dark, brooding eyes but couldn't tell if it was wisdom or cunning.

Standing behind his desk, Finn pointed to a chair when Leonardo walked in. "Mind if I call you Leo?"

"That's fine."

"Miss St. Martin referred to you as *Dodo*." Finn grinned.

Leonardo rubbed his eyes. "Yes, a nickname she contrived the first summer I came to Seattle. She was thirteen at the time."

Finn took in Leonardo's slumping posture. "Did you murder Dan Whiting?"

Leo's eyes widened. "No. I was walking to the lake when I heard the shot."

"Anybody see you?"

"I don't know."

"Do you have a local address?"

"No, I've been touring the world the past two years. I came to Seattle today from California. I took off the month of August to vacation."

Finn felt a pang of jealousy at the mention of vacation. "How'd you know about Miss St. Martin's wedding?"

"I read the announcement in *The San Francisco Chronicle*."

Finn scribbled a note. "Where were you before going to the lake?"

"In the carriage house with Julia."

Finn crossed his arms. "Well, young man, you'd better explain."

Leonardo nodded. "After meeting Whiting tonight, I couldn't believe Julia loved the man. Knowing my fascination with automobiles, she'd mentioned earlier that her mother had a Ford Model S. I used that as an excuse to speak privately with her—by asking her to show me the car. It was my only chance to dissuade her from marrying him."

"You were sweet on her?"

"I loved her." Leonardo gnawed his lip. "I came hoping to convince her to marry me."

"I see. How long were you in the carriage house?"

"Not long. She thanked me for the pearl necklace I'd sent her as a wedding gift. She looked beautiful in it."

Finn recalled that Julia was not wearing pearls when he questioned her. "Then what?"

"I asked her to come away with me. When she turned me down, I asked how she could marry a louse like Whiting. She said she'd promised her father. She alluded to bad investments and the disastrous drop in stock due to the banking panic two years ago. I concluded Whiting had rescued the governor from financial ruin, and Julia was payment."

"Anyone see you there?"

"I don't think so. After she told me she intended to marry Whiting, she suggested I go, saying Whiting had watched her leave the house and had probably seen me, too. She said he was very jealous. She was nervous about being seen with me, so I left. I walked toward the lake."

"Did anyone see you?"

"I don't think so."

"Why the lake?"

Leonardo rubbed again at his eyes. "To say goodbye to a lot of happy memories."

Finn squinted at Leonardo and snorted. "You had a powerful motive to murder Whiting. Plus, you were discovered beside the body with his blood all over you. Tell me about the gun."

Sweat glistened on Leonardo's forehead. "I didn't see a gun." His hands shook when he gestured. "I simply tried to help the man but it was too late."

"How'd you get there so fast?"

"I hadn't gone far when the shot rang out. It sounded like it came from the barn and I was afraid for Julia. I took off on a run, hoping to get to her in time."

"Did you see anyone else when you ran into the building?"

"No. A couple minutes later the men arrived from the house. I shouted for them to call the police—that Whiting was dead."

THE next morning, Finn returned. First, he walked the lane from the home to the carriage house. It took nine minutes. Then, he walked the grounds, jotting down the distance and angle of slope from the lake to the carriage house. He supposed if a man were strong and fast, he could cover the distance before someone from the house arrived. And, equestrians usually have strong legs.

Finn stepped into the carriage house and noticed the victim's blood had been absorbed into the brick flooring, leaving only the stain. He created a detailed sketch of the building and its interior, noting the telephone hanging above a row of cabinets, probably the one used to report the shooting. Then he examined each vehicle, especially the *S.* Finding nothing more of value for his investigation, he left for the barn.

The elegant, walnut-paneled barn contained four box stalls along one wall. Each was occupied by a tall, handsome

Saddlebred. Working methodically, he sketched the layout, marking the placement of the closed door to what he suspected was the office. He added the cabinets along the opposite wall next to a workbench, crossed the room and opened each one, finding only well-kept tack. Above the bench hung another telephone. He thought it curious that there was a telephone in the barn. It pleased him to have one in his office because very few people had them in their residences. But, in a barn? He took down its number in case he might need it.

Then he noticed on the work bench the wadded cleaning rag partially covering a mahogany pistol display case. He pushed the rag aside. Beneath the glass lid, a silver single shot dueling pistol rested in a red velvet-lined, custom-fitted bed. The depression for a second gun was empty. Along the bottom, a small box of bullets was embedded in the velvet. Lifting the lid, he read the inscription engraved in the pistol's grip. Count Leonardo Di Franceschi.

Finn grabbed the earpiece of the telephone and dialed the station. "This is Finn. Tell the Duty Officer to start the paperwork. Di Franceschi is under arrest for murder."

As he hung up, a voice behind him ordered, "Don't move."

Finn slowly turned.

An elderly man, thin and a bit stooped, stood in the office doorway pointing the missing gun at Finn's chest. He glared angrily, and the gun quivered in his grip as he moved closer. "Did Whiting's people send you?" he asked through tight lips. "Move, and I'll shoot you."

Sergeant Andy's warning about Mercury retrograding flashed through Finn's mind. He raised his hands in a steadying motion. "I'm Chief of Detectives, Captain Finn. Are you Dominic Di Franceschi? I'd like to talk to you." He gestured to the gun. "Would you put that down?"

"When I'm ready." He aimed a little higher. "I'm Di Franceschi. I don't see you wearing a badge."

Finn's hand went to his breast pocket. Di Franceschi widened his stance and pointed the gun at Finn's head. "Slower, if you please, detective."

Finn, holding his breath, gently removed his badge and held it face forward. The old man's expression softened. He stepped closer and eyed the badge. With a slight nod, he offered the pistol, grip first, to Finn. "Sorry. You don't look like a policeman."

Noticing the gun was not loaded, Finn laid it in the display case. "Can we talk?"

Di Franceschi motioned to two leather chairs in the far corner. As they crossed the room, Finn said, "That's a fancy set of firearms."

"Leo gave them to me." Di Franceschi lowered himself into a chair. "I wondered when you'd come."

"What do you mean?"

"I'm told you're a smart man. I figured it wouldn't take long to realize I shot that vicious swine."

Finn was astonished. He'd never met a sane person willing to admit to murder. And, the old guy seemed completely sane. *Was he trying to save his nephew?*

"I was told you weren't here last night, Mr. Di Franceschi."

"Please, call me Dom." He rubbed his hands together as if they were cold. "I wasn't supposed to be. I brought the pistols to mount on the wall in my office."

Finn studied the man. "You don't seem upset over killing Whiting."

Dom coughed violently for several seconds. "Please excuse me. It's my lungs." He wheezed. "No, I'm not upset. I did what I had to."

Finn felt puzzled. "What do you mean?"

"He was trying to kill Miss Julia. I had to stop him for Mrs. St. Martin's sake. I couldn't let him murder her daughter."

"Start from the beginning."

"I was polishing one of the pistols when I heard Miss Julia's screams. There's not much space between these two buildings. I loaded the gun, praying it would fire. I wasn't certain it was a real firearm. As I came through the back door of the carriage house, that despicable man took a swing at her. She dodged his blow, but his fingers caught her pearls. I don't think he meant to break them. But it didn't stop him. He grabbed her by the throat, strangling and shaking her like a rag doll. That's when I fired." Dom shook his head sadly. "I couldn't let Julia die. How would I explain it to Mrs. St. Martin?"

"Then what?"

"I started for Miss Julie, but she ran out."

Finn stared at Dom, finding his story hard to believe. This case was getting crazier by the minute. Dom had just confessed to murder and was accusing Whiting of attacking his bride.

"Have you talked to Julia?" Dom asked, his voice agitated. As he spoke, he slid open the drawer in the table next to his chair and reached inside. Immediately, Finn drew a gun from beneath his coat. "Stop," he commanded. "Remove your hand slowly."

Dom did as he was told, but when his hand cleared the drawer, it held a leather pouch. He handed it to Finn. "I collected these this morning. When they flew from her neck, they bounced all over like golf balls on concrete. Most settled along the far wall. Miss Julia may want them restrung."

Laying his gun in his lap, Finn opened the pouch and examined the pearls. "Did Miss Julia or Whiting see you before you fired?"

"No. Her back was to me and he never looked my way."

Finn jostled the pouch in his hand. "Why should I believe your story? You could be covering for your nephew."

"Take a look at Miss Julia's neck."

"I will." Finn studied the old fellow, wondering why, with all his class, he chose to spend his life working in a barn. "We took Leonardo into custody. Why didn't you come forward last night?"

"I couldn't. I had a terrible coughing spell right after I shot the blighter. I tried to get back to my office for my medicine but passed out before I reached my desk. When I woke up, everyone was gone. I'm telling you, Leo didn't do this. I did! He couldn't—not the way he loved that girl."

"Did she love him?"

"Oh my, yes. The lad was foolish to stay away so long.

Miss Julia and I often talked about him, until one day she said she no longer wished to."

"What do you think happened?"

"She became convinced he wasn't coming back. Then, I heard St. Martin had financial problems. Next thing I know, she's marrying that black-hearted scoundrel."

Finn squinted at Dom. "How could she not know Leonardo was an Italian Count?"

"He wasn't when she knew him. He received the title before his first European concert two years ago."

"From who?"

"From me. It was my title. Only I could hand it down."

"You? Why did you work here as a barn man? Surely, you didn't have to."

He shrugged. "To be near the family, and the horses," he said in a near whisper.

Finn crossed his arms and stared at Dom. The old man, seeming uncomfortable, looked away. Suddenly, Finn understood. "You were in love with Mrs. St. Martin."

Dom closed his eyes and nodded. "I couldn't be a count and a barn man, too."

"So you both kept it a secret. Is Julia your daughter?"

"Don't I wish. I love her as though she's mine. After she was born, I drove her and her mom home from the hospital." He smiled. "I held Miss Julia in my arms when she was eight days old—a week before her father did." His eyes misted. "Mrs. St. Martin is a wonderful woman—a good wife and mother."

Finn nodded. "She was more important to you than your title."

WHEN Finn entered the house, a maid escorted him to the solarium where Julia, dressed in black, sat behind a lady's desk, penning a note. She greeted him politely, apologizing for her behavior the previous evening.

Assuring her that her apologies were unnecessary, he explained he'd found Whiting's killer and also discovered her fiancé had tried to kill her. "Is that true?"

Tears filled her eyes. She nodded as if she were ashamed.

"Tell me about it."

Julia left her desk and paced the length of the room. She kept her eyes diverted as she spoke. "Dan stormed into the barn shouting that he'd seen Leo leave and accused me of cheating—said I was just like my mother."

A sob escaped her as she pulled a handkerchief from her sleeve. "My mother would never cheat on my father! I don't know why he said that." She blew her nose. "He said I wanted a lover in the barn, just like my mother had. I told him Dom and Mother were not lovers, that he had an evil mind." Her eyes blazed. "That's when he tried to slap me. I dodged his hand, but he still broke my necklace."

Finn interrupted her. "May I see your neck?"

She shyly turned from him and lowered her high lace collar. Finger marks were clearly evident in the bruising.

Tears slipped down her face. "I tried to catch the pearls, but his hands were around my neck, choking me. I remember struggling. Mostly, I remember him shouting and me screaming. He seemed out of his mind." She took a deep, shuddering breath. "Then I heard the shot. He let go of me, stepped back and collapsed. It happened so fast, I didn't realize he'd been hit."

"Did he say anything more?"

She shook her head. "He just stared at me with such despising eyes—from the time he grabbed me until he fell. I've never seen such hatred. It was horrible, Captain. I wanted to help him but I was afraid." She shook her head. "I'll never forget that look."

"What did you do?"

"Like a coward, I ran to the house."

Finn took her hand. "You're no coward. You did the right thing. Whiting might have killed you." He guided her to a chair. "Why didn't you tell me this last night?"

She shook her head. "I felt so humiliated in front of my parents. They had gone to great expense for the wedding—guests had come from far away. How could I face them?"

"But, none of it was your fault."

When she seemed calmer, Finn relayed Dominic's story, leaving out the old fellow's feelings for her mother. When he finished, he gave Miss Julia the bag of pearls.

She seemed relieved. "Thank you." She raised her eyes. "Will you be arresting Dom? I don't think he can survive in prison."

"You needn't worry. After seeing your neck, I'd say it's a clear case of justifiable homicide. I doubt charges will be brought. I want you to have a tintype made of those bruises today—in case we need it later for evidence. If you're able, I'll take you with me now to the prosecutor's office so he can see your bruises first hand."

"Absolutely. What about poor Leo? Will he be released?"

Finn smiled. "As soon as I return to the station."

IN April of the following year, retired captain, Patrick Finn, found a booth in the coffee shop on board the ferry, *Arthur A. Denny,* on his way to Orcas Island to purchase a summer home.

Through the salt-sprayed window, Finn noticed the waters of Puget Sound, dazzling in the morning sun. He sipped his coffee and opened the newspaper. When the society section was all that was left, he flipped through it. If the ride to the island was shorter, he'd have missed the article. He smiled as he read:

> *Miss Julia St. Martin and Count Leonardo Di Franceschi were married in Seattle on April 21St with her parents, Governor and Mrs. St. Martin, and the groom's uncle, Dominic Di Franceschi, attending. Following their Paris honeymoon, the couple will return to America on board the Lusitania. Count Di Franceschi's first performance upon his return will be a Chopin concert for President Taft and his guests at the White House.*

MERLE McCANN, award-winning author, is best known for her *Longjohners' Mystery Series* for young adults, a literacy project to which she's devoted the past seven years. Born in the Yukon, raised in Seattle, she traveled the United States and Europe with her husband, pursuing their thirty year Arabian horse business. Before settling down to write serious fiction, McCann worked as a scenic photographer. She lives with her husband in Scottsdale, Arizona.

CHECKMATE
DIANA MANLEY

Tiffany was no fool. If she had learned anything in her twenty-seven years, it was that no one wins all the time. The trick was to bide your time. But only if it was something worth fighting for. Certainly nothing as trivial as chess.

She glared at her husband. Stephen was killing her again. She hated chess but he insisted on teaching her. The reason? He had taught his daughter, Jordan, when she was five.

Well, she wasn't Jordan. Tiffany swept her blonde hair behind her ear. Thank God for that. Who would want to be her? Sure, Jordan was smart; she had to be, saddled with a horsey face that even plastic surgery couldn't fix. Jordan had hated her from the first time they met, the day she and Stephen returned from their honeymoon. Tiffany didn't know why. She hadn't stolen Stephen from her mother…his second wife had.

"Darling, you have a move," Stephen said.

She peered up at him. "I do?"

He nodded.

Frowning, she studied the chessboard, considering every possible move. Ah, there it is. She sent him a pouty air kiss and moved her bishop.

He raised his eyebrows. "Ah…that wasn't it."

Surprise flooded her face. "It wasn't?"

He shook his head then slid his queen forward. "Checkmate."

"Ohh." She slumped back in her chair. "I'm just not good at this, Stephen."

"You're getting better, darling. You need to focus."

"But I don't like chess." She folded her arms against her chest, scrunching her eyes together. "I don't have to win at *everything…*like you…or Jordan."

Stephen set up the chessboard again. "Darling, winning is survival. The first rule of life…the only one that matters."

Sulking, she stared at the board, tempted to upend it, flinging the pieces everywhere, hopefully lost forever.

"All right, darling. No more chess today." He took her hand and raised it to his lips. She glanced down. Blue veins and wrinkles crisscrossed his hand, sending a jolt of revulsion through her. "Now, close your eyes."

"Why?" She was in no mood for more games.

"Just do it. No peeking."

Tiffany sighed. "All right."

She felt her fingers separating and then something cool slide over the ring finger of her right hand.

Opening her eyes, she saw an enormous diamond ring, four carats at least, fifty thou minimum. "Oh! You are sooo good to me." She held up her hand and watched the light dance off its facets.

"Let's never say that evil word 'divorce' again," he said.

"Never ever." She waved her hand through the candlelight, mesmerized by the beauty of the ring.

"Do you like it?"

"I adore it! It's the most beautiful ring I've ever seen… except for this one." She raised her left hand. Stephen had purchased the five-carat emerald diamond at Tiffany's in New York. It was flawless. She knew because she had used the jeweler's loupe to check it herself.

To be fair, life with him wasn't all bad. He was crazy about her, gave her everything she wanted—three homes, expensive vacations, a Porsche. And, he had married her without a prenup, certainly proof of true love.

AFTER dinner, she sat next to him on the sofa while a fire blazed in the fireplace and Chopin's sonatas floated through the air. She sipped her champagne then snuggled up to him.

"Tired?" he asked"

"Content."

"Even though I made you play chess?"

"You ask so little of me. It's the least I can do…" She

glanced up at him, a teasing look on her face. "Just not too often."

Stephen laughed and raised his wine glass. "Agreed."

She smiled and clinked her glass against his.

He was in good shape for a man his age. He worked out every morning, watched his diet, didn't smoke. Unlike her father, who with his beer-belly, double chin and a face mapped by wrinkles looked ten years older than Stephen, though her dad was five years younger.

Stephen had few lines in his face. Botox she suspected. Everyone over thirty should use it. His only flaw was his butt. Wrinkled, saggy and almost flat. Couldn't he Botox it? Or, get implants? It wasn't something you could ask your husband. Instead, she learned to avert her eyes when he padded around the bedroom naked and imagined her first love, Tony. Her mouth curved upward as she remembered his broad shoulders, his flat stomach and his...

"Darling?"

His voice jolted her back to the present. "Yes, Stephen?"

He bent down and kissed her on the cheek. "I said, pack your bags. I'm taking you away for a romantic weekend."

"Wonderful! Where are we going?"

"It's a surprise."

"How will I know what clothes to pack?"

He laughed. "Bring your bikini and your passport."

A slow smile inched across her face. "Can you promise me one thing?"

"Anything."

"You won't ask me to play chess."

He chuckled. "Not on our vacation."

She thought for a moment. "What about Mitch. Isn't he your favorite partner?"

Stephen nodded. "Mitch is the only one who ever beat me. But he'll be leaving as soon as he flies us in. He's got a hot new girlfriend."

"He does?"

"Won't tell me anything about her, says he's not sure I'll approve."

"Probably a bimbo."

He shrugged. "Probably." He drained his wine glass. "I can get by without playing the game for a few days. Besides, there'll be other things to do." He took her arm, caressing it with his fingertips. "I'm a lucky man."

She smiled. He was sweet. Then she looked down at his hand, spotted like a reptile. If only he wasn't sixty-four. The doubts surfaced again. She sighed. It was certainly easier to be loved than to love.

For eighteen long months, she had been patient, trying to ignore his snoring, his stomach growling and his knees creaking when he walked up stairs. True, she had agreed to stay with him, but how much more could she take?

His father hadn't died until he was eighty-three. Well, she'd given him a chance, asked for a divorce. He'd refused.

Now she'd have to kill him.

TIFFANY slept most of the six-hour flight, thankful the company jet had sleeping quarters, glad she had insisted on silk sheets.

As the plane approached the landing field, Stephen rubbed her shoulder. "Wake up, darling, we're almost there."

She pushed up her sleep mask, yawned and stretched. "Where?"

He raised the window shade but all she could see was a sea of green foliage. "Where are we?"

"Tagala."

"Tagala?" she repeated. "What is Tagala?"

"A speck in the Pacific. North of the equator, south of Hawaii."

How big was a speck? It didn't matter, as long as there were enough boutiques and shops.

The plane bumped down the runway and skidded to an abrupt stop, throwing her forward then yanking her back against the seat. Tiffany gasped and put her hand to her heart. "That was a terrible landing. You need a new pilot."

Stephen shook his head. "Mitch is a good pilot. It's a short runway. We could have taken the other plane but you wanted sleeping quarters."

Next time she'd check the length of the runway. If there

was a next time.

She stepped down from the plane and looked around. The jungle, dark and forbidding, began a few feet from the runway then circled around a small tin building. A white SUV waited in front. To the left, a red-dirt road snaked off into the jungle, swallowed up almost at once by dense foliage.

She wrinkled her nose. Nothing about nature appealed to her. "It looks like one of those islands on *Survivor.*"

He chuckled and put his arms around her. "It's not. One of my clients has a home here. It made the cover of *Architectural Digest.* You'll love it."

AD! She adored the magazine. That's where she found her designer. Things were looking better.

Overhead, the brilliant sun hung high in the flawless sky. Behind her, the raucous sounds of exotic birds filled the air. She could smell the damp earthiness of the jungle mixed with the sultry fragrance of exotic flowers. The humid air made her skin feel like silk.

"This has got to be the smallest airport in the world."

"It's his private landing strip. He owns the island."

Her eyes widened. "The whole island?"

"It's small, about five miles by seven."

She glanced around, noting that there was only the one road. "How far is the town?"

"No town."

"No town?"

"Just the caretaker and his wife. Their quarters are down the road from the main house. The next island is thirty minutes away by boat."

A shiver ran down her spine. She was afraid but didn't know why.

"Don't worry." He wrapped his arms around her, squeezing her hard. "No one will bother us. We'll be alone."

Two whole days? Alone with him? Then she smiled and squeezed him back. "That's ever so perfect!" She looked over his shoulder toward the distant mountains. *Oh yes, it could be ever so perfect.*

Mitch set their luggage down at their feet and held out a pink Chanel satchel. "Your purse, Mrs. Chambers."

She acknowledged him with a slight smile.

The pilot looked to Stephen. "Will that be all, sir?"

"Yes. We'll see you at five on Sunday. Enjoy your time off."

Mitch nodded and turned back toward the plane.

Tiffany's forehead crinkled as she watched him.

"What's wrong, darling?"

"I don't like the way he looks at me."

Stephen shrugged. "You are a beautiful woman. Of course he's going to give you an appreciative glance." He came up behind her, put his arms around her and rocked her gently. "Men have looked at you like that all your life. You know how to handle them."

"He doesn't know his place. When you're not around, he acts like he's cock of the walk."

"Mitch? He's been with me…" His forehead furrowed in thought. "Well, forever. I would trust him with my life." Stephen took her chin in his hand. "Ignore him."

She started to say something but stopped. She smiled. "You're right. You know I'm always cranky after a nap." Reaching up, she pulled his head down and kissed him.

THE house was magnificent, a celebration of teak and glass that sprawled over a broad cliff jutting out over the ocean. Wide windows wrapped around the house, erasing the boundaries between indoors and out. A negative-edge pool and cabana nestled to the right. Clusters of tall palm trees rustled in the breeze while blood-red hibiscus and feathery ferns softened their vertical lines.

The interior, furnished with simple pieces of bamboo, rattan and wicker, revealed a sense of peace and order. Tribal accessories—woodcarvings, statues and pottery added drama. A tang of incense lingered in the air.

Tiffany felt they were in paradise. They swam in the salt-water pool, dozed on chaise lounges and grazed on lobster, fresh pineapple and papaya and sipped Mai Tais. It was a lazy day, a perfect first day.

By noon the second day, Tiffany was bored. She'd had her swim and finished reading her celebrity/gossip magazines. Now what? There was no TV, no one to talk to but Stephen. She sighed. She could only lie around so long.

She glanced over at him, half-asleep on the rattan chaise. Well, he had napped long enough. "Sweetheart," she whined. "I'm bored."

"Hmm?" He opened his eyes then shaded them with his hand. "What did you say?"

"I said I'm bored."

"What do you want to do?"

"Let's walk around the island."

He reached over and took her hand. "I didn't think you were the exploring type."

She arched her left eyebrow. "You don't know everything about me."

"Yes, I do."

She sat up, swung her legs over the side of the chaise and leaned toward him. "Who was my third-grade teacher?"

"Well..." he laughed. "Almost everything."

She jumped up. "Come on. Bet I can change faster than you," she said, running into the house.

TEN minutes later, Tiffany adjusted the chinstrap on her safari hat and struck a pose. "How do I look?"

"Like *Indiana Jones's* girlfriend," he chuckled. "Where did you get the hat?"

"Found it in the closet. There's another one..."

He shook his head. "Don't need it." He slid open the patio door. Fifty feet of green lawn spread out before the cliff tumbled down to the ocean. The crashing sound of the surf and the calls of the sea gulls were loud but had a certain restful rhythm. He glanced around. "Which way?"

"Let's explore Secret Beach."

He looked puzzled. "Where's that?"

"The housekeeper told me about it." She took his hand and led him to the edge of the cliff. "Look down there." She pointed down to a small beach, shaped like a crescent. Huge black lava boulders dotted the white sand, a few stumbling out into the ocean. Wild blue-white waves crashed onto the shore, the spray rising up like plumes of airy smoke.

Stephen followed her gaze, frowned and shook his head. "It's too treacherous. The path, what's left of it, only goes halfway down. We'd have to climb over those lava boulders. They're bound to be slippery from the surf."

She gave him a teasing look. "You can do it."

"Darling, I'm worried about you, not me."

"*Darling*, I work out every day, just like you."

He said nothing, merely stared down the trail.

"Let's go before the tide swallows it up. The housekeeper says it comes in early today." She headed toward the overgrown footpath, pushing aside the huge green leaves from banana trees.

Halfway down, they reached the boulders. The small ones they easily skirted while the larger ones, they had to grasp the damp sides and clamber over them.

Behind her, she could hear his labored breathing. She moved faster.

"Darling," he called, "let's stop for a minute." He leaned against a boulder, his face flushed, breathing hard. Pulling up his shirt, he wiped his perspiring face.

She hurried up to him. "Are you okay, sweetheart?"

"Think I have a touch of the flu. I didn't say anything earlier, didn't want to ruin our weekend."

"It's all right. We'll rest here as long as you like." She stared down the rocky slope to the beach. She had to get him down there.

Turning around to face him, she gazed at him through lowered lashes, eyes narrowed so that everything was blocked out…everything but him.

"Let's go swimming," she said.

"We didn't bring our suits."

She ran her hand up his thigh and in a husky voice, said, "Who needs a suit?"

He bent down to kiss her. "You have the best ideas."

Suddenly, she stiffened. "Don't move," she whispered. "There's a huge snake behind you."

Stephen's face turned the color of ash. He didn't move. She didn't move.

After what seemed an eternity, she said. "It's okay, it's

gone now." She threw her arms around him, squeezing him with all her might. "I was so afraid for you!"

He twisted around, scanning the area. "Are you sure it's gone?"

"Positive. Didn't you hear it slither away?"

"I heard something."

She pulled on his arm. "Come on. Let's go before it comes back"

LATER, they lay down on the white sand, drying off in the sun, a gentle breeze whispering over them. Above, the sapphire sky, stippled by wispy clouds, stretched over the endless turquoise sea.

Tiffany reached over and stroked Stephen's stomach. "Lying here, just you and me, and no one else. It's like we're Adam and Eve in the Garden of Eden."

He bent over and kissed her forehead. Sitting up, he checked his watch then grabbed his shirt. "We should get going. Mitch is picking us up at five and we have to pack."

"He can wait. I want us to enjoy as much of today as we can."

"Another time. The tide will be coming in soon. It'll take longer climbing up than it did coming down."

Maybe not, she thought as she slipped on her thong.

"Come on, darling," he said.

She glanced up at him, and then with sleepy eyes and a seductive smile, she crawled over to him and walked her fingers up his leg.

He laughed. "You're insatiable. But we don't have time." He grabbed her hands and pulled her up. "Mitch will be here soon."

She glared at him then picked up her clothes.

"Darling, don't be mad. We can come back in a couple of weeks."

Without another look, she ran toward the slope, scrambling over the rocks, moving fast.

About a third of the way up she heard him call.

"Tiffany! Wait."

She ignored him, continued climbing, increasing her

speed.

"Tiffany!" He called, this time, an urgent, desperate tone to his voice.

She turned around. He lay sprawled over a boulder, gasping for breath. She ran toward him, jumping over rocks, pushing aside branches and had almost reached him when she tripped over a tree root. She pitched forward and slammed onto the ground with a thud.

"Tiffany!" he yelled. "Are you okay?"

Stunned, she lay on the ground, excruciating pain shooting through her left leg.

"My leg. My leg. It's broken!"

He stood up, no longer breathing hard. "That's too bad. Though it will make things easier."

"What?" she asked, her mind still hazy from the shock.

He walked over and looked down at her.

Strange, she never realized how cruel his mouth was. He really had no lips, just a thin, crooked line stretching across his face.

Whimpering, she raised her hand to him but he ignored it.

"Stephen, what's wrong?"

He crossed his arms over his chest while a sardonic smile slid across his face. "I told you I knew everything about you."

"What? What do you mean?" The pain played tricks with her mind. She couldn't make sense of what he was saying.

"You were planning to kill me, you little bitch."

"No!" she cried in disbelief. "I just saved your life. The snake…"

"There are no snakes on this island. Just like Hawaii."

"No, no!" she cried, terrified. "There was one. A giant spotted one. I swear!"

"Was that part of your plan? Or, something to throw me off?"

"Plan? What are you talking about?"

"Mitch told me everything. How you planned to kill me. How you offered him five hundred thousand dollars to help you."

"That's not true. He's lying!"

"Is he?"

"He wants me, said we would be together after he killed you, but I said no! That I loved you."

"I have the recording."

She shrank backward, hands tightly clasped to her chest.

"And, after I gave you that four carat diamond."

Her hands flew to her mouth.

"Ah, yes. The rings. Give them to me. Both of them."

Terrified, she stared at him, unable to move.

He held out his hand, his eyes blazing. "The rings. Now!"

She slipped the rings off and held them up for him.

Grabbing them, he said, "You won't need them where you're going."

"No," she whispered.

He grabbed her arm and yanked her to her feet. "And, now darling, it's time to say goodbye."

She screamed in pain, struggling to stand on her good leg. "But you love me. I know you love me." She gasped. "You didn't ask me to sign a prenup."

He shrugged. "I didn't ask my second wife, either. Have you forgotten how she died?"

She frowned, thinking. "Misty fell…" Her heart plunged to her stomach. "You didn't."

"I did."

He wrenched her arm behind her back. "Ahh!" She screamed, collapsing back against him.

"Goodbye, darling. Focusing was never your strong point."

Behind them, they heard the sound of a branch breaking and rustling noises. Stephen whirled around. "Mitch."

"Mitch, Mitch! Help me," Tiffany screamed. "He's going to kill me."

Stephen laughed. "I'd say it was self-defense."

Mitch walked slowly toward them, his dark aviator glasses hiding any expression.

"Can you imagine?" Stephen said. "She thought she was smart enough to kill me."

Mitch tilted his head and studied Tiffany. "She's not dumb but she's no match for you. Or Jordan."

"Darling will soon be no more. Say goodbye to her, Mitch."

Mitch turned back to Stephen. "Jordan is brilliant. Just like you, sir"

Stephen rubbed his chin, considering. "She's more ruthless."

"Right again, sir." Mitch pulled out a gun. "Your turn."

"What?" Surprise spread across Stephen's face. "Why?"

"Jordan and I were married yesterday."

"Married?" Stephen whispered, disbelief glazing his eyes.

Tiffany snickered. "And, you said I didn't focus enough?"

Stephen ignored her, his eyes locked on Mitch.

A cruel smile crept across Mitch's face. "It's been a pleasure working for you, sir. This was Jordan's idea. Playing up to your wife, pretending to go along with her plan."

"Mitch, I know you love me," Tiffany cried, stepping in front of Mitch.

"But, you're like a son to me," Stephen pleaded.

Mitch's face darkened. "Jordan said to tell you goodbye— Dad."

Stephen's face crumpled. "Jordan…?"

Mitch's laugh, loud and diabolical, rang out. Then he sneered, "Turn around, both of you."

Slowly, they turned. Tiffany looked back, opened her mouth to say something.

"Turn around, bitch!" Mitch said. Then with his foot, he kicked Tiffany then Stephen over the side of the cliff.

Their screams followed them to the boulders below, then silence, except for the cries of seagulls and the relentless roar of the incoming tide.

"Checkmate."

DIANA MANLEY, a former interior designer and journalist, now spends all of her time writing mystery fiction. Her first novel, a thriller set in Mexico, is near completion. She wrote "Check-mate" after visiting her son in Kauai, Hawaii where she plans to return soon for more inspiration.

SINS OF THE FATHER
Susan Budavari

IN the dimly lit hospital room Abby Evers sat by her dying husband's bedside. Over the span of the last two weeks Ben's health had rapidly deteriorated. Despite multiple tests, the doctors were at a loss to explain the cause. He had gone from a seemingly healthy forty-four-year-old with a minor back problem, to an ICU patient, kept alive by machines.

He opened his eyes a slit and mumbled, "…take care…"

Abby leaned her ear closer to his lips straining to hear his voice. "…son…Bar Har…"

It took a moment for the words to register. "Son? Did you say *son?*" she whispered back.

The slightest nod.

"Bar Harbor? Take care of…your…son in Bar Harbor?"

Ben closed his eyes for the last time.

DURING the days following Ben's death Abby struggled to hold herself together. She broke out in tears without warning. Ben's last words haunted her. As she notified the few friends they had of his death and arranged for his funeral service, she replayed his words in her mind. At first she'd passed them off as deathbed delirium. If Ben had a son, she had to find him.

They'd married late. Each had baggage from the past that they'd shared. Why would he have kept something so important from her?

Maine. Ben had insisted that every year they vacation in Bar Harbor on the northeast shore of Mt. Desert Island, explaining that the only happy memories of his childhood were from his summers there. *Did he have another reason for going to Bar Harbor?*

They always stayed in the same cottage. She remembered

their agreement early on—at Ben's insistence—that they'd give each other space during their time there. She caught up on her reading; Ben took long walks by himself and disappeared for hours each day. Why hadn't she questioned him about his long absences? Had she been afraid of the answers?

Although they weren't close, she had immediately called his brother, Scott, in Philadelphia to tell him of Ben's death. Scott voiced shock, made some trite remarks and asked about arrangements. He and his wife Cindy would fly to Phoenix for the services and remain for at least a week.

Then he asked, "Who's your lawyer?"

"Why?"

"Ben's will."

Abby gulped. "We always meant to get around to writing them, but—"

"Whoa. Better check Arizona's inheritance laws." Then more quietly, "I hope we can settle things quickly."

"What do you mean?" Abby had taken for granted that everything Ben had would pass to her.

"The family trust money," Scott said. "Our parents are dead and Ben didn't have any kids. I'm his closest blood relative..." Abby thought she heard suppressed elation in his voice.

Abby knew Ben wouldn't want his brother to get any part of his estate. Ben had made remarks about how Scott squandered money. He'd discouraged Abby from inviting Scott and his family to visit them in Phoenix. After a while, Abby accepted that Ben wanted little to do with his brother.

Even more reason she needed to find out if Ben really had a son and heir.

AT the funeral service, Abby overheard Scott speculating with Cindy about the size of Ben's estate and how fast it would be settled. Abby realized she must have grimaced because when Cindy glanced in her direction, she slipped away from Scott and approached her. Although she'd only met Cindy on a few occasions in the three years she and Ben were married, they'd had an instant rapport.

Cindy reached for Abby's hand and said, "I'm sorry if Scott offended you. He has a big mouth. Ben didn't know, but last year Scott lost his job in the pharmacy and my salary is barely keeping us afloat."

Abby wondered how she'd handle it if Ben actually had a child and hadn't told her. He'd called her his first and only love and lavished her with expensive gifts. Said he'd never wanted to get married before meeting her. Was that a lie? She thought she knew him. Had he fooled her?

She needed to find a private investigator.

ABBY asked around. Through Laura, her college roommate, she found a Boston P.I. named Herb Nesbitt. Laura had used him and assured Abby that Herb was an ideal choice to conduct an investigation in Maine.

Abby contacted Herb and gave him the limited information she had. When he asked how old she thought the son could be, she admitted she had no idea, but assumed he must be more than three.

"I'll need more to go on," he told her. "Go through your husband's things for any financial records he's hidden from you. If he had a kid, there's a good chance he's been funneling money to him."

Herb also told Abby, "Write down everything you know about your husband including his social security number, birthdate, names of relatives and friends, schools and jobs." When she went to do that, she realized how little she really knew. The only members of the Evers family she'd met during their marriage were Scott and Cindy.

It took Abby days to perform a thorough search of the house and to wade through Ben's papers. She discovered several bank statements locked in a secret compartment in his desk. Without her knowledge, he had transferred thousands of dollars to a bank account in Maine. She also discovered receipts for premiums paid on insurance policies she hadn't known about. *How did he manage to keep all this secret from me?* Her hands shook as she faxed the documents to Herb.

ON the night before Scott and Cindy were to return to

Philadelphia, they invited Abby to a small French restaurant in downtown Phoenix.

Throughout dinner Abby plied Scott for information about Ben. Other than sharing some memories of their childhood in Boston, he offered very little about Ben's life. Because Scott was four years younger than Ben, and they had lived in different cities from the time Ben finished college, they'd always led separate lives and rarely spoke to each other. Apparently that was agreeable to both since neither Ben nor Scott had ever made overtures to change things.

Scott wrung his hands. "I'm sorry Cindy and I didn't get to spend much time with Ben and you over the years. We never expected to lose him so early."

After he finished his coffee, he stared at Abby's emerald cut diamond bracelet for a long moment before he asked, "I wonder if you could see your way clear to give us a loan against our share of Ben's estate?"

Abby cringed inside. Once she received the payout from Ben's life insurance policy, she could easily afford to give Scott the advance he'd requested. However, she wasn't sure she wanted to give him anything.

"I'm leaving for Bar Harbor next week and will be away for a while. I'll look into it when I get back."

"Actually, it's critical that I get the money pretty fast. I'd appreciate it if you could move quickly."

"Let me think about it, Scott."

His eyes narrowed. "May I ask why you're leaving so soon after Ben's death?"

Abby took a deep breath and debated what to tell him. She resented Scott pressuring her. "Ben and I were supposed to go to Bar Harbor on vacation later this month—our yearly trip to Bakers' cottages."

Scott nodded.

"I've contacted them and I'm going up a couple of weeks earlier than planned." Abby caught herself thinking about how alike the brothers seemed despite the difference in their physiques—Ben had been husky with middle-aged spread, whereas Scott was still slender and youthful in appearance.

Scott cleared his throat, commanding Abby's attention.

"You were saying…"

"I'm taking Ben's ashes with me and…"

"Not what I'd call a vacation, but…" He was silent for a moment and Abby sensed he had something on his mind.

He gave his wife a nod and then said to Abby, "Maybe Cindy should go with you."

To watch me?

"Won't it be hard for you there without Ben?" he asked.

"Thanks for your concern, but even if I agreed—which I haven't—who'd take care of your kids?"

"My mom," Cindy said. "She's with them now while we're here." She looked down at the tablecloth and brushed away a crumb. When she looked up at Abby she blinked back tears. "We'd be very grateful to you if you saw your way to help us. It's been so hard on our family ever since Scott—"

Scott glared at his wife. "Abby knows we'd appreciate her generosity. We shouldn't trouble her with the details of our problems."

Cindy nodded sheepishly. "I'm sorry, Abby. You have enough on your mind." A moment later she regained her composure. "Scott's right. It could be too soon for you to go alone to a place with so many memories."

"I'm as ready as I'll ever be and I've made up my mind to go now."

"Well, if you reconsider and want Cindy's company, let us know," Scott said. "Be sure to give me your contact information before you leave. Just in case."

Abby had no intention of telling Scott the other reason for her trip and planned to delay responding to him on the money issue as long as she could.

She thought about what her lawyer had said when she told him that Ben might have a son and that she'd hired a private investigator: "Without hard evidence, we need to proceed as though there are only two potential heirs to Ben's estate, you, the major beneficiary, and his brother. I'll file for a court date, but realize, this process could take a year or more."

"What happens if we find Ben has a son?"

"We negotiate with Scott to avoid a lawsuit."

THE next morning, Abby flew into Boston and rented a Mercedes sports car at the airport. She took the same five-hour route to Bar Harbor as Ben always had. Although apprehensive at first, she'd never driven there herself and would arrive in Maine in darkness, she found the ride pleasurable.

Abby pulled into Bakers' Dozen on the Water, thirteen cottages arranged in a horseshoe that faced Frenchman Bay. She stopped in front of the white clapboard cottage on the left, closest to the water. The cottage, marked with an O on the front door, served as both the office and the summer home of Ted and Rona Baker. The Bakers had bought the cottages thirty years ago.

Ben had known them for a long time, having stayed there before Abby and he met. He'd brought her there once they started seeing each other. *Ted and Rona must know some things about Ben's past that I don't.*

The Bakers greeted Abby with hugs and condolences. "We've just finished dinner and were about to have coffee. Come join us," Rona said.

"I'd love to. Give me fifteen minutes to unload my car and I'll come back."

They gave her keys to cottage twelve where she and Ben always stayed, and she moved her car in front of it. Although too dark to see the bay, the smell of the salt air brought her comfort. The Bakers told her she was the first renter of the summer season and no one else was due before the end of the month.

When Abby stepped into the cottage, she found the place toasty and inviting. She put her suitcase in the bedroom and re-familiarized herself with the surroundings. As always, the kitchen and bathroom sparkled and the hardwood floors were waxed. A new coat of paint had even been applied to the walls. The Bakers had clearly prepped the place for her, even added some new space heaters in the bedroom. She felt welcomed as she unloaded the groceries from the car then headed back to the Bakers.

As she sat down in their kitchen, she said, "When I

stopped at the general store for groceries, Ray reminded me that you've known Ben for quite a long time."

As Rona and Ted nodded back at her, Abby noticed Rona's eyes glass up.

"I hope you don't mind my questioning you about him," Abby said softly. "Since Ben's death, I've realized how little I know about his life before I met him." She sighed. "The details were never important before."

Rona reached across the table to pat Abby's hand. "We understand."

After pouring coffee for Abby, Rona exchanged glances with her husband and said, "It's been well over twenty years since we met Ben. He was barely twenty and quite the restless one. Can you imagine, he talked about body-building all the time and going off to Australia?" Everyone chuckled.

"When he and I met, he was thirty-nine and a vice-president in the insurance company where we worked. By then he was more interested in crunching numbers than doing body crunches." Abby took a sip of her coffee. "Did you ever meet his parents?"

"No. But his brother Scott would come around. Ben acted like a father to him."

The conversation continued with the Bakers sharing a few stories about the youthful adventures of the brothers. Then Abby said, "I'm curious. Did Ben have a girlfriend way back?"

"Many," Rona said with a smile. "Both the brothers did."

"Any one in particular for Ben?"

"Julia. Julia Coelho," Ted said, "but she was older. Probably more of a friend than a girlfriend. Sad story there."

"Ben never mentioned Julia?" Rona asked.

"I don't recognize her name. What happened?"

"A bad car accident." Rona's expression darkened. "It was raining hard. Julia was driving. The car went off the road into a tree. She didn't make it and her boy was seriously injured. Ben was the only one not hurt."

"Her parents insisted Ben had driven," Ted said. "But the police found out that wasn't true. After that, Ben stayed away from here for a couple of summers."

Could that have been Ben's son? "How old was the boy?"

"Little, five or six. He'd be over twenty now," Rona said. "Do you know what happened to him, Ted?"

"No. I think after the accident he went to live in New Bedford with a grandmother or an aunt."

"What was his name?"

"Billy or Bobby—something like that," Rona said.

"His last name?"

"Coelho, same as Julia's."

"Do you happen to know if his father's still around?"

Rona looked at Ted and said, "Hard to say. We never really knew who his father was."

"Could it have been Ben?" Abby tried to sound calm.

"That's a funny thing to ask, Abby." Rona furled her brow. "Why would that even occur to you?"

"No reason." Abby fiddled with her five-carat diamond engagement ring, her hands resting in her lap.

Ted said, "I doubt it. Julia was the friendly sort and collected men."

"Hey, that's not nice." Rona tapped Ted on the arm. Turning to Abby, she said, "Don't pay attention to him. Julia wasn't a bad sort and her boy was well-behaved."

"But neither of you know what happened to the boy?"

Both shook their heads.

Soon after she left the Bakers, Abby called Herb and filled him in.

"Yeah, I know about the accident. Lots of headlines in the local newspapers. But the Coelho boy didn't make it. He died a couple of months after the accident. We found his father. It wasn't Ben."

Abby felt her body slacken and wondered if it were in relief or disappointment. "It would've been too easy if that were the answer," she lamented. "What now?"

"I actually think I've figured it out," Herb said. "I'm following a promising lead. I also expect to hear more from my banking contact today about Ben's account."

"Call me the minute you have something—day or night."

THE following morning Abby rose at sunrise and walked

down to the bay. She carried Ben's ashes in a brass urn. The wind blew her hair into her eyes. She drew her jacket closed and put on the hood. May mornings were cold in Maine and the wind brisk, a sharp contrast to Arizona where temperatures were already climbing into the nineties.

After meditating for several minutes at the waterside, she said a short prayer and dispersed Ben's ashes.

ABBY'S cell phone rang at 7:15 a.m. the next day.

"I'm coming back to Bar Harbor later today to talk to a few people," Herb said. "By tonight I should have some answers for you."

"Any chance you could stop in so we could meet each other?" She gave him the address and brief instructions how to find the cottages.

"I'm not sure of the timing. I'll call before I head over. Watch for a red Chevy pickup."

ALTHOUGH she'd visited Bar Harbor many times with Ben, she'd never walked the famous Shore Path. She began the walk near the town pier continuing for close to a mile along the eastern shore of Mt. Desert Island, invigorated by the salt air and captivated by the cawing of seagulls, and chattering of sea lions on the off shore rocks.

She photographed the stunning mansions with manicured lawns on one side of the path and the awesome views of Frenchman Bay on the other. At one point, out of the corner of her eye she spotted someone who looked eerily like Ben from the distance. Her heart skipped a beat. When she turned back, trying to get a better look, the man had disappeared. The words of a neighbor, also a recent widow, came back to her: "Don't be surprised if you see Ben's face in a crowd. The mind plays weird tricks on you when you lose someone close."

It was near dark when she returned to the cottage to shower and change clothing. While in the bathroom she thought she heard her phone and found a message waiting from Herb. He would be on his way over soon. Noticing her cell phone battery was nearly dead, she plugged it in to charge then laid down for a few minutes to rest.

Abby awoke to a pounding on the front door. She glanced at her watch. 8:05. Almost an hour had passed. She peeked out the window and saw a red pickup in front of the cabin. She rushed to open the door. "Welcome—"

In the shadows stood a slender twenty-something man in jeans, definitely not Herb. She did a double-take. The features seemed so familiar. *Is he the man I saw on the path?*

"Abby?" he muttered.

"Who are you?"

Babbling, he shouldered her out of his way and stepped into the room, then kicked the door closed. At first she couldn't understand his words. His manner frightened her.

"What did you do to Ben?" he shouted, frenetically moving around the room, as if looking for something.

She expected him to lunge at her any minute. If he did, what chance would she have against someone inches taller and much younger? Abby eluded his grasp and darted to the bedroom, locked the door and wedged a chair top under the doorknob. *Who is this guy?* Several moments of silence passed, then he began banging furiously on the door, screaming unintelligible words. Any minute he would break through. She had to get help!

My phone. Where is it?

It took her a few moments to remember. Grabbing the phone from the charger, she climbed on the bed and tried to open the window. It wouldn't budge. Painted shut! Her hands shook. Murmurs and cries slipped from her throat. *Am I going to die here at the hands of a maniac?*

She froze at the sound of a car pulling up, doors slamming, people rushing into the cottage. Loud arguing and scuffling. Then Herb's voice. "Abby, it's Herb Nesbitt. It's okay. We've restrained him. You can come out now."

Heart thumping, Abby moved the chair away from the door, unlocked it and opened it a crack. She saw the intruder slumped in a chair. Herb and another man hovered over him. As she eased into the front room, Herb came over and took her arm. He nodded toward the other man, "Wilson, here, is a nurse from Mark's group home. He gave him a sedative to calm him down." Herb gestured to the young man in the chair. "Abby, this is Mark Evers."

"Ben's son?"

"Nope, Scott's." He signaled Wilson and ushered a trembling Abby to the kitchen where they sat down at the table. "Better we talk here." He leaned forward and said in a soft voice, "Mark's bipolar. His mother was also bipolar and overdosed when he was a little boy. He witnessed what happened."

Abby could see Herb's sympathies lie with Mark. "What a dreadful start in life," she said. Her mind raced. Thoughts of relief conflicted with new questions. "But what's this about Scott?"

"Scott abandoned him. Mark spent his childhood in institutions. When he was in his early teens, they got his meds right and released him to a group home. He's been there ever since."

"How did Ben get involved?"

"The state contacted him looking for Scott," Herb said. "When Scott refused to have anything to do with his son, Ben went to see the boy. After getting to know him, he assumed financial responsibility and visited him on a regular basis. He set up an annuity to take care of him." Herb stopped for a moment and stared at Abby. "In case you're wondering—he didn't adopt him. He's not Ben's son in the legal sense."

"When did all this happen?" Abby quivered waiting for Herb's response.

"From what I discovered, about eight years ago. Mark's twenty-two now."

Long before Ben married me. "So he knows Ben's dead?"

"Yes. I'm not sure when he found out, but he took it badly. Wilson thinks he stopped taking his meds."

"How did he escape to come here?"

"He's not imprisoned, Abby," Herb said, annoyance resonating in his voice. "I've met with him twice. We sat together for quite a while today and I explained why I was there. When I stepped out of his room to talk to Wilson, he slipped out." Herb shrugged. "I was careless with my keys and he *borrowed* my truck. Resourceful."

"I don't understand how he knew where to find me."

"I made the mistake of telling him. To prepare him in case you wanted to meet him. I called to warn you, but got your voicemail. I couldn't reach the Bakers, either."

"I was charging my phone." Abby thought for a moment. "Why didn't you call nine-one-one and get the police out here?"

Herb shook his head. "Wilson was sure he could handle him."

"That was reckless. He could've hurt me!"

"Look, I'm sorry," Herb said. "We weren't far away. I figured we'd get here faster than the police."

"At least you've gotten him under control."

Herb's face darkened. "There's something else you should know. Wilson said Scott called Mark yesterday and also earlier today."

"I wonder if what Scott said agitated him. What happens now?"

"Wilson will take him home and contact his doctor. The rest is up to you—whether you want to press charges."

"I need to think about it."

Abby walked over to Mark. He appeared to be asleep. *He certainly looks like an Evers.* She felt sorry for the rough deal he'd gotten out of life, but was it her problem?

She now understood Ben's disgust with Scott, but why hadn't Ben confided in her about Mark? Had Ben attempted to make up for his brother's failings? While she felt she could never have abandoned her own child, she didn't owe anything to Mark, but how much did she owe to Ben?

Had Ben kept this secret from her because it was a burden he'd assumed freely and didn't want to impose on her...until he had no alternative? She thought back to her conversations with Cindy and wondered if she knew about Mark. *Is that what had troubled Cindy?*

After Wilson and Mark left, Herb remained behind. He told her he'd looked into Ben's insurance policies and there was a large one with Mark as beneficiary. He advised Abby to think about the kind of future, if any, she might want to build with Mark.

Taking on a new responsibility wasn't a smart move for her. Suddenly staying in the cottage for another two weeks might be too dangerous. She debated about getting into the car and driving to the airport, but decided to sleep on it.

Shortly after Herb left, Ted Baker knocked on her door. "I saw a pickup in front of your cottage when we came home. I just wanted to be sure everything was okay."

Abby explained what had happened.

"I don't know, Abby," Ted said, "this sounds like there could be big trouble. Look, program my number into your speed dial and call me if you ever need help. I keep a gun in the house ever since we had a break-in years ago."

THE next day Abby stayed inside to read a book and putter around the cottage. By the time she turned in for the night, she'd decided to remain in Bar Harbor to vacation as she'd planned. She deserved some peace and quiet after all that had happened. After placing her cell phone under her pillow within easy reach, she quickly fell asleep.

A scraping sound roused her. She opened her eyes but saw only darkness. Heart thumping, she listened but heard nothing else.

She flipped on the lamp. Mark sat in a club chair facing her, his eyes shut. She pulled the covers under her chin. Her gaze jumped to a man crouching by the space heater, a pipe wrench in his hand. He stared at her as if he'd been watching her all night.

Scott!

"What are you doing here?" she shouted as she slid her hand under the pillow to press the speed dial on her phone. "How did you get in?"

He put down the wrench and in a sinister voice, said, "You're confused. I'm not here. Only Mark is. He can't stay away from you. He's good with locks but not good at following instructions." He took something from the pocket of the jacket lying next to him on the floor.

"What did you do to Mark?"

"Gave him something to sleep." He laughed. "Too bad

you woke up, but I've got something to put you back under." He glanced at the heater. "Such a crummy heater. Don't people realize carbon monoxide can kill them while they sleep?"

"Stop it! You're not making any sense," Abby said, anger overcoming her fear.

"You brought this on yourself. All you had to do was give me the advance I asked for. No matter. With you and Mark gone, I'll have all the money I need."

Scott started toward her, brandishing a syringe. Abby sat rigid until he reached the side of her bed and then she thrust the bed covers over him, leapt from the bed and dashed toward the door. Before she could get past the door she felt a sudden push from behind propelling her forward, her head slamming into the door.

ABBY lay on the floor of the brightly lit bedroom. She opened her eyes and blinked. It took several moments for her to get her bearings. Ted and Rona, both in pajamas and robes, hovered over her.

"You're safe, Abby," Ted said. While he went to get one of the paramedics administering to Mark, Rona knelt beside Abby and answered her questions.

After checking Abby out, the paramedic gave her an icepack for the lump forming on her forehead, helped her to a chair, and left to wheel Mark out on a stretcher to the ambulance.

Abby flinched at the sound of Scott's voice coming from the kitchen area. "Scott?"

"The police have him handcuffed and are questioning him," Ted said.

"Thank God you came in time."

"When I got your call I didn't take any chances. I grabbed my gun and ran right over. Rona called nine-one-one." He glanced toward the bedroom door. "Found you there, out cold, with him holding a syringe over you, ranting about some insurance policies. Didn't realize who he was at first." Ted took a breath and sighed. "Stopped him from injecting you and doing whatever else he planned to do."

OVER the remaining time she stayed in Bar Harbor, Abby spent long hours reflecting on everything that had happened since the day Ben first took sick. In the end, despite some unforeseen obstacles, it had all worked out as she'd planned. She'd inherit Ben's entire estate. Scott and Mark, both under arrest, were no longer a threat to her.

Abby felt certain Ben realized she would go to look for *his* son and what would happen as a result. Ben knew Scott would stop at nothing to get at his money.

Ben figured out I poisoned him.

She almost chuckled when it finally hit her what Ben actually meant by his last words: "*...take care...son...Bar Har...*"

The son in Bar Harbor will *take care of you.*

SUSAN BUDAVARI has written two psychological suspense novels, more than thirty short stories and co-edited and contributed to several award-winning mystery anthologies, including three from Red Coyote Press: *Medley of Murder, Map of Murder,* and *Medium of Murder.* She has worked in chemical research and scientific information management in the pharmaceutical industry and was Editor of *The Merck Index,* a bestselling encyclopedia of chemicals, drugs and biologicals. She is an avid portrait painter and photographer of the desert landscape.

NIGHTFALL ON BLACK BEACH
Martin Roselius

THE motorboat pushed through deep swells and the small speck on the horizon grew into a range of towering mountainous rock surrounded by a tangle of thick tropical growth. Coconut trees burst skyward like natural fireworks. As we nosed into the cove facing a crescent of black sand, a cluster of thatch roofs sprouted among the palms in a wash of color reminiscent of a Gauguin painting. It seemed as advertised: idyllic and peaceful.

The old black man navigating the powerboat hadn't spoken a word, his stoic face hardly a welcoming for what had been promoted as a plush twenty-four hour retreat. The pamphlet the local boy had handed me on the streets of Soufrière advertised a *free* promotional package, a day at the luxurious Black Beach Resort, a newly remodeled timeshare.

I knew from experience nothing's free. I would end up suffering through a two-hour sales presentation, but having vacationed on St. Lucia for the past two weeks in budget accommodations, it was an offer I couldn't pass up. Besides, this would provide an opportunity to visit one of the neighboring islands of St. Lucia, my ancestral home. A descendent of African slaves brought to the Caribbean to work the sugar and coffee plantations, this vacation had been all about walking in the footsteps of my ancestors.

After I reluctantly accepted passage aboard a weathered wood motorboat, we left the pier at Soufrière trailing a stream of thin blue exhaust during our one-hour jaunt.

There were five of us. Ted and Bonnie appeared to be in their early thirties and would make the perfect poster couple for the yuppie nation. He wore a ball cap from the East Sound Yacht Club.

I didn't get Harold's story, but if I had my guess I'd peg him to be a visiting professor on a specimen gathering expedition for some prestigious university's biology department.

Carissa, a twenty-something, appeared fit and ready to climb that pointed pinnacle of rock in the center of the island with only her bare hands.

And then there's me, Guame Washington, twenty-nine and counting, ex-military and reasonably fit, although a slight beer-bulge around the beltline belies that fact.

The surf rose up in one last surge lifting the boat and laying it gently upon the black sand. I stood up, held a firm grip against the side of the craft to steady myself and lifted my duffle, timing my jump as the surf receded, landing on the coarse ebony surface born of previous volcanic activity.

I tossed my bag farther up the beach then turned back to the boat. "Give me your hand." Carissa dropped her bag into my arms, catching me off guard as I scrambled to grab hold, keeping *it* dry while *I* dropped to my knees. I glanced up and caught her sheepish grin.

With no one to greet us, we headed for the nearest bungalow set among the palms. The thick brush appeared unkempt and wild, but I assumed it was their way of maintaining a natural setting.

"Hello! Anyone here?" I shouted. Other than a few wild birdcalls, silence greeted me. I moved into the brush and approached the first building. A mild shock registered when I observed the condition of disrepair. Wood siding had popped loose, the thatch roof had thinned to bare spots and windows displayed broken glass, if any at all. Hardly the postcard-perfect vision presented in the brochure.

"What's with this?" I heard Ted ask from behind, his voice registering slight confusion.

I turned and shrugged in disbelief. "Plush? Newly remodeled?"

Bonnie curled up her nose and glared at Ted.

The building had no door so I stepped inside.

"Hey, take a look at this." Sitting on the grass floor mat was a long banana leaf piled high with fruit. A handwritten note lay next to it. EAT. DRINK. BE MERRY.

Despite the food, a feeling of uneasiness began to take hold. I turned, looking through the doorway and noticed our humorless boatman had left without so much as a goodbye. His plume of smoke dissipated in the breeze.

"Check this out." I turned to see Ted shaking a wooden barrel. "It's full. And we have cups and a ladle." He lifted the lid, leaned down and sniffed. "Punch." He sniffed again. "Of some kind."

He picked up a cup, stared at it with a cautious eye, wiped it clean with his shirttail, then filled it with the rum scented liquid and took a sip. "Hmmm. Not bad."

I took a slice of papaya while slipping out the back door to have a look around. When I returned my fellow timeshare adventurers had seated themselves on the worn floor mat, chatting, eating fruit and drinking punch.

I sat down with my legs folded. "Place is deserted. Think he brought us to the wrong island?"

Carissa reached for a banana. "Certainly he'd know these islands."

Harold held up a star fruit and examined it. "Strange, I'd say. Surely they knew we were coming?"

Ted raised an eyebrow while sucking on a piece of cut pineapple. "The resort's probably on the other side of the island. I bet someone will show up before long. More punch anyone?" He rose with two cups in his hand, filled them and reached for the others.

We continued to devour the fruit. The punch tasted refreshing and encouraged conversation. Everyone confessed they had taken this tour based on the pamphlet the village boy had passed out. We agreed the flyer had not appeared professionally produced, nor our mode of transportation to the island as expected from a newly remodeled luxury resort.

Small talk that began with a light nature shifted as we ventured to share our thoughts on the oddity of our arrival and the absence of any sign of civilization, soon realizing none of us *really* knew anything about the resort other than what we had read in the brochure. Had we been enticed to the island by the offer of a free promotion for some unknown reason? As time passed and no one showed, a pall began to set in.

The eating slowed, but with nothing else to occupy us, the drinking continued.

What was it about this punch? Time and space began to blend into one indiscernible blur, my mind became a blank slate as I heard mumblings I could not comprehend. I rocked back and forth staring. Who *are* these people? My head became thick, my eyes heavy. I struggled to keep them open. As my body became limp, my muscles gave way to my heavy frame. I leaned back on my elbows, a final attempt at maintaining any semblance of balance, then I tipped over and fell flat on my back. A rush of swirling palm fronds danced overhead before everything went black.

SUNBEAMS hit my face, jarring me awake. I blinked, lifted myself up and fought to refocus. Glancing around I observed blurred figures sprawled awkwardly across the grass mat. I shook my head, attempting to clear it. Thoughts began to form. Then I remembered the previous night. The fruit. The punch. We passed out and spent the night here. What was *in* that punch?

I rubbed my face, as my vision cleared, revealing a startling sight. Four bodies stripped down to their underwear. Then I looked down. I had on my white boxers while everyone else was attired in various colors and styles of undergarments. Their chests rose with each breath as they continued in a state of deep sleep. I blinked and stared, confused. What happened last night?

The underwear didn't alarm me as much as the large white bull's eye target I had discovered on my chest and abdomen, which I could clearly see branded on my companions as well. A chill raced up my spine. Painted? A target? On my chest! By whom? When? It had to have happened as I slept. *This*…freaked me out.

I stumbled to my feet in mild panic. What in hell's going on? I rubbed at the white circular target but it would not wipe off. My eyes darted about the hut. My bag. Where's my bag? Where's everyone's bags? They were gone. Somebody had been here. How'd they get here? I ran outside and looked toward the beach, searching, finding nothing. Seeing no one.

A voice from behind startled my already frayed nerves.

"What happened?"

I whirled around to see Ted standing there in his striped boxers, rubbing his head in an apparent daze.

"Someone took our clothes. Our bags are gone too." I pointed at my chest. "And what the hell's this?"

I heard the others stirring. I ducked back inside. Bonnie had scooted back against the wall and clasped her knees. "Where are my clothes?" She began to choke up.

Carissa crossed her arms over her chest. "Is this somebody's idea of a sick joke?"

"What's going on?" Ted asked.

I studied each face as reality set in. "Someone other than the five of us was here last night. Took our clothes. Painted this thing...this target thing on us." I paused. "Something was in that punch. There's no way someone could have done this without our knowing...if we hadn't been drugged."

"Oh, my God!" Bonnie whimpered. "Drugged?"

Harold stood up. "It's the only logical explanation. But why? Is this some kind of ritual?"

Ted moved to comfort Bonnie. "There is no resort, is there?"

"Apparently something's going on we aren't aware of yet. Let's stay calm and see what happens. Ted, you and I should take a closer look around. Harold, why don't you stay with the ladies?"

Carissa jumped up, defiant. "I'm going with you guys."

I studied her a moment. "Fine. Let's go."

We headed for the edge of the beach and waded in to wash the targets off our body. "What *is* this stuff? It's not coming off." I glanced up, my eyes scanning seaward when my heart jumped. "Look! Someone's coming!"

I stared anxiously, my hopes rising, my attention focused beyond the surf. Cutting through the waves beyond the cove a sleek white yacht headed our way at a fast clip. Carissa and I began jumping up and down, waving our hands, shouting. "Hey, over here! We're over here!"

Ted expelled a loud cheer, then turned and headed back in the direction of the shack.

A shrill whistle zipped past me, making a thump into the packed sand, sending a spray of stinging black grains against my legs. Something hit the water in front of me, raising a thin whoosh of salt spray. "What the hell!"

I instinctively jerked my arms up, covered my face and ducked. My eyes and ears told me someone was firing a gun at us, but for a moment my mind wouldn't accept the reality. A third shrill *zip* whizzed by and a burst of sand jarred me out of my state of disbelief.

"Jesus!" I screamed. "They're shooting at us!"

A few more bullets zipped past with a thud as they hit the beach. It was only then that I heard the crack of gunfire above the rhythmic roar of the powerboat's engines.

Carissa had remained frozen in one spot as little sprays of sand pelted her. "Carissa! Get the hell out of here!" I turned to run toward the trees as Ted, Bonnie and Harold appeared, heading our way. They stopped in their tracks. I caught their blank stares.

The projectiles continued to ping and ricochet around us, pelting the sand, the low brush and the solid trunks of the coconut palms, scattering thatch and black grains into the breeze.

"Get out of here." I managed to scream. "Into the trees!"

I turned back and saw that Carissa hadn't yet moved. I grabbed her arm and yanked. "Let's go." She looked at me with a stunned look. "Now!"

Ted and Bonnie were ahead of me, arms covering their heads, staggering through the soft sand. More tiny explosions rocked the ground around us. I dashed up the beach and dodged my way through the trees, pushing and urging everyone forward.

An amplified voice through a megaphone blared over the crack of gunfire. A raspy voice. Laughing. "Let the game begin!" Then more laughing. More shooting.

I shuddered. My mind confused. What's going on?

"Move it, guys! Move it!" I counted heads. There were three. I made four. I stopped and turned, then started back. A figure emerged from a clump of low palms. Carissa. "Come on! Move it!"

She nodded as she passed, her face white. I noticed she had a tight grip on one arm as it hung loosely at her side. Blood had begun to seep through her fingers. I took a deep breath, exhaled and fell in behind her.

The firing continued as we pushed through the jungle, eventually finding ourselves on higher ground at the base of a rock outcrop. From this vantage point I could see the yacht had now anchored near the entrance to the cove. A small inflatable dinghy was heading ashore with two men aboard. I looked around at dazed faces staring back with looks of fear. I checked Carissa's arm. It appeared to be a messy flesh wound, painful, but not serious. She bit her lip as I examined it.

Bonnie trembled, her face buried in Ted's chest, small muffled sniffles added to the sound of our heavy breathing.

Ted stared toward the cove. "They're still coming."

Harold looked up, false hope in his eyes. "Maybe if we can just talk to them."

I stared at him, incredulous. "They *don't* want to talk."

"Did you hear the loudspeaker?" Ted asked. "The laughter? My God. They're killers. They tried to kill us."

Carissa had remained quiet. "You okay?" I asked.

She nodded with a grimace.

I lifted myself up so I could follow the progress of the dinghy as it rode the surf to the beach. The two men jumped out carrying backpacks and rifles slung over their shoulders. They began pulling the dinghy up to higher sand. I glanced around at our group and the targets on our chests.

It didn't take much imagination to determine what they would do when they found us. The voice on the megaphone unnerved me. The laughing. "Let the game begin," the voice had said. Was this just for sport? Some insane, perverted and barbaric game? A manhunt? And *we* were the hunted. A shiver sent chills down my spine. I had survived a tour of duty in Iraq. *This* made less sense and presented greater danger.

I studied the territory and decided it best to keep

climbing, working our way through the jungle growth. "Come on. We need to keep moving." I glanced down at their pampered feet that weren't prepared to traverse anything tougher than an Oriental carpet. "And watch your step."

We moved out at a brisk pace, my eyes constantly searching for the surest path though not always the most obvious. My army jungle training would be put to good use. We walked for about two hours. By the position of the sun I assumed it to be near midday. We stopped and rested a few moments by a creek that provided much needed hydration.

Harold and Bonnie seemed to be weakening, nearing the end of the adrenalin rush that had kept them pushing so hard at the start of our ordeal. The looks on their faces told me they wouldn't be able to proceed much farther. "Wait here. I'm going to have a look around."

Among the brush were dark, rugged boulders piled against one another. I probed among them and found a tight crevice a person could squeeze through. I slipped in and found a protected area, with a space large enough for our group. I knew we couldn't continue to climb or we'd be beyond the jungle growth and exposed among the higher peaks.

I returned to the creek. "Look. We have two options. We can keep running, but I'm concerned some of us may slow the rest down. We don't even know where we're going." I pointed over my shoulder. "There's a cave of sorts back among the rocks. We can hide there."

Ted spoke up. "Then what? We need to get help."

"I don't think we'll find any help on this island. And *nobody's* going to be looking for us anytime soon...*if* anybody even knows we're here. We have to take care of ourselves."

Ted frowned. "How? These guys have guns!"

"You have any ideas?" Harold asked. "A plan?"

"Maybe." I studied their anxious faces. "I don't think we have many options." I explained my plan to them.

Harold squinted and stared. "You some kind of Rambo?"

"I've had some army training. If I can keep the element of surprise, I..." I didn't finish. I knew my plan was a long shot. And I wasn't sure I believed any more than they did that it had a chance to work. If nothing else it would divert the shooters' attention away from the others, buying them some time.

"What about us?" Ted asked. "What can we do?"

"You need to stay together. I can do this better by myself."

I retraced my steps to the rock formation and everyone followed me in. After preparing a futile plan of response if the gunmen showed up, an attempt to surprise and overpower *them* with a barrage of rocks, we sat in silence. Each person dealt with the uncertainty and fear in their own way.

As I watched the sun lower toward the western horizon, I stood up and prepared for my departure, reminding them once more what they needed to do. If they didn't see or hear from me by tomorrow, mid-morning, they were on their own.

IT took a couple of hours to make my way through the brush before I reached the black sandy beach. The sun had begun to set and the last essence of daylight lingered among the trees. Along the water's edge, a few hundred yards farther up the beach, I could make out the dinghy resting in the sand. Seeing that, I knew the two armed men were still on the island. More than a hundred yards in the distance, toward the cove entrance, the yacht bobbed in the gentle tide, tugging against a taut rope that held the anchor firm.

I glanced around at the vegetation, then gently pulled and snapped thin green limbs and leaves until I found a tall tree from which rope-like vines draped the jungle floor. It produced leaves the size of a man's palm, and when snapped clean, oozed a thick yellowish resin. I tested the consistency, then began gathering them, snapping stems off at the base and dabbing the resin against my chest everywhere the white bull's eye had been painted. My body became a glob of tacky residue.

After covering the entire target I crept back to the tree line fronting the beach. I watched for the gunmen as I knelt down, scooping up handfuls of black sand. Filtering it through my fingers, it stuck to the sticky goo. Within minutes

I had camouflaged the white bull's eye, blending it with my ebony skin. I looked down at my white boxers. Wearing them would be akin to waving a white flag. I shrugged, dropped them to my ankles, stepped out and buried them.

After nearly an hour, Black Beach had settled into nightfall. The complete darkness of the evening sky told me the lunar calendar might be in my favor. The dinghy had disappeared from my vision but there'd been no sound of an outboard so I knew it still rested in the sand some distance away. Red and green running lights reflecting on the water's surface remained the only visible indication of the yacht's position.

For one last moment I listened for any sounds rising above the surf, but heard nothing to alarm me. It was time.

I dashed for the water's edge, crouching low, kicking up sand in a silent sprint. Forty yards. Thirty. Twenty. The sand became compact, damp and cool before my feet drove into the surf. Saltwater lapped against my legs with a cold chill. My feet gripped the firm bottom, pushing me forward. As the water rose against my body I tucked my head and began a hard stroke.

I kept a steady pace but eventually slowed as exhaustion began to set in. Within thirty minutes I had closed to within ten yards of the bobbing yacht and began treading water, watching for any sign of movement. The white sides loomed over me, nearly forty feet in length. The cabin remained dark and appeared to be empty. I circled the craft with caution, my breath coming heavy as it mixed with ocean salt and frothy saliva in my mouth.

Paddling toward the stern, I lifted myself up onto the attached platform floating just above the waterline. Crouching low, I crossed the deck, heading for the sliding glass door. Unlocked, it slid open. I felt my way through the dark cabin. Red and green lights from electronic controls threw a faint ambient light across the room. I identified a seating area that surrounded a dining table on my right and two cushioned chairs on my left. Moving forward I found and searched the kitchen and then checked out the raised area on the opposite side where the captain sat to pilot the boat.

In front of me a stairway led down to another door. I opened it and a cloud of stale air tainted of mildew escaped the cabin as I peeked into the darkness, finding what appeared to be a bedroom. I located a light and turned it on briefly while I continued my search. A clear hatch in the ceiling provided a view of the star-studded sky. I pushed it open and lifted myself out onto the bow, inhaling a deep breath of the fresh ocean breeze. The stainless rail led me back to the sliding door at the stern and steps that led to an area above the cabin. I climbed up, studied every detail, looking for anything that might be useful, as I finalized my plan.

Coming back down my knee rubbed against something attached to the wall. I bent over and discovered a long wood pole with a metal hook attached to a pointed end. I remembered from a fishing trip I once took that the crew had called it a gaff. Having searched and found no guns, I carried this makeshift weapon back into the salon. Preparations now complete, it was time to begin phase two.

After rinsing my mouth out with a few refreshing swigs of cold beer from the fridge followed by a handful of pretzels, I stepped up to the captain's chair, took a deep breath and exhaled before flicking switches at random, turning on and off lights and electronics until eventually locating the ship's horn. I hit the horn a half dozen times before shutting everything off and taking up my final position.

I had nothing to do but wait.

I stared off into the darkness, thoughts rushing through my head, visualizing in my mind my plan, my backup plan and my escape plan in the event neither of the first two succeeded. The enclosed cabin felt warm and stuffy. My hands became clammy, my brow moist. My heart kicked into a higher gear. The waiting became agonizing. Had they heard me? Would they come? Twenty minutes later I heard the sound I had been nervously anticipating—the high pitch whine of the dinghy motor approaching at a rapid pace.

I could see nothing.

I crouched down and prepared myself. The engine grew

louder as it neared, then soon puttered at a slower idling speed accompanied by the sound of waves slapping against fiberglass. The engine coughed, went silent and I heard the distinct sound of the inflatable craft rub against the floating platform. I swallowed and tensed as I heard a thump, a groan, then a series of quick footsteps against the fiberglass deck. I braced myself, gaff at the ready.

The door slid open with a quick jerk. A shadowy face and a body dressed in black burst in, an automatic rifle pointing directly at me as I crouched in the dark.

With the flick of my wrist I sent a ceramic cup crashing against the stainless table leg. The figure turned in response and I sprang forward, rising up with a quick leap, thrusting the metal barb into the fleshy chest, twisting, forcing it deep into bone and muscle. A gunshot broke the silence as an agonizing scream curdled the night air.

Yanked from my hands, the long pole jerked upwards and swung about wildly as the body flailed and jerked. His arms flew backwards, the gun dropping to the deck beyond the doorway, out of my reach. A deep moan escaped as the body shuddered and finally collapsed.

A raspy voice called from the direction of the dinghy. "Sam! What's going on! You kill the bastard?"

Without hesitating, I turned, dashed toward the kitchen and down the steps into the bedroom, where I reached up and grabbed the edge of the hatch, then pulled myself topside.

Picking up the long kitchen knife I had placed on the bow earlier I scrambled up and over the windshield putting me in the area above the cabin. Silently creeping to the back edge I peered over toward the stern. The dinghy was secured to the floating platform, but no one was there.

Knowing I only had a few seconds to maintain the element of surprise, I turned in one quick motion, lifted a large ice chest above my head and tossed it over the side into the blackness. It hit the water with a loud splash, sending up a shower of spray, leaving a growing ring of small whitecaps.

I crouched along the edge as footsteps sounded beneath me. The second man emerged from the cabin and flung himself against the railing, his gun aimed in the direction of the splash. Taking a deep breath I leaped downward, my arms stretched outward, the knife leading the way.

The blade plunged deep into his shoulder along the base of the neck. His gun exploded with a loud crack. Fiberglass shattered. He screamed. The impact of my fall threw me to the deck, but my knife remained deeply embedded in flesh. He grabbed the handle. Blood squirted between his fingers. He turned to face me wild-eyed, gasping, staggering on his feet. The gun barrel dropped and clacked onto the deck. I kicked at his knee with all the force I could muster. It snapped and he buckled, falling face forward across my legs.

I thrashed my feet, kicking him off, scooting backward, then jumped up, tense, watchful. My heart raced and my chest heaved. Hot breath rushed through my lungs. Everything had happened quickly. I had acted on instinct, but now I began to tremble. Nothing in my army training had prepared me for this. I waited, my eyes darting back and forth between the body and the cabin, but saw no movement.

After a few moments, I stepped closer, reached down cautiously and felt for a pulse, finding none. I looked up at the sliding door and moved a few guarded steps toward it. Looking in, I saw the first man lying prone, his eyes open, the steel hook still impaled in his chest. The tip of the wood shaft grazed the ceiling. I stared, mesmerized, as the pole swayed with the rolling surf.

I placed the two bodies out of sight in the bedroom, knowing I would have to spend the night on the boat. When darkness lifted and the new dawn broke, I would return to the mountain to lead the others down.

Ted would initiate phase three. With his boating background he'd try to contact the authorities using the yacht's communications systems, then pilot us safely back to St. Lucia.

Exhausted, my emotional bank totally drained, I sank down into a cushy chair, staring out into the darkness. Today I have seen hatred and a callous disrespect for life found in the worst of the human spirit. Today I have walked in the footsteps of my ancestors.

MARTIN ROSELIUS, following a career in graphic design/ illustration artist, has channeled his creative energies into the art of writing, having completed a memoir, SAND IN MY SHOES, ROCKS IN MY HEAD, and his first novel, an espionage thriller, YELLOW BLOOD, RED FEVER. He has written numerous children's stories and recently had a travel article printed in *Caribbean Travel + Life* magazine.

WISH YOU WEREN'T HERE
CHANTELLE AIMÉE OSMAN

"**THIS** is not what I consider a vacation…"

"Pardon me?"

"Oh, um, this conference is almost like being on vacation!" I covered brightly, as I finished my signature with a flourish and handed the autographed book back, smiling. Had I really said that out loud?

My agent, Grace Chiklet, had described this as a free trip to sunny California; all expenses paid, a ritzy hotel, near the beach…only a couple hours of work. "It'll be like a vacation," she'd promised, and man, did I need one. I'd endured non-stop speaking engagements and signings since my book came out six months ago. But what had been sold as no work all play was turning into an all-day-every-day nightmare.

I had to be at the signing tables between every panel, be seen in the workshops by the right people, and linger near my book in the makeshift bookstore when I wasn't signing. I didn't even have my nights free. Grace had insisted I attend all the cocktail parties, dinners and other prearranged activities. Vacation? It was closer to being in jail—or summer camp.

I glanced longingly out the window. White sand, waves rolling in, beautiful people frolicking under the beautiful sun. It hadn't even had the decency to rain so I wouldn't regret being trapped inside.

"Umm…" A high-pitched nervous voice interrupted my reverie. "Francesca, could you sign this?" she asked holding out a book.

I squinted at her name tag. A multitude of cat stickers made it difficult to read SHEILA MERTZEL, outlined in florescent purple marker. I looked up at a huge linebacker of a woman engulfed in purple ruffles, wearing a pair of glasses that made her look like one of those fish with six eyes. She was exactly why I didn't want to take this job.

When my editor asked me to write a cat-themed mystery/romance series, I wanted to run screaming. But Grace—she does seem to be behind all of my bad decisions—reminded me I needed the money, and my name on anything in print would help my "real" book, an international espionage thriller, get published. After all, my editor had insisted there only be a little romance—it didn't have to be between the cats. I was here promoting the first in the series. The second was already complete and in the hands of my editor.

"Of course," I replied, and read aloud as I wrote: "To Sheila—"

"No!" the woman yelled, jerking the book away, my felt-tipped pen trailing off the page and marking the cloth on the table where I sat. "I wanted it to Mr. Sparkles!" She flipped over her badge and poked her finger at the photo she had taped there of a clearly overweight feline wearing what looked like a feather boa in, what else, purple.

I tried my best not to laugh, I really did, but I couldn't help but smirk when I offered to cross out her name, and add Mr. Sparkles'.

"Mr. Sparkles does not want a ruined book, does he? No!"

I started to respond when I realized that, in fact, she was addressing the photo of the cat, not me. I looked to my left at the super famous, and rather devastatingly handsome, Stöss Majeur, author of the Mariner Ranger thriller series, signing books at the table next to me. Did he go through this before he made it big?

He glanced up at me, eyes widening when he saw Sheila the ruffled terror looming over me, waving my book. In my head I could hear him retelling the tale in his clipped accent to his New York Times-Bestselling-Author cronies, and I suddenly recognized that this situation could turn into an item of gossip at the cocktail party tonight if I didn't handle myself correctly.

Pulling it together, I whipped out a brand new copy of the book from the box at my feet and offered it to her. "Please, take a new copy. Shall I make this one out to Mr. Sparkles? Or would he prefer to have it to his first name?" Honestly, I was being completely serious and merely trying to humor the heaving behemoth before me, but she turned red and started to shriek, tears rolling down her face.

"Now you're making fun of me! I can't believe you treat your fans this way! I hope you're happy! I'm never reading one of your books again...And I'm going to make sure no one else ever does either! Don't think I can't!" With that, she began tearing pages out of the book, rolled them up, and proceeded to toss them at my head. Of course, she used the pristine copy, not the ruined one.

I sat there, a frozen statue, the tiny missiles of my prose battering me as the other attendees stared at the spectacle. Finally, after she had destroyed chapter five in its entirety—the longest chapter in the book—she stormed off. Before I buried my face in my hands, I caught a glimpse of her cornering Mickey Gunner, the conference chair. This is one hell of a vacation, I thought, as I struggled between laughter and tears. I'm going to kill Grace. That prospect cheered me somewhat. I stood to gather my things and saw my friend Blythe, author of the Food to Die For series, elbowing the now-dispersing crowd aside and rushing toward me.

"Oh my God, Frankie! What happened?" she panted. "I just finished my panel and saw that purple thing pelting you!"

"I don't want to talk about it, let's just go up to the room. I want to wash the bits of paper out of my hair, and get ready for the cocktail party. I am really ready for a glass of wine. I'll tell you all about it then." We made our way to the bank of elevators. "How did your panel go?"

She started to tell me, when my elbow to her ribs stopped her mid-sentence.

"Hey, ow! What did you do that—?"

"Shh!" I hissed, and pointed.

"Is that...?" Blythe mouthed. I nodded. Not a foot in front of us stood Stöss Majeur in all of his Edgar Award-Winning glory.

"He was signing at the table next to me," I whispered. "For a minute I actually thought he was going to come to my rescue and stop that horrid woman, but I guess I imagined it."

"Yeah, I imagine Stöss rescuing me almost every night myself," Blythe said with a wink. We collapsed in a fit of laughter. Silently, of course. We wouldn't want to appear immature.

A ding announced the elevator's arrival, and we collected our dignity. All the conference goers were eager to hurry and change for the party, so it was a crush to get in. I had to fight to maintain my place and not be shoved out by the hoard.

Once safely inside, I looked up and found myself in what, anywhere else but in an elevator, would have been considered an intimate embrace with Majeur.

I studied my feet, praying he hadn't heard what Blythe had said, and that if I stood still he wouldn't notice me. I decided to focus on getting my key card out of my wallet. Oh crap! Was that his thigh I just brushed?

"I see you made it out alive," a deep baritone said from above me. I could feel his breath on the top of my head. Did I mention he was 6'4"?

"Yeah, I guess everyone's as eager as me to get to the open bar." I kicked myself the moment it came out of my mouth. Now he'll think I'm some kind of wino groupie.

"I was referring to your brush with Sheila," he clarified, drawing out the syllables in an attempt to help me to understand this time. I had a feeling he would abandon me as a lost cause if he had to give it a third go.

"Oh," I sputtered, blushing, trying to recover from my faux pas. "There's always one fan like that out there, right? Do you know her?"

"She and her little outbursts are a fixture at this conference. Been around since I've been coming, anyway."

"This is my first time." I realized what had come out of my mouth. "At this conference. My first time at this conference…I've been around. To other conferences." I just couldn't stop myself from talking. Fortunately, fate intervened at that moment and the elevator doors opened.

"Well, this is me. See you at drinks." He squeezed out from next to me and was gone.

The elevator doors slid closed again, and since his body was no longer supporting mine, I fell back against the buttons, my purse hitting the one that read EMERGENCY CALL. The car jerked to a stop, and everyone glared at me as a siren wailed. I swiveled around, trying to press something that would silence the blaring. Blythe shoved me out of the way and pulled back out the call button.

"I can't take her anywhere," she explained to the crowd. There were a few titters of laughter, but I was certain they were planning to lynch me the moment she left my side.

I finally reached the safe haven of my hotel room. I bolted inside and threw myself face-down on the fluffy white bedspread in abject humiliation. After a few moments, and a rather vociferous pep talk, smothered as it was by the feather comforter, I felt a bit better. I got up, reassured that the day could not get any worse, and showered. I quickly applied my makeup and slipped on my confidence-boosting little black dress. Within the hour, I was on my way back down in the elevator, keeping my distance from the buttons this time, a new woman.

Blythe met me in the lobby. "Wow, no one's going to remember the 'incident' this afternoon when they see you in that dress!"

"That's the plan," I replied, smiling. "Ready?"

She took a quick look in a nearby mirror and patted down a stray hair. "Ready."

The hotel had set up a bar in each corner of their grandest ballroom, crystal chandeliers sparkled from the ceiling, and the dais at the front overflowed with flowers. Writers and fans milled about in literary bliss, nibbling on crackers and cheese. Although we were fairly early, many had already scoped out seats at the linen-covered tables. Since we'd both been sitting most of the day we made our way to one of the taller ones without chairs that had been placed around the perimeter of the room.

"I'll go brave the bar line," I said. "You watch the table. Red, right?" She nodded, and I left her territorially guarding our spot while attempting to make eye contact with a waiter passing with a tray of cheese.

The line wove halfway through the room and I took my place in the rear. Knowing I had a long wait ahead of me, I scanned the crowd for familiar faces. Hearing Grace's insistent voice in my mind, I made a mental checklist of the people I must make an effort to mingle with before the night ended. It was then that I saw a mountain of lavender ruffles stomp through the doorway like a lioness stalking her prey, obviously searching for someone in particular. Sheila. I gasped.

I had convinced myself her earlier scene would have humiliated her enough that she wouldn't have the nerve to show up tonight. Then it hit me: Maybe it's me she's looking for. Please don't let her see me, I prayed, whirling around so I would be facing away from her. In my haste, I lost my balance and fell right into the person in front of me. He turned around, wiping a bit of brie off of his suit jacket.

"Do you mind?" Majeur! Would there be no end to my embarrassment? I smiled sheepishly. "Oh, it's you again," he said. "Can't stay out of trouble, can you?"

"I'm so sorry, it's…Sheila walked in, and I didn't want her to see me."

"Sheila?" Majeur's head snapped up and he looked around. "Where?"

"I don't know, she was just by the door. Look for yards of purple ruffles, you can't miss her—" I turned to help him look, his presence making me bolder. After all what could she do to me when he, a bestselling author, was around? He cut me off.

"Would you excuse me? I see someone I need to speak with."

"But you're next in line," I said, but he had already walked away. "Sorry again," I yelled at his retreating form.

His hasty departure struck me as a bit odd, but then I remembered I was the neophyte cat romance author who kept invading his personal space, and realized he was probably trying to escape my presence.

I got our drinks and went back to the table. Blythe and I

kept our eyes peeled for Sheila but we didn't see her again. Eventually I forgot about her and began to enjoy the party. I even regained my self-assurance after several fans interrupted to ask if I would sign their books while I was chatting with Ann Wolf, one of the top New York agents. No one mentioned the "incident" and I felt it was a pretty safe bet that I'd be asked back next year—and maybe be on the bestseller list by then and asked to be guest of honor. Well, okay, maybe just asked back. A girl can dream.

I was trying to follow a monologue on drop stitching by Nettie Carson, author of a popular cozy series about knitters, when Blythe interrupted and dragged me away.

"What? The chair is about to toast the guest of honor and I don't want to miss it."

"I saw the oddest thing! I was running up to the room to grab my lipstick, and I would swear I saw your purple assailant talking to Stöss Majeur out on the balcony."

"Maybe she's stalking him and followed when he snuck out? He implied she does things like that at every conference."

"I couldn't hear what they were saying, and it was pretty dark, but it seemed like the other way around."

"Oh my God! It looks like you're about to get your answer," I said, horrified.

"What? Where?"

I pointed toward the front of the room. Sheila staggered through the ballroom doors and unsteadily climbed the steps of the dais. Mickey went to grab her arm and guide her offstage, but she was faster. She elbowed him in the stomach, and took the live microphone out of his hand.

"I have an announcement..." Sheila slurred.

Every head turned to her, and the room that was a cacophony of voices only seconds ago immediately became quiet. No one wanted to miss the train wreck that would, no doubt, be fodder for the conference circuit for years to come.

"There are some authors here..." she continued. My stomach dropped. No. This couldn't be about me. She could ruin my reputation and my career with a few choice words. Blythe looked at me, eyes wide. We both sensed what was going to come next. But we were wrong.

Sheila raised her hand, ready to point out the offenders of whatever "crimes" she was about to elucidate, but instead her hand continued up to her throat and she emitted a small cough. Suddenly, one of the humungous chandeliers came crashing down onto the dais, crushing her in a cascade of glass, flowers and ruffles. Someone screamed.

Luckily, the hotel was only blocks from the Santa Monica PD headquarters. The police arrived less than ten minutes later. They cordoned off the dais, and announced that no one was to leave. Fortunately, the bar was still open, and these were mostly mystery writers and fans, so no one minded too much. I got another glass of wine and hung back to watch as the CSI technicians examined the frayed chandelier cord. Was this some kind of strange accident, or did someone intentionally loosen the chandelier?

Fiona Blackburn, writer of paranormal mysteries, interrupted my murderous musings. "Have you heard?" she asked, waving her glass of white wine excitedly. I shook my head, and waited for her to tell me that a ghost had been sighted in one of the conference rooms. "They're questioning the chair. Mickey's going to be arrested any minute now!"

"Really?" I found this hard to believe. I barely knew Mickey, but he had seemed very mild-mannered and eager to please the participants. I guess in this crowd you never knew, though.

"Well," she whispered. "Kerr Goldcross—she knows absolutely everybody—anyway, she told me that Mickey's complained for years about how that woman has ruined his conferences. He tried everything, but since he legally couldn't prohibit her from coming, maybe he took the matter into his own hands."

"Mickey was on the dais with her," I shot back. "He couldn't have dropped the chandelier."

"He's the one who makes all the hotel arrangements. We've had the conference here for years, so he's had plenty of time to get friendly with the staff. He could have bribed any one of them to rig it to fall."

Fiona's willingness to convict poor Mickey without a trial

made my head spin, and I thought I may have begun to hallucinate when Stöss Majeur unexpectedly appeared at my elbow with two glasses.

"Here's your wine. Do you have a moment to discuss that conference opportunity you mentioned outside?"

"Sure," I replied. I couldn't help looking confused. I had no idea what he was talking about, but I followed him, happy for the escape.

"Sorry, you looked like you needed rescuing," he said, once the crowd was safely behind us.

"Thanks, did I ever." Apparently I had been wrong about him avoiding me. He seemed thoughtful, not at all cold and distant like he had appeared before. "Fiona is certain that Mickey rigged the chandelier to fall on Sheila, which makes no sense at all. I mean, how could he know that she would choose that exact moment to hijack the microphone? It could have just as easily fallen on him as her." Majeur opened his mouth to reply, but I was still ranting. "She says they're about to arrest him, but I think that's ridiculous!"

"Oh?" He leaned casually against the railing. "Who do you think murdered her?"

"Who said it was murder? I know we all have death on the brain, considering what we do for a living and all, but chandeliers just don't fall on bad people in real life."

"Point taken. But, hypothetically. If this were a crime, who do you think would be behind it?"

"Hmm…" I mulled this over for a moment, sipping my drink. "Well, if I were the police, I suppose the first person I'd suspect would be, well, me. I mean, everyone heard her threaten to ruin my career this afternoon. As a new writer, maybe I took her seriously?"

I was really getting into the swing of this game. "Embarrassing me like she did in front of my fans and peers would be motive enough for me to want to kill her." I grinned at my own perceptiveness. "Jeez, I've almost convinced myself I did it. I sure hope the police don't reach the same conclusion," I joked. If I played my cards right, my plotting skills would impress him so much he'd want to read my "real" book.

"Funny, I was thinking along the exact same lines," he purred, moving closer.

Whoa. Maybe he thought my klutziness today was some kind of awkward attempt to hit on him? Little did he know that very few of my actions have that much forethought.

"Were you?" My words came out in a squeak. I scooted farther away. I didn't want to lead him on—merely pick his brain. "I'm surprised, I would have thought knowing Sheila as you do that you could have come up with a list of suspects with far older and bigger grudges."

"What do you know about me and Sheila?" He leaned in and loomed over me.

"N-nothing," my heart raced. This felt menacing, not like someone intent on romance. "Only what you told me—that she's been attending the conferences as long as you have."

He laughed, low and deep. He stood close enough that I could feel his breath ruffling my hair. "I gave you the clue in the elevator and you didn't put it together. I don't think you'll have a very long career as a mystery writer."

Clue? What clue? What was he talking about? I was on a balcony alone with the Stöss Majeur—and instead of being thrilled, I was terrified.

"I don't know what you're talking about," I tried to push away from him, but the railing dug into my back.

"Sheila and I go way back. I told you she's 'been around since I've been coming.' She only started coming to the conferences because I did."

I got a feeling of déjà vu, but couldn't put my finger on why. Oh, no! I've written this scene before! This is where the killer confesses! I looked around frantically for a way out of this mess. I could see the party still going on inside—compounded by the police investigation. No one was looking in my direction. Was it only this afternoon that I was praying to be outside?

"I met her when my first book came out," he continued. "It was an erotic mystery, under a different name, but the first of my Mariner series was already in the hands of a publisher. My agent had assured me I'd be on the bestseller list by next year. Then Sheila pulled a little trick like she did on you today.

The publisher got wind of what happened and killed the deal—said I wasn't fan-friendly. It took me five years to find someone else willing to publish it. In the meantime I had to return my advance. I lost my job, my house, my wife."

"But that was eons ago. You're one of the most popular writers in the world, you must have bags of money. Can't you, well…get over it?" Me and my big mouth.

"I had. But Sheila wouldn't let it go. She showed up at every signing and conference. I found out she was contacting my agents, publicist, manager and all my friends—stalking me, trying to ruin my career again. Her antics annoyed me, but eventually I learned to live with it. Until now. Somehow, Sheila found out that I hadn't actually written the Ranger series…"

The magnitude of what he had said hit me like a ton of bricks and I forgot about the precariousness of the situation. "What? You're kidding," I shrieked. "You don't write the Ranger series? I am so disappointed! Hold on, was that the announcement Sheila was about to make?"

"If anyone found out, it would ruin my career, and start a million lawsuits. I was about to lose everything again, all because of Sheila. I knew I had to stop her from making the announcement—stop her from making my life miserable, once and for all—then when I saw her threaten you, I knew it was the perfect opportunity…"

"What if the police arrest me? I'll tell them what you told me!" This isn't happening. This isn't happening.

"Like I said before, you don't have a long career ahead of you…merely a long fall." He bared his teeth as he nodded toward the balcony, and the fifteen story drop below. "They'll think you felt remorse for killing Sheila and jumped."

I squeezed my eyes closed. Well, at least I'll be famous now. Once I'm dead—and at the hands of one of the most famous writers of our time, no less—sales of my stupid cat series will go through the roof. Grace will love that. I wondered if I could survive if I landed on the portico awning—and if I should try to take Majeur with me when I went over the edge.

"Stop right there! Put your hands up and back away from

the girl!" a voice roared.

I forced open one eye and saw what must be the entire police force, guns drawn, pointing straight at Majeur. I collapsed as they cuffed him. Blythe came running, and enfolded me in a hug.

"You always did have a great sense of timing," I quipped feebly.

"Is this the man you saw, ma'am?" the officer interrupted, pointing at Majeur.

"Yes, that's him." Blythe answered. "He killed Sheila right here on this balcony."

"Wait...what?" I asked. "The chandelier fell on her in the ballroom."

Blythe took a deep breath. I can't believe this. I don't even get to do the brilliant reveal in my own life story? Then she continued, "I saw you leave the ballroom with Stöss, but I didn't think anything of it at the time except '*lucky girl.*' A few minutes later, the police took me aside so I could give them my statement. The CSI team leader interrupted to tell the officer that despite Sheila's obvious injuries, she had certain symptoms—swollen, discolored tongue and the like—that pointed to being poisoned, though, of course, they couldn't be sure until the ME looked at her. That backed up what Kerr told me earlier—she knows absolutely everything about everyone, you know."

I rolled my eyes as she continued on. "She said she'd never seen Sheila take a drink of wine all the years she'd been at the conference. When the policeman asked if I had seen Sheila talking or arguing with anyone that evening, I remembered seeing her with Stöss on the balcony—a perfect opportunity to slip something in her drink. The dropping chandelier was a red herring—an extremely well-timed coincidence. The cord supporting it was past due to be replaced and gave out, that's all. But when it fell, Stöss thought he'd gotten away with the perfect murder—"

I finished for her, trying to get my moment in the spotlight: "Until he overheard me talking to Fiona, and realized it wouldn't take the police long to discount the whole chandelier thing..."

"Exactly. And you were the next logical suspect for the police, so he took the first opportunity to get you alone. If you were dead, the case would be closed." Blythe finished with a self-satisfied smirk. There was a smattering of applause from the bystanders and colleagues who had gathered to witness the excitement.

"Excuse me, ma'am," the officer holding Majeur's cuffed arm interrupted. "Have you ever considered writing mysteries?" he asked Blythe.

That was all I could take for one day. I fainted. I remember thinking as I lost consciousness: This is not what I consider a vacation...

CHANTELLE AIMÉE OSMAN's flash fiction and short stories appear in anthologies, literary journals and e-zines. She is a founding member of The Sirens of Suspense, a group of authors who blog on all things writing and publishing (sirensofsuspense.com). In her other life, she is an attorney and owner of the script editing and consulting company, A Twist of Karma Entertainment (twistofkarma.com). Chantelle speaks on film and screenplay writing at conferences across the country. Her non-fiction book on screenwriting *Keys to the Kingdom* will be released October, 2010.

MOUNTAIN GETAWAYS

THE TRIP OF A LIFETIME
KRIS NERI

ROTTEN kids, Babs Frich thought. *Bunch of unappreciative brats.* She would make them pay for their ingratitude. She'd make them all pay. She was just one day away from finally getting back at this whole damn town.

Tomorrow, Babs would retire from thirty years of teaching at the Park Lane Elementary School. *More like serving a life sentence. Hard time.*

Well, maybe it hadn't been that bad at first. She had to admit she'd really loved it in the beginning. She'd gone into teaching with the hope of opening eager young minds, secretly dreaming of being honored as a great teacher. Only somewhere along the line, she ceased to care. Dreams, she learned in the course of this lousy life, don't come true. No sooner did she think she'd captured one, than someone came along and snatched that dream away.

Babs couldn't say when the decay set in, nor why exactly. Maybe it was seeing generation after generation of the same faces moving on with their lives, while she remained stuck in that dreary classroom. She'd taught a good many people in this town in her time, certainly many of the parents, possibly even grandparents, of her present students. Or maybe it was that there was nothing else in her life. No husband, no family of her own. Those dreams hadn't been realized, either.

After Principal O'Halloran's wife died, Babs thought there might have been a chance for something between her and "Dearest Peter," as she called him in her dreams. Sure, he was a few years younger than Babs, but sometimes she would catch him looking at her with such longing, and when they talked, he seemed to hang on her every word. It was still not too late for them to build something of a life together. Too bad he never even asked her out.

She took to nursing her wounds with vodka. After a while, Babs saw everything in life through that blurry glass. Now, tomorrow, thirty years of that pain would end.

And wouldn't you think *someone* would notice? No one had even mentioned her impending retirement. Not a single one of her students. Sure, she hadn't given much of an education to the ones she'd taught in recent years, and maybe she did take out her frustrations on them, but at least she gave them easy grades. She'd done a better job with their parents—what was their excuse for ignoring her? Didn't any of them look back fondly on their favorite teacher?

What about her colleagues? Wasn't she the one who always filled in for them when they couldn't make their after-school activities? Good old Miss Frich with nobody waiting at home could always be counted on in a pinch. Sure, the vodka got her through it. She didn't know how she'd have survived without a thermos of the stuff to sip throughout the day. Didn't they owe her, nonetheless?

Wasn't there anyone in this whole town who cared that she'd be retiring tomorrow?

The fear that they might all ignore this milestone in her life had been in the back of her mind, or revenge schemes wouldn't have kept surfacing in the final weeks. Still, the plan would not have come together if the perfect opportunity hadn't dropped in her lap the week before.

She should have noticed that she'd sipped a bit more vodka than usual that day when the thermos bottle ran dry by early afternoon. Yet she hadn't realized she'd tippled too much until she almost hit that high school boy, a real troublemaker, with her car on the way home from school, when she failed to see him in the crosswalk. With screeching brakes, her bumper came within inches of his legs and caused him to fall before the car. She threw open the door and raced around to the front of the car, horrified by what she'd done.

The close call had sobered her up instantly. She would have been ruined if she'd killed, or even hurt, a child. A near miss was bad enough. If the police came and realized she'd been drinking, she was sure to lose her miserable job and the pension that was all she lived for.

For once, luck was with her. When the boy tripped, a plastic bag filled with his stash of marijuana flew from his jacket pocket and landed on the street. When he finally noticed the bag, he grabbed for it. Fortunately, Babs reached it first.

She saw instantly how his pot could be the instrument of her revenge. But she had to make the deal quickly, before someone summoned the police to the near-accident. And she couldn't let the boy know how much it meant to her. Well, she hadn't spent thirty years pushing kids around for nothing!

She told the boy she would let him off with just a warning. Relief flooded his features. As wild as he was, he was still young and hadn't learned to hide his emotions. With his record, the least the little twerp could expect was to be expelled from school. Still, his insolence returned quickly.

"You're not as awful as I remembered," the boy said.

So this brat was one of mine. Good grief. Now she couldn't even remember them. Time to get out. His remark hadn't surprised her, either. She knew that behind her back they called her, "Miss Frich, the bitch." Naturally, the kid didn't protest when she confiscated his stash. She might have let him off easy, though a teacher wasn't about to give it back. The rude little bastard even recovered enough to suggest she try it. *No thanks, kid.* Vodka was her numbing agent of choice. Besides, she had other plans for that bag of dope.

Babs waited until the last minute to put her plan into effect, when she'd given up any hope of the getting the recognition she deserved. The afternoon before her final day, her anger gave her unaccustomed vigor as she rushed straight home from school. The kid she took the stash from had had enough marijuana for her to bake it into six pans of brownies. With only twenty-three kids in her class, she was able to cut a big piece of the tainted treat for each student.

She wrapped the pieces in gaily-colored wrapping paper left over from Christmas. After buying the paper, she'd decided she hadn't liked anyone well enough to buy a gift, so she had plenty left. She addressed each package to a particular child and signed them all with the anonymous tag, AN END-

OF-SCHOOL GIFT FROM A FRIEND. Babs packed the gift-wrapped brownies in a cardboard box that a case of vodka had come in and put it into her car.

The last day of school before the summer break was always a trial. The kids, normally too hyper to control, were worse than usual today. Yet Babs found herself drifting off, soul-searching. Didn't even load up on her usual quantity of vodka; by the close of the school day, her thermos was practically full. She kept asking herself whether she'd regret it if she allowed those tainted brownies to be delivered. When not one person remarked on her retirement, she decided this town deserved a scandal the likes of which it had never seen. She debated whether she should stay and watch her plan unfold. However, it seemed safer to make herself scarce.

She had planned to give herself the trip of a lifetime as a reward for making it through thirty years of teaching. She hadn't taken a vacation since those early years when she first started at the Park Lane Elementary School. She asked the local travel agent about a glamorous cruise along the Mexican Rivera. She thought she might even get her hair done and buy some new clothes, maybe even use a touch of makeup. But there was only one cabin left, and by the time she decided to book it, someone else had already taken it. Another dream snatched away from her.

It still seemed like a wise idea to leave town before the effect of those tainted brownies hit the fan. She'd just get into her car and keep driving. It didn't matter where she ended up. Maybe she'd never come back. Let her landlord close up the shabby house she hadn't cared enough to make into a cozy home. It would still be a vacation, yet it wouldn't be the trip of a lifetime that she'd hoped for. Someone had denied her that. *Crappy life.*

It occurred to Babs that if she'd done some of those things before—like fixing up her appearance or rewarding herself with a vacation—maybe she wouldn't feel so bitter now. No, she wasn't the problem. Her lousy students and this ungrateful town were. People were just too self-involved to thank a teacher who'd devoted her life to them.

Still, the doubts distracted her. After school on that final day, Babs tossed her thermos into the car, and it landed in the box of packaged brownies. Not wanting to take the time to remove it, she left it there, while she raced to the delivery service that one of her former students had opened downtown.

The shop was as crowded as she hoped. Even with an assistant, her former student was so overwhelmed by customers, he didn't seem to notice her at the end of the line. He was never a bright boy.

Babs lifted the box onto the end of the counter. She remembered to take her thermos from it and placed it on the counter beside it. Couldn't leave that thermos behind to give the game away. She was famous for carrying that thermos bottle wherever she went, and the cool "water" people probably assumed she sipped from it. She took a moment to tape an envelope to the outside of the box, which she stuffed with delivery instructions and a wad of cash.

When she reached for her thermos, she knocked it over and the cap came off, spilling vodka onto the counter. Fearful of attracting attention, Babs grabbed the thermos and left before anyone noticed her.

During her drive home, she seethed with anger at her colleagues' and students' lack of regard. But she really got them all this time. What a brilliant plan. Since most of her students' mothers worked, many of the kids would be home alone when those packages were delivered tomorrow. By the time their parents returned home, the little monsters would be stoned out of their already-inadequate minds.

She hoped they liked the experience so much, they'd all turn into hardcore drug addicts, though she knew that wasn't likely. At the very least, it might make them sick. Whatever the outcome, it would terrify their parents, and that fear would be their punishment. The students themselves would be shamed. With a little luck, it would all come down on Principal O'Halloran—*Dearest Peter*—since the enclosure notes on those gift-wrapped brownies referred to the school.

Babs noticed an unusual number of parked cars on her street when she went home, but didn't pay much attention. She drove into the garage and reached for her house key.

Funny, it wasn't on her key ring. She tried the doorknob, and it turned in her hand. The door was unlocked. Fearful of an intruder, Babs crept into her house.

"Surprise!" an orchestra of voices shouted.

Countless numbers of people jumped from hiding places: Teachers from school, her students, many of their parents, her neighbors, even *Dearest Peter.*

"You didn't think we'd let you retire without a party, did you, Babs?" Peter O'Halloran asked. "We even have a gift for you. We pooled our money and bought a ticket for a Mexican cruise that leaves tomorrow. You'll be able to make it, won't you?"

Babs stammered her thanks. She felt the blood drain from her face, leaving her woozy. If anyone thought she looked pale, she hoped they attributed it to pleasant surprise.

Once people drifted to other parts of the room, Peter took Babs aside. "I never thought it would be right to get involved with one of my teachers," he said, flushing. "Couldn't be impartial. Now that you're retired, do you think we might have dinner together sometime?"

Dinner with Peter? Babs couldn't believe it. *Why now?*

He reached into his jacket pocket for the cruise ticket. "That is, unless you have one of those wonderful shipboard romances with someone else."

The cruise! That was the perfect escape. Nobody would question her leaving, since they bought the ticket. Babs reached for it as the telephone rang. Peter offered to answer it, insisting that she go enjoy her party, taking the ticket with him. When he returned, his eyebrows were knitted together in an angry scowl.

"That was the young man who owns that new delivery service, Miss Frich," he said with cold formality. "Some liquid on the counter damaged the box you left there. When he moved it, the bottom broke and the packages opened. Since they were destroyed anyway, his assistant ate a brownie and discovered what you put in them. How could you, Babs? You tried to drug *children!*"

Fortunately, she still had her wits. Not too much vodka today. "I don't know what you mean. What makes you think that was my box?"

"It was just your bad luck that a former student of yours runs the place. He recognized the handwriting on your note. Said he could hardly forget the writing of his best teacher, the only one who took the time to help a slow student succeed. The police are on their way here, I'm sorry to say."

Principal O'Halloran glanced at the ticket envelope he still held in his hand. With a sigh, he tucked it back into his pocket.

Another of her dreams snatched away. It hit Babs how wrong she'd been. But it was too late. Now her trip of a lifetime would be to jail.

KRIS NERI's latest novels are *High Crimes on the Magical Plane* and *Revenge for Old Times' Sake*. Her novels have been nominated for such prestigious honors as the Lefty, Agatha, Anthony and Macavity Awards. She has published some sixty short stories, and is a two-time Derringer Award winner and a two-time Pushcart Prize nominee for her short fiction. Kris welcomes visitors to her website: KrisNeri.com.

HELL TO PAY
Barbara Goodson

A scream of fierce emotion and raw passion made the tiny hairs on the back of Tami's neck quiver.

"What the hell was that?" she asked.

"Elk," Clay answered, looking back at her. "In the fall they bugle. Sounds kinda like someone screamin'."

She held a hand over her eyes to shade her face against the morning sun and looked down the valley. Gold aspen leaves shimmered against the deep green of the spruce forest. The late August wind from the west carried another shriek. She shuddered and jammed her hands into the pockets of her jeans.

"Get movin," he growled through clenched teeth.

The stream they followed trickled over stones that looked as sharp and cold as broken glass.

"Maybe there's nothin' there," she said pulling her jacket tighter.

"It's there. He said it was didn't he?"

"Maybe he lied."

"He wouldn't lie to you. You're too pretty to lie to."

Too pretty to lie to. What a joke. Clay lied to her all the time. She wouldn't point that out. There'd be hell to pay if she did. A month ago he'd punched her square in the face because he thought she was being disrespectful. In the five years they'd been together he'd cracked two of her ribs, sprained her wrist, broken her nose and she'd suffered more bruises that she could count.

If she wasn't careful she'd be a blonde, green eyed forty-year-old with no teeth. Or a corpse. Tami knew he wasn't kidding when he said if she ever left him, no matter where she went, he'd find her…and kill her.

The morning sun splashed across the harsh, rocky trail. The thin light brought no warmth. She dipped her head and kept moving. Breathing was an effort at 9,000 feet.

"Can we stop?" she asked, shivering, wishing she'd worn gloves.

"We'll stop when we get there."

The smell of dust and rotting wood billowed around her. "He said he'd be there Friday."

"Never mind what he said."

THREE nights earlier, Clay had been comfortably slumped on his recliner, his eyes half open watching TV. He wasn't expecting a visitor. Certainly not a kid named Burnet who seemed like he might be kinda high. Not out-of-control high, just buzzed and talkative. He said he was some relation to Clay's Uncle Elliott. Clay couldn't remember ever hearing his name. But there were lots of relatives. In Clay's opinion they were all worthless.

Burnet had knocked on their door with a twelve-pack of beer and a story about needing a place to crash. Just for the night he said. He'd be gone in the morning.

Clay wasn't sure if Burnet knew he owed Elliott a couple thousand dollars. Collecting on the debt wasn't likely, at least not for a while. Elliott had recently begun a three to five year stay in the Arizona State Prison at Florence. So, even though Clay didn't care much for maintaining congenial family ties, he didn't want to get any hard feelings going. And the beer was welcome.

"Okay, you can stay." Clay said, rubbing one hand across his sagging belly. Then he added, "Just for the night."

"Thanks," Burnet said.

Before Burnet could say anything else Clay snatched the twelve-pack, ambled across the room, and flopped back onto his chair. With a contemptuous glance in Burnet's direction he set the beers on the floor, pulled one out, popped the top and sucked down half the can. He didn't offer one to Tami or Burnet.

Burnet didn't seem to care. He let the door slam shut behind him and started pacing around the room.

Tami kept her face turned toward the TV game show while surreptitiously watching Burnet. He was taller than Clay, and in better condition, like he lifted weights. She noticed he still had the watery eyes and twitchy moves of a doper. It didn't look like he'd dropped any of the old, bad habits.

Dragging his fingers through his tangled brown hair, Burnet wandered into the cramped kitchen. Tami sat on the couch without speaking. Having Burnet in the house could be dangerous. Even when he began to tonelessly hum, Tami continued to ignore him. Clay shot him a pissed-off look and turned up the volume.

Burnet kept moving, circling around the room. Every junky piece of furniture and random knickknack seemed to distract him. Eventually he came to the frayed couch. He leaned over the back and looked down at Tami. She kept her eyes straight ahead, adjusted her tank top and self-consciously pulled her hair back behind her ears.

"What's that?" he asked, pointing to a tattoo on her left shoulder.

Tami shrank back into the corner of the couch and ignored the question.

Clay's eyes narrowed. He stared at Burnet with feral intensity. "That ain't your concern."

Apparently, Burnet didn't catch the threat in Clay's voice. "Looks like a dog. Like a puppy dog."

Glowering at Burnet, Clay drained the beer and slammed the empty can down on the scratched coffee table.

Burnet prattled on. "I had a dog once. He was a stupid little thing, but I liked havin' him around." He paused, as if lost in happy reminiscence. A second later he shook his head sadly. "Somebody shot him. I think it was Elliott, he hates dogs." Burnet's mood shifted again and he grinned with crackbrained pleasure. "I'm gonna get me a puppy soon as I collect my money from Elliot."

Tami looked over at Clay. Hearing the word "money," he was suddenly, and dangerously, alert. He grabbed another beer and held it out.

"Want one?" he asked, ignoring the fact that, technically,

the beers were Burnet's.

"Sure."

Clay tossed him the can and pulled out another for himself.

"So, what's old Elliott got you doing?"

At that point Burnet seemed to realize that he might have said too much. He dipped his head and stared at the floor. Finally, scratching the back of his neck he gave Clay a cautious look, took a pull on his beer, and shrugged, "I don't know. Nothin' really."

"Don't give me that," Clay said sharply. "What're you doing for Elliott?"

A petulant tone crept into Burnet's voice. "Don't know for sure. He said I should go up to the ranch. Wants me to keep watch on some stuff. *I don't know what!*"

Clay shook his head in disbelief. "How you gonna watch something if you don't know what you're watchin'?"

"I forgot what he said. It was a couple days ago when he called."

Clay held Burnet in a slow and steady stare. Burnet shifted his weight from foot to foot. He stood directly under the ceiling fan but he was sweating. A tight smile crossed Clay's face. He dropped the empty beer can on the floor. Taking his time, he adjusted his T-shirt and got to his feet. Burnet opened his mouth to say something. Clay held up a hand to stop him and took a step in Burnet's direction.

Stumbling backward, away from Clay, Burnet stammered, "I don't know nothin'."

Clay gave Burnet a one-handed shove and stepped around him. With a sneer he pointed down a narrow hallway. "I gotta pee. When I come back I'll tell you what we're gonna do."

Burnet jammed his hands into the back pockets of his jeans and tried, unsuccessfully, to look nonchalant.

As soon as Clay was out of sight Tami twisted around and leaned over the arm of the couch. "You know what you've done?" She spoke in a scared whisper.

Burnet frowned in concentration. "What? What'd I do?"

Speaking louder, but still whispering, she pleaded. "Get

out of here."

Running a hand through his hair he squeezed his eyes shut. He seemed to be struggling to figure out his next move. A moment later he opened his eyes and gave an uncertain grin. "It's no big deal."

"What? What's no big deal? You better be ready to tell him what you're doing for Elliott. If you don't you're gonna get a serious ass kickin.'"

"It's no big deal," he repeated, creasing his forehead. "It's just that Elliott says there's some gold coins up at his ranch. Place was his Grandpa Ben's. The story he told me was that in the old days Ben ran with the Butch Cassidy gang. When them boys robbed the bank in Telluride they headed up the mountain to Ben's place. The gold they carried was real heavy so they hid some on Ben's ranch. Elliott says some of it's still there and he don't want nobody goin' through his stuff and findin' it."

Tami rolled her eyes and shook her head.

Burnet began to crack the knuckles of his left hand, "Could be true I guess," he said, avoiding Tami's gaze. "Then again Elliott mighta made the whole thing up. I wouldn't put it past him. I don't really care. I'm gettin' a ride up to Telluride on Friday. When I get there I'm just gonna drink beer and do nothin' till Elliott gets out. When he does, he's givin' me a thousand dollars."

Tami shook her head in frustration and repeated, "Get out before Clay comes back."

Burnet licked his lips and tried to chug down the rest of his beer. His hand shook before he got the can to his mouth and he spilled some down the front of his shirt. He sheepishly put the can down, shrugged defiantly, and gave Tami a nervous smile.

Tami didn't return the smile. "Unless you're suicidal, you better get the hell outta here."

Burnet shook his head as though that might clear out the booze and the drugs. "Okay, then I'm goin'." But he didn't move.

Tami twisted her hands together and almost yelled. "Move your butt. I mean it."

Burnet strolled across the room, opened the door and stepped across the threshold. He stopped, turned back and gave Tami a dopy grin and a thumbs-up. With that, he quietly shut the door.

Tami collapsed back on the couch and pretended to be engrossed in the TV show. Before she could get her breathing completely under control, Clay wandered back into the room. He dragged a hand across his lips, adjusted his drooping jeans and looked around the room. Shaking his head he returned to his recliner.

Tami waited for Clay's reaction. She expected violence. Clay surprised her. He didn't seem to notice, or care about, Burnet's departure. She burrowed deeper into the saggy couch and let herself pretend nothing bad would happen. Clay opened another beer and ignored her.

Two beers later Clay burped loudly, then announced, "We're goin' on vacation. Leavin' tomorrow. Headin' up to Telluride."

Tami looked at him for a long minute. "You heard?" she finally asked.

Clay smirked, "Course I heard. In this place you can hear a fly fart from the backyard. I knew that dumbass little tweaker'd tell you everything." He adjusted his wide butt on the recliner and muttered, "We're goin' on vacation and if there's any gold up there we're getting it. Gold coins from the eighteen eighties? To the right guy they'd be worth some major bucks."

TWO days later Clay led Tami up Mt. Emma, heading for a shack that Elliott called a ranch. She'd made this trip before, two years ago when Clay thought there was a warrant out for him in Phoenix. She remembered the route. Now she struggled to negotiate a narrow section of the trail that clung to the side of a steep gorge.

Clay was well ahead of her, moving along the switchbacks that followed the canyon wall. In the spring a torrent of snow melt would plunge down the nearly vertical drop. Now, after a dry summer, water barely trickled over the rocks.

Ten yards ahead Clay moved toward the shade of a

massive granite outcrop. Tami stopped. For a single second she thought she saw something metallic glimmer in the shadows. As she watched, Clay came to an abrupt halt. He leaned forward, peering around the shoulder of the great rock. He seemed unable to make sense of what he was seeing.

Tami scrambled up the narrow path until she came up behind him. Clay wasn't alone. Burnet stood blocking the trail with an automatic pistol aimed at Clay's head.

"Sonofabitch," Clay said.

Burnet stood motionless, silhouetted against the clear Colorado sky. The gun gleamed as he gave a tight-lipped grin. "I hear you been beatin' on my big sister." He nodded at Tami and continued. "I been away down in Florence for a while, but I'm here now. You gotta' know you can't get away with that. Sooner or later there's gonna be hell to pay."

Clay hunched his shoulders and took a menacing step forward. "Gimme that gun."

Without any visible emotion Burnet shook his head, gripped the gun with both hands and squeezed the trigger. The sound of the shot boomed around them and reverberated down the canyon like a clap of thunder. Clay jumped back as the bullet smashed into a piece of granite a few feet away. Shards of the rock went flying, ripping into Clay's legs.

In less than a second, Clay wheeled around, shoved Tami into the bushes, and began a desperate retreat. Burnet followed. Clay slipped and slid fighting for balance on the rocky path. He was surprisingly agile. But the race was over before it was run. Burnet was younger, faster and he had the gun. Burnet took his time, letting Clay scramble like a bleeding, injured animal through the rubble and loose stones.

Clay struggled on until, twisting around to cast a panicked glance over his shoulder, the stony soil slipped beneath his feet. He lost his footing, lurched backward, stumbled and teetered on the edge of the precipice. In desperation he flailed wildly at the thin air. With one swift motion Burnet stepped forward and smashed his fist into Clay's face. Clay toppled back, off the sheer rock wall.

A scream of fierce emotion and raw terror echoed down

the canyon and made the tiny hairs on the back of Tami's neck quiver. She looked up. High above, a small black bird caught an updraft and soared over the canyon.

Tami smiled.

BARBARA GOODSON is a graduate of the University of California, Irvine. She has contributed a travel article to the *Chicago Tribune* and has recently completed a contemporary mystery, EARTHQUAKE WEATHER. Over the years she has worked as a graphic designer, illustrator, and teacher. Barbara now lives in Arizona and is a member of the Desert Sleuths chapter of Sisters in Crime.

COWGIRLS DON'T CRY
JUDY STARBUCK

"There comes a time when you're gonna get bucked and you're gonna need to know what to do so you don't get stepped on."

- Betsy Swain, 1875

MY name is Annie O'Dell, and I've rafted the Rogue River in Oregon, bicycled through New England, hiked the Appalachian Trail, and kayaked in Kauai. When I heard a cowgirl described as "full of sass, strong as a bull, and proud as a peacock," I knew the Wild West was the perfect spot for my next adventure vacation.

I made reservations to attend the World's Oldest Rodeo in Prescott, Arizona over the Fourth of July. My flight from Minnesota arrived in Phoenix mid-morning and I walked from the terminal into a wall of dry summer heat. Dry as a four-hundred-degree oven. I cranked the air conditioning up full blast in my rental car and headed for Scottsdale to get outfitted at the local western wear store.

The saleswoman at Saba's Western Wear showed me a variety of outfits. Each expressed a different attitude, anywhere from sexy to subdued. I chose a few items that showed off my shape, but when I told her I was going to the rodeo alone, she said, "Why honey, let's tone it down a bit. There are some cowboys you need to watch out for. They aren't there for the rodeo. A pretty little thing like you ought to be real careful."

"Thanks for the warning. I intend to keep to myself and see what this rodeo business is all about. I've never been to Arizona, so after Prescott I'm going to Sedona, the Grand Canyon, and Monument Valley."

"Well, I'm sure you'll be fine." She paused then added, "Just don't go anywhere alone at night."

I bought a black top embellished with rhinestones, a pair of Justin aged bark boots in a cognac ostrich print, two Vintage snap front shirts in red and turquoise, and the requisite cowboy hat. My favorite purchase was a pair of Rock and Roll Cowgirl jeans with rhinestone peace signs on the back pockets.

The drive from Phoenix to Prescott was a four thousand foot climb. The dusty colorless terrain outside of Phoenix changed dramatically when I reached the Verde Valley. It was a "wow" moment. The dry desert suddenly was covered with grassy mounds. Cottonwoods and lush sycamores edged the winding streams. Tall rock formations seamed with rusty red jutted straight up out of the desert. I lowered the car window and breathed in cool air that held a faint smell of pine.

At the Cordes Junction turnoff, the procession into town turned painfully slow. Folks from all parts hauled horse trailers around the bend leaving little opportunity to pass. I took a deep breath, settled back, and cranked up my iPod. Garth Brooks got me in the spirit with "Rodeo" and "The Dance," and Reba McEntire twanged, "I Want a Cowboy."

In Prescott I stopped first at Courthouse Square. The grounds of the historic courthouse were adorned with large shade trees. Surrounding the square were restaurants, shops and Whiskey Row. The lady at Saba's recommended the Jersey Lilly Saloon which was right next door to the famous Palace Bar. The sign outside stated, A PROPER DRINKING ESTABLISHMENT FOR GENTLEMEN AND LADIES. I climbed the stairs and sidled my way through the crowded bar to a tiny table by the balcony overlooking the square, a perfect spot to observe the local color. Wedged between families, couples, and rowdy cowboys, it was easy to get into a conversation.

In the background Hank Black and the Ropers played a live version of the Brooks and Dunn song, "Cowgirls Don't Cry." When they got to the refrain, the crowd joined in.

One particular cowboy seemed to draw a lot of attention. Two teenage cowgirls held out rodeo posters for him to autograph. He signed them with a flourish then flashed a million-dollar smile at the crowd in general. They wriggled and giggled all the way down the stairs before letting out squeals.

I turned to a lady sitting near me and asked, "Is he a celebrity?"

"Heck yes, honey, that's Hollywood Haynes, the famous rodeo clown. His real name is Craig, but he's so handsome everybody calls him Hollywood. He refers to himself as a bullfighter, but he can sure entertain the crowd with his clown antics when he's in the ring."

After waiting for some time, I realized I'd have to get myself over to the bartender if I wanted some food. I edged my way up to the bar and placed my order. About ten minutes later, with a cool tall one in one hand, and a huge cheeseburger platter in the other, I headed back to my table.

As I passed Hollywood, he swung toward me. "Well, hello, darlin'. Haven't seen you around."

I gave him a tentative smile. "I haven't been around," and kept walking.

I took a slow satisfying swig of beer and saw Hollywood moving toward me. He took a chair from a nearby table and sat down across from me.

"You're mighty purty to be here alone, darlin'. Waitin' for someone?"

"Yes. I'm meeting friends." I wasn't about to tell this arrogant rodeo Romeo that I was alone.

"Are they as good lookin' as you?"

Talk about cow dung, but I played along. "No, not nearly."

He put his hand on mine. "Well, in that case, my name is Hollywood Haynes. I always go for the best."

I pulled my hand away. "Well, I always wait and check out the choices." I took a whopper-sized bite of my cheeseburger. The long drive had left me ready to do some serious eating. Besides, with my mouth stuffed I didn't have to deal with this phony. He gave me his trademark smile and told me he'd see me around. I nodded and finished my meal in peace.

When I picked up my backpack and worked my way out of the bar, Hollywood followed me down the stairs. He obviously knew how manly he looked, packed just right into his Wranglers. He had mastered the art of holding a gaze with his sky-blue eyes that made a woman feel warm clear down to the soles of her boots. Just the kind of guy the woman at Saba's had warned me about.

Standing much too close, he asked, "Where you stayin', sweetheart?"

"With a friend." I moved back to put some space between us. "Those purty women in the bar are waiting for you."

He sneered, "We call 'em buckle bunnies. Like I said, I always go for the purtiest."

"Well, good for you." I turned and walked away. My car was parked a block from the center of town. As I got in I looked back and noticed Hollywood stood with a group of men and stared at me. I locked my doors, backed out, and hit the gas.

The cabin I had reserved was twelve miles from town in an area called Skull Valley. Off the highway, I turned onto Tough Country Trail, a twisting, bumpy road that took me to a forty-acre ranch tucked beneath Granite Mountain. When I finally reached my destination I was awestruck by the rustic beauty of the place and let out a relieved sigh.

"Welcome to Spirit Ranch," said my cordial host Dave when I walked into the office. He and his wife, Linda, showed me to an isolated cabin at the far edge of the property. "You're lucky you made reservations last fall. Rodeo Days are mighty busy and we fill up early. This is the choice spot here at the ranch. We call this cabin Granite Rose. It has the very best views."

The centerpiece of the one room cabin was a stone fireplace with a mantle that showcased a well-used cowboy hat, a lariat, and an antique leather mailbag. A distressed-leather couch, draped with Navajo blankets, faced the fireplace. I set my bag down and Linda showed me how to use the gas stove and work the shower.

A fully equipped kitchen with a farm table was placed at one end, and I unloaded the food and drinks I had purchased on the way. The bed featured a tooled-leather headboard and footboard and was angled into the other corner. It was covered with an overstuffed quilt and serape print pillows.

I glanced around the room. "I don't see a phone."

"We don't have them in the cabins but you're welcome to use the office phone for local calls."

I looked down at my cell phone. The display read NO SERVICE.

LATER, on the porch, I listened to the breezes sweep through the thousand-year-old junipers. My dinner consisted of cheese and crackers, fruit and chardonnay. When a wave of tiredness came over me I decided to call it a day.

Closing the shutters, I locked myself in as tight as possible in the old cabin. The creatures of the desert serenaded me as I slid under the covers with a book and dozed off into a deep dreamy sleep.

THE next morning at the rodeo, I found the stands packed with people of all ages excitedly waiting for the show to start. They shouted and clapped. I settled on my seat and took in the unique smells of broncs and bulls. Soon the crowd stood and cheered as the Rodeo Queen rode in carrying a huge American flag. The men held their cowboy hats to their chests and the women placed their hands over their hearts as everyone sang the national anthem.

A tall and lean cowboy caught my attention as he walked up the aisle then stopped at my row. He looked at the empty seat next to me and worked his way over. After he tipped his hat, he smiled, held out a calloused hand, and said, "Levi Carter. Folks call me Lightning."

I shook his hand and smiled back, captivated by his clear blue eyes and sun-streaked hair pulled into a ponytail. "My name is Annie."

The competition began and after I told him I had never gone to a rodeo before, Levi gave me a blow-by-blow description of each upcoming event. First on the docket was the bareback bronc riding then calf roping. I flinched when the lariat jolted the calf to a stop and the cowboys flipped it on its back and tied three of its legs together. I felt sorry for the animals, but Levi assured me that the rodeo animals were better cared for than most house pets.

"So Annie, I'm gonna guess you're not from around here. Your accent gives you away. I'd say North Dakota or Minnesota."

"You're right on the mark. Where are you from?"

"All around. I used to rodeo. Got banged up pretty good." He showed me the scars on his arms. "After the bull got me the last time, I took some time off." He grew quiet.

I watched the events on the edge of my seat. The cowboys mounted their rides in the chute, and when the gate opened, they burst out. Some stayed mounted for the allotted time. Some didn't. I closed my eyes when they fell, expecting spilled blood or broken bones.

Finally the bull riding began, the main event of the day. The excitement of the crowd grew. The announcer warmed up the crowd. "Ladies and gentlemen, welcome the one, the only, Hollywood Haynes, the world famous bullfighter."

The crowd laughed as a potbellied clown-faced cowboy entered the ring, dressed in a red and white striped shirt and green pants held up with huge yellow suspenders. I never would have guessed this clown in heavy makeup was the hunk from Jersey Lilly's. He waved his hat to the crowd and began performing his antics accompanied by shouts and whistles of approval.

When the bulls exploded out of the chutes and their riders were bucked or they jumped off at the sound of the buzzer, Hollywood moved in with split second reflexes to divert the bull's attention away from the fallen cowboy. He rolled a bright red barrel from the side, jumped inside and waved his arms at the bull. Just at the last minute he ducked down as the bull charged it. Levi called the barrel a "clown lounge" or "Porta-Potty."

The announcer bellowed. "Look at what Hollywood just did. He risked his life to save that rider from sure death at the horns of that half-ton bull. He has the most dangerous job at this here rodeo, folks." The crowd roared.

I turned to Levi. "What did you do when you competed?"

With a resigned look on his face he said, "A little of this, a little of that." He paused. "They called me Lightning cuz I moved so fast."

"Well, I'm sure you were just as good at what you did as Hollywood. And a whole lot nicer."

"You met up with him?"

"Let's just say I caught his act over at Jersey Lilly's."

Levi nodded, seeming to get my point.

Hollywood continued to protect the riders from the testosterone-charged bulls as he entertained the crowd. Competing in a rodeo wasn't an adventure I ever planned to pursue, but was impressed nonetheless by the athleticism of the cowboys and the enthusiasm of the crowd.

At the end of the festivities, the announcer reminded the crowd about the Rodeo Dance. "At seven o'clock tonight at the dance you might meet some of the rodeo contestants and clowns, and you lovely ladies can enter the Prescott Goes Nuts for Wrangler Butts Contest." That sounded like something you wouldn't see in Minnesota.

"Do you plan to go to the dance tonight?" Levi asked.

"For a little while."

"Are you staying around here?"

"No. Out in Skull Valley."

"Well, nice to meet you, Annie. Hope you enjoyed your first rodeo."

WITH two hours to spare, I drove back to Courthouse Square. The aroma of spicy beef, popcorn, salty pretzels and sweet pastries lured me over to the food vendors set up on the grassy square. I sampled the BBQ beef sandwiches and Indian Fry Bread, washing them down with Arizona Tea.

The crowd began to gather at Matt's Saloon for the biggest rodeo party in town. When the music began, I watched from the sidelines. People of all ages streamed in and began to dance to the sound of the band, Western Fusion. Mindful of the warning from the lady at Saba's, I wanted to leave before it got dark and the crowds got drunk and unruly.

Edging my way toward the door, I watched a young couple "kick it" in the middle of the dance floor. I was startled when strong hands gripped my shoulders from behind. I whirled around, looked into Hollywood's eyes and smelled the whiskey on his breath.

"Why there you are, darlin'. I knew I'd get a dance with you."

"Sorry. I was just leaving." I turned toward the door.

He grabbed my arm. "You'll be sorrier if you say no again."

"No. Again." I shrugged his hand off my arm, spun around and hightailed it out of there. I wasn't great at sprinting in my new boots, but gave it all I had. By the time I reached the car my lungs burned and my calves were cramping.

THE road out of town was bumper to bumper with other rodeo folks. I drove to Spirit Ranch and spotted a group sitting around an open fire in front of the main house. I parked at my cabin and took the trail back to join them. Linda and Dave introduced me to some friendly folks who had rented the other cabins. The blazing fire and upbeat conversation elevated my mood and I stayed until the last of them left.

A couple from Wickenburg walked me to my isolated cabin and we agreed to meet in the morning and ride to town for some breakfast at the Iron Springs Cafe. I mentioned the cowboy who had been following me and they told me the town was full of guys looking for a good time.

The husband assured me that the creep would move on to another woman. "I hear that guys around here are outnumbered. The town's full of lonely women."

"Yeah, but he's not just any cowboy. Ever heard of the rodeo clown called Hollywood Haynes?"

"Sure have. All the more reason he'd have his pick of women."

We said goodnight. The husband took his wife's hand and they headed toward their cabin.

I let myself into Granite Rose, locked the door, and went into the bathroom. I washed my hands and was about to take off my boots when I heard the sound of gravel crunching outside my cabin. Peeking out the tiny window, I saw a man stumble out of a dark pickup. A sick feeling shot through me.

Looking for something to defend myself with, I yanked open the linen closet. The arsenal consisted of an iron, ironing board, a hair dryer, and various aerosol cans. I settled on the wasp spray. Maybe it could buy me some time if shot directly into someone's eyes.

Switching off the light, I walked to the fireplace and reached for the poker, then turned toward the open shutters on the front window. The smiling face of a clown was pressed into it.

Suddenly there was a loud slam and the flimsy door flew open. The clown rushed at me, spun me around and pushed me face-first into the stone fireplace, scraping my skin, cracking my nose, and blurring my vision. The wasp spray and poker flew from my hands. Blood streamed from my nose and my brain reeled.

"City gal thinks she's too good for a cowboy?" He slurred. "Well, this cowboy'll show her." His foul whiskey breath blasted me. "There's no horse 'cain't be broke. Same goes fur a woman."

Hollywood yanked me back around, pressed himself against me, and ran his hands up and down my body, then tore open my shirt. I pounded at him as cool air shocked my bare skin. I tried to push him away but he held tight. He slid his hands down to the back pockets of my jeans. "I'm havin' me a piece of that," he muttered.

I tried again to fight him off but he worked his hands up to my neck. As he squeezed the air out of me, rage replaced my fear. I stomped on his foot with my boot, twisted to the right, and sent a mean jab of my elbow into his ribs. Caught off guard, he released me. I whirled around and kneed him in the groin. He bellowed, bent over, and lost his footing.

Down on one knee, he clutched his crotch, and glared at me through bloodshot eyes. "You little bitch. You're gonna pay for that." He struggled to stand.

I picked up the wasp spray and let him have it right in his red eyes. He howled and covered his face with one hand while he came at me blindly with the other. I grabbed the fireplace poker and slammed it onto the back of his head with all the angry force I had. He staggered and fell, hitting his head on the stone hearth, then lay still.

Determined to keep him from getting away, I grabbed the lariat on the mantel and tied his hands and feet together just as I'd seen them do in the rodeo.

"Not bad for a city girl," I muttered as I stumbled out the front door. I looked down. What remained of my shirt was torn. His red, white and black clown paint was smeared all over me. My face felt like a thousand bees had stung it and I could barely swallow. My new boots had blistered both feet and my tight jeans chafed against my thighs. Fear propelled me forward, but the rocky path tripped me up. I landed on the ground with a painful thud.

On hands and knees, struggling to stand, I saw a truck coming toward me. I didn't know who to trust around here so I crawled to the side of the path in case this was yet another drunken cowboy. I wasn't fast enough. The driver slammed on his brakes and jumped out.

"Whoa, Annie. Is that you?"

Squinting through swollen and gritty eyes, I saw Dave. Another man with dark hair and eyes got out and came over with him. Still on hands and knees, I backed away.

Dave held out a hand to help me up. "Oh my Lord, girl, what happened to you?"

His partner kept repeating, "Madre de Dios," as he stared at me.

"This is Vincente. He was cleaning up around the fire pit when he saw a truck swerving erratically and headed toward your cabin. He came to find me. What happened?"

I choked out the words. "Back in cabin...man... cowboy...attacked. Clown...Hollywood." I held my torn shirt to my chest as I struggled to catch my breath.

"Are you telling me a cowboy attacked you?" Dave handed me his jacket so I could cover myself.

I nodded and pulled in a deep breath.

"In your cabin?"

I nodded again.

"Where's he now?"

My breathing began to slow and my heart settled a bit so that I could speak. "Still there. Call the sheriff…"

Dave ran to his office and made the call then he and Vincente helped me back to my cabin. When they walked in and took a look, Dave shook his head. "Whoa. How did a little thing like you handle this big guy?" Vincente stood open-mouthed.

I shrugged.

Just then we heard crunching on the gravel. Dave said, "The sheriff couldn't get here this soon." He stepped outside to check.

Dave didn't come back in alone. Hollywood Haynes was by his side.

I gasped then pointed at the man tied up on my floor. Who's that?"

My attacker began to wriggle and groan. His eyes flashed open and he glared at me with hate. "You little bitch." He tried working out of his restraints, but I must have tied them plenty tight.

Hollywood moved over to take a better look. "It seems you had your own private rodeo with Lightning Carter."

I looked down at my rodeo seatmate. "Why would he do that?"

"It's a long story, but the short version is that Lightning's never gotten over losing his job as a rodeo clown. This isn't the first time he's tried to impersonate me. I've had to fight off rumors for some time over some unfortunate incidents where he used my name. He saw me talking to you at the dance and confronted me. I figured you might be in trouble when he called you Annie and said you were staying in Skull Valley."

"But why did he go after me?"

"You were convenient. He still hopes to get his job back by discrediting me," Hollywood said. "He probably didn't expect to meet his match in a bitty thing like you. I had a bad feeling and came out to check on you. And to apologize for my rude behavior."

Even through the pain I couldn't hold back a smile. I had tamed two bullfighters in one night.

AN hour later, after a Sheriff's deputy questioned me, he carted Lightning away. Apparently I wasn't the first city girl this clown had tried to charm using Hollywood's name. When asked if I would press charges, I said, "Absolutely."

The deputy handed me his digital camera so I could see the extent of my injuries. My eyes were already ringed with yellow and I figured they would soon turn black. Blood and paint smeared across the chafed skin on my face. My neck showed purple impressions from Lightning's grip.

The sheriff suggested the emergency room, but at the moment all I wanted was a hot shower and Motrin. Pain radiated from my chest and shoulders and it was hard to swallow or talk through my bruised throat. My nose throbbed. I figured this was how cowboys and cowgirls must feel after a rodeo.

Linda offered me another cabin, free of charge, for the next few days so I could recuperate. I accepted her offer to stay on, but told her I wanted to stay in Granite Rose. Although anxious to get on with my trip, I needed to stay right here and process what had happened. I certainly could say I'd had an adventure vacation of an unexpected kind.

Hollywood had hung around and just before he left, paid me a compliment any western woman would like to hear. "I have to say, you were one tough cowgirl. You never shed a tear."

"Well, you know what they say... 'Cowgirls Don't Cry'."

JUDY STARBUCK is a Scottsdale teacher, handwriting analyst, and mystery writer. Her short story "The Sun Also Sets," is included in the award-winning anthology, *Map of Murder,* and "Neither Rare Nor Well Done" in another award-winning anthology, *Medium of Murder.* "The Christmas Stalking" is included in *How NOT to Survive the Holidays,* and "Liar" in *Mystery in the Wind.* She is involved in adoption search and support groups, is an Arizona-certified Confidential Intermediary, and an active member of Sister in Crime.

MURDER AT THE TOADSTOOL CAFÉ
CONNIE FLYNN

"WATCH out!" Clara warned, bracing herself against a pixie attack.

I ducked, flailed my arms in an unmanly way, and caught one of the metal and plastic beasties on the fly. A flattened and brightly painted face flashed a grotesque smile at me. "Damn pests." Resisting an urge to squash its triple A battery powered body, I raised my hand to cast it into the morning air—hopefully to outer space. It joined its pesky buddies and swooped down on a bunch of giggling school children, who declared the mechanical monstrosities "cute" and "adorable."

I guided Clara past a for-sale sign, up a flower-edged path. We were at Faerie World, an amusement park with a theme of Old World magical creatures. We headed to the Village Commons, a circular group of buildings that included a large gift shop—*ka-ching, ka-ching*—the Faerie Dell Chapel, the Gaol—aka the jail—the Olde Ice Cream Shoppe, and the Toadstool Café. Various costumed characters roamed the paths and cries of joy and terror came from the busy rides.

In the center stood a stone cottage where visitors bought entrance tickets and were given maps of the grounds. I guided Clara inside, feeling *pixied* by nagging thoughts that I really should tell her why we were here in the owner's office.

A large, loose-limbed guy with a slightly receding hairline almost dwarfed his antique desk and the cramped office it occupied. His nameplate read Hank Carmichael. He waved us over and I introduced myself as Derek Shriver, co-owner of Christmasland. When I introduced Clara, his pen slipped from his fingers and he almost knocked over his coffee cup. I smothered a smile as we sat down across from him. Clara affected men that way, and I generally tried not to gloat. A few minutes later, Hank and I sank deep into negotiations and I forgot all about my lovely bride-to-be.

"I'm leveling with you, Derek." Hank leaned closer, his voice low. "Ignore the P&L end numbers. We did make a profit last year."

"Yeah?" I said. "Maybe you should've plowed some of it back into the park."

On our walk through the Commons, I had spied a few closed attractions. Many of the ticket booths were long past needing paint. Admitting the unclaimed profit was a risky thing to do, but not all that strange. Most amusement park owners were kids in adult bodies when it came to managing a business.

The minute I'd spotted the sign I knew this was an opportunity not to be missed. Just think, Clara and I would own Christmasland *and* Faerie World. A grand beginning for an amusement park empire. I gently nudged my lovely companion. "What do you think?"

Clara turned a slick brochure over in her hands. FAERIE WORLD it read. LAND OF THE MAGICAL. The text claimed it was a premier attraction of the Arkansas Ozarks, which my fact checking had proven reasonably true—I mean, some exaggeration was expected.

Looking unimpressed, Clara whispered, "But we're on vacation, Derek. Our wedding is tomorrow."

I frowned, puzzled. "Did you think I forgot?"

"What? No! It's just that…" She pushed her chair back and leapt up. "Do what you want! I'm going to find a ladies room."

"Clara…"

But she'd already raced out. I looked back at Hank, who stared through the open door. "Doesn't your girlfriend like the property?"

"I don't think that's the issue," I said, the accountant in me warring with my need to soothe Clara's ruffled feathers.

A loud bang ripped through the air. A startled scream followed.

"Clara!" I bolted for the door and ran out of Hank's office.

Outside, I vaulted a low fence. People were pouring from

the Toadstool Café, shouting, "He's been shot! Help! He's been shot!" Park medics rushed up the path, but Clara was the only thing in my mind. I saw her standing amid a crush of people at the edge of the huge mushroom canopy that gave the Toadstool its name. My heart started beating again and I hurried toward her.

Yelling would have been pointless over the noisy confusion, so she shook her head, mouthing, "Stop him, stop him." She pointed to the heavily wooded dell behind the café. "He's getting away."

A scarecrow of a figure dashed toward the woods and, idiot that I am, I took chase. I should know better by now. These things never turn out well.

"Stop!" I shouted. "*Now,*" as though he actually would. But, no, on he went and my legs pumped like crazy to catch up.

When we entered the dell I was right on his heels. The ferns and branches grabbed at me like living fingers. The light had nearly vanished beneath the huge trees. The pixies sped down at me with maniacal glee, then veered up just before colliding with my scalp. My quarry brushed them away with ease, but I felt like I was being swarmed by gnats. Those pests would be the first thing to go after I bought this place. While I was having that misplaced thought, the man disappeared. What the hell? Where had he gone?

The path hadn't veered. I considered slowing to a walk, but something told me he was ahead. Maybe there was a fork just around the bend.

A shrill wail sent a centipede of shivers down my back. Then I realized the banshee cry came from the roller coaster so I kept on running. Sure enough, the path split. Going on pure instinct, I took the left fork. The wail sounded again and a skeletal man stepped from behind a tree. Tall, inhumanly thin, he stared at me with empty eyes. My ears vibrated in protest and I clamped my eyes shut for an instant. The next moment, cold steel pressed against my hand and my index finger automatically slipped through the trigger.

When I opened my eyes, the apparition had flown the coop and I was holding a mighty heavy Colt forty-five.

The long barrel of the revolver was still warm to the touch. I sniffed the acrid scent of gun powder. The murder weapon for sure.

And the last thing I wanted was my fingerprints all over the place. Since the hammer wasn't cocked, the gun wouldn't discharge accidentally and I held it loosely as I circled back toward the park.

"DEREK! Derek!" Clara raced toward me, dark curls bouncing around her lovely face, I was struck once more with gratitude that this matchless beauty wanted to marry me. If I hadn't still been holding the Colt I would have broken into a gallop to meet her.

"Are you okay, sweetheart?"

She nodded, hurrying to me. Capping my face in her hands, she murmured, "I was so worried," then she kissed me...as only Clara can kiss. I wanted to crush her in my arms. Unfortunately, I still held the humongous revolver and I didn't want to accidentally shoot my beloved in the foot.

"Clara," I whispered against her lips. "You are the *light* of the light of my life, but..." A tiny waggle of the gun caught her attention.

"Oh..." She stepped back and stared down. "Oh, that's huge. Where did it come from?"

"The guy I chased shoved it in my hand."

"Uh-oh."

"That's all you have to say?"

She shrugged. "What're we going to do with it?"

We. I loved the reassuring sound of that. "Turn it in to the police."

"Say again."

I tried to figure out what might be causing the compressed white line around my darling Clara's luscious red lips.

"The wedding," she clarified, looking very unhappy. "What about the wedding?"

Our Faerie Dell Chapel ceremony was scheduled between two and four tomorrow. We'd reserved the back room of the Toadstool Café for the reception. A faerie queen would officiate and our relatives and closest friends would witness the blessed event.

"You were the one who sent me after the guy," I accused, purposely missing the point.

She gasped. "Dear God, that poor man. It was horrible, Derek. I found him—"

"*You* found him? Where?"

"In the ladies room. I'd just walked into a stall when I heard the door crash open, two gruff voices arguing, then the gunshot. I screamed. *Did* I scream? I think I screamed." I nodded and she lifted her hand to her mouth. "So stupid. He might've shot me, too. But he ran out and I waited a second to come out of the stall. That's when I saw the body."

"How horrible for you, sweetheart."

She bobbed her head furiously. "He, uh, had a big hole in his forehead and, oh God, the wall behind him—" Grabbing my shirt collar, she buried her face and whispered against my chest, "I don't even want to know what that was."

No argument there. We were here to get married, not relive traumas from the murder at Christmasland. "You're okay now, Clara. You're okay."

I mumbled my next question into the top of her head. "What should we do with the gun?"

"Gun?" She jerked away, stared at me with wide eyes. "Oh, lordy, the gun. If we turn it in, you could get arrested. You know how cops think. 'He who has the gun is usually he who shot the gun.'"

"Oh, yeah."

"That'll really screw up our wedding."

"Oh yeah."

"Is that all you have to say?"

"Oh. Yeah."

"All right then." She jerked her handbag off her shoulder and shoved it at me. "Drop the dang gun in here. I'll throw it in the woods."

"What? No! He's probably still out there. If anyone does that it'll be me."

"And leave a double set of your footprints? Derek, you aren't thinking clearly."

"Neither are you if you think I'll willingly let you go."

"Then it will have to be unwillingly because I'm going." She wiggled her purse. "Drop the gun, mister."

I shook my head. "Sweetheart, we're at a crime scene. My guess is that the Toadstool Café, maybe even the whole park, will be closed down for several days."

"What? Are you saying we'll have to postpone the wedding, anyway."

"There you go. That's what I'm talking about." Plus, no way would I let her put her lovely neck on the line for me. A pixie buzzed me, a friendly reminder to maybe keep that thought to myself. Clara, delightful as she was, could be argumentative at times.

"All right, Derek. Let's go back to the café."

"Good call."

As we walked, fallen leaves crunched beneath our feet, a cool breeze brushed our backs, and not a single pixie troubled us. A good omen. I hoped. I needed it.

A dirty black Crown Victoria idled in the driveway, its six-point star and block letters proclaimed ARKANSAS CONSTABLE. A short, square-shouldered man stood outside the open driver's door writing something on a clipboard. A patch on his black shirt read CONSTABLE MORRIS MCMANN.

His head lifted when Clara and I emerged from the dell. "Hey you," he yelled, pointing at me. "You got a permit for that thing?"

I assumed that the technical term *thing* referred to the Colt. "Nope," I yelled back over the car's rumbling engine. "Stole it off the man who shot your victim." I thought better of admitting how it really ended up in my hand. "You ready to accept some evidence?"

"Take it over to the jail. Got a deputy there interviewing folks."

"You want me wandering through the park with a small cannon in my hand?"

"Park's closed."

The small gasp beside me drew the constable's attention

and even his oversized aviator sunglasses failed to hide the rise in his eyebrows. "She with you?" His pointing finger veered to Clara, whose cozy spot beneath my arm should have answered the question. Then again, it had taken the good constable quite a few beats to even notice her.

"Yep."

"Well, then, both of you to the jail. Now."

THE Faerie World jail was halfway between the ticket-slash-business office and the café. The sign stated GAOL and I was impressed that a lawman who clearly operated in the Barney Fife tradition actually knew that gaol meant jail. We opened the door to a blanket of cigarette smoke.

"Gotta guy bringing in a gun!" squawked a Walkie-Talkie.

The deputy sprang from his chair. Clara coughed genteelly and said she'd wait outside.

"Put out your smoke," someone else said, alerting me we weren't alone in the cloudy room. I squinted and saw Hank lounging on the bench of a single cell with thick bars.

"What're you doing in there?" I asked.

"They think I shot my tax man. Would you tell this Roscoe idjut that you and me were together when the shot was fired?"

"You offering a discount on the property for that?"

"Very funny, Shriver. Just tell him."

I peered at the deputy. "True, Roscoe. We were talking in his office."

"About what?"

"Me buying the park."

"That right?" Roscoe eyeballed me. "Where's the gun Morris radioed about?"

I lifted my arm and he started to reach for the Colt, then must've thought better of it. A gallon size plastic bag materialized from somewhere and he held it for me while I lowered the gun inside. It didn't quite fit, but the bag served its purpose.

"You might want to find someone to put on the safety," I mentioned.

"It's n-not on?"

I rolled my eyes. "It's a revolver, man, and the hammer's not cocked. My prints are already on the gun."

I considered walking out, getting Clara, and driving away from Faerie World. But, God, the amusement park was a fire sale opportunity too good to pass up. Another part of me interjected, *no good can come from staying.*

Every time I ignored that voice bad things happened, so while Roscoe occupied himself with logging in the evidence I eased out the open door. Clara was nowhere in sight but I knew where she'd be. I headed straight toward the Village Square Gift Shoppe, passing the Selkie River Rapids and Pixie Ferris Wheel. Ahead I could see the famously enormous Banshee Roller Coaster and the Gnomes' Mining Camp. All eerily quiet and motionless without the rowdy push and shove lines. Even the pixies were gone.

"Hey," someone shouted and I turned. A tall man bristling with frenetic energy raced toward me. "What're you doing here? The park's closed today."

"Maybe tomorrow, too, if the esteemed constable has his way."

The man looked toward the low-slung cruiser. "Well, he's not the brightest bulb on the Ferris wheel. So why're *you* here?"

I would have asked the same thing if he hadn't been wearing a felt faerie cap. "I'm a witness."

"That so. What did you see?"

"I haven't given my statement yet."

"It's my guess Roscoe's waiting for it."

"I saw him. He showed no interest in my statement. Right now I'm looking for my fiancée."

"Ah, the knockout. Slender brunette, medium height?"

"That would be her."

"She went into the gift shop with Iris."

"Iris?"

"Hank's partner. The one who's not in jail. She's the financial brains behind the outfit and Hank's the mechanical genius. Works well for them, I guess."

A glance around reminded me of the contrast between the indifferent grounds upkeep and the immaculately designed and maintained rides. Iris got the better deal. "And how do you fit in?" I asked.

"You sure you don't work for Morris?"

I laughed and shook my head. I kind of liked this guy. "God forbid. My girl and I were scheduled to get married in the chapel tomorrow. Everything's screwed up now. She found the body and we both saw the killer. He was taller than Shaquille O'Neal but skinny as a skeleton." As soon as the words came from my mouth I thought it was a mistake to have said even that much.

"Sounds like the Horseman." He stuck out his hand. "Welcome to Faerie World—Home of the Magical. Name's Andy. I supervise the ride ticket booths".

"Derek." I accepted his handshake. "Who's the Horseman?"

"The Headless Horseman. You know, Sleepy Hollow, Ichabod Crane…Each night just before sunset he rides through Faerie World with his head on the saddle in front of him out to kill Ichabod. But the Horseman doesn't roam during the day, so how'd you see him?"

"Maybe I should save that info for McMann." Andy nodded agreeably, so I added, "Who plays him? Although that's one guy who's in the clear. No one would be so stupid."

"Glad you think that, since I play him on Wednesdays and Saturdays, and alternate Sundays."

I lifted an eyebrow. "There's more than one Horseman?"

"Hank, Iris and me. We take turns pulling on the platform boots and ratty robe with the false shoulders. Then we climb on Bridget, slap the fake head on the saddle horn and gallop around the commons. I think it's fun, and so does Hank, but Iris is always trying to weasel out of her nights."

"Well, Hank was with me, so that clears him."

"I was working the ticket booth, which makes me good."

I grinned. "I haven't met Iris. Maybe she did it."

Andy laughed. "Iris? No way. She's got the voice of a longshoreman and sits tall in the saddle, but don't let her looks deceive you, she's mousy and shrinking. If a gun went off near her, I'd wager she'd scream for a week."

"The screaming woman was my bride to be, and she was tastefully brief."

"Yes, she was. And there she is now," Andy said, then faded away.

I raced toward Clara, who waited for me on the wood plank sidewalk outside the gift shop. "You've got to meet Iris."

She dragged me inside and made introductions.

"Hello," Iris said, her smoker's voice proving Andy didn't lie. She straightened as she shook my hand, but clearly this was a woman who usually walked stoop-shouldered to look shorter.

"Tell him what you told me," Clara requested.

"Well, er, I mean this must be upsetting to you both. A man murdered on the eve of your big day. However, if you stay over until the investigation's complete, we can significantly reduce your room charge. Plus, we'll waive the chapel fee."

"Isn't that super?" Clara gushed. "We don't have to hurry back, so all I'll have to do is phone our guests. She's thrown in a suite to use as a hospitality room, haven't you, Iris?"

"Wow," I said, the accountant in me jumping with glee. But… "Have you talked to Hank about this? Last I saw, he was locked up."

Iris stiffened and her voice turned icy. "Hank and I are partners. I don't need his approval. Besides, I have to do what's needed. We're all upset. The victim is…er…was, our H&R Block man. Did our taxes for years. To know he was…well, to have him murdered like that, inside our Toadstool. It's, it's just terrible. Why did you know his brain—"

"Yes!" Clara said sharply.

"She found him, Iris."

Iris touched Clara's arm. "Oh, of course, I heard. I'm sorry."

"It's okay, honest. So what do you think, Derek?"

The shift in mood took us to a point of decision.

"Let Clara and me talk about it more, Iris."

"I'd prefer a quick decision." When I didn't respond, she

nodded. "But get back to me soon. I have to make arrangements."

I nodded agreeably. In truth, I just wanted out of Faerie World. The murder of the tax man, the weirdly unprofessional constable, this strange little big woman, and the damned pixies. Something else troubled me, but I couldn't put my finger on it.

I nudged Clara toward the door, then stopped when a thought occurred to me. Looking back, I asked Iris, "You have any clue what your H&R man was doing in the woman's bathroom? Seems odd for a middle-aged tax accountant."

"Yes, doesn't it? I have no idea why."

"You were close by," I commented. "In here, minding the store, weren't you?"

"No, no, I was in my office. I ran out when I heard the shot."

Giving Clara a gentle nudge, I resumed walking. You know, this just wasn't my problem. Or Clara's. When we'd closed the shop door behind us and were standing safely on the wooden walks I turned her to face me. She wasn't going to like what I had to say.

"**SEVEN** states, Derek. *Seven*. Sixteen venues, three months of searching for just the right place." Clara pulled our car out of the park, then onto a narrow public road that led to Faerie World, or in our case, *away*. "We can't discard perfection without a backward glance."

"I understand, sweetheart, and I was on your side until the murder. I'm telling you there's something wonky going on in the land of the magical and it ain't Puff the Magic Dragon. We can come back after it's all settled."

"Postpone our wedding?" she wailed. "Oh, Derek, that breaks my heart."

"Then let's stop in Vegas on the way home. I have a friend who's an Elvis impersonator and a minister. We can have a classic Graceland wedding."

"Why do you always joke?" Stiff anger replaced her tears and she stared straight forward. "I want Faerie World and you know it. So don't even talk to me."

Clara has shorter legs than me and I'd been leaning forward to see her face. Now I flopped back, feeling as pissed as she did. For one thing, I wasn't joking about Vegas. Plus, the way she acted, you'd think I'd murdered the tax man myself. Still fuming, I happened to glance in the rearview mirror. The reflection of flashing red lights did nothing to lift my mood.

"Sweetheart," I muttered, "It looks like you're getting your wish."

CONSTABLE McMann shoved us into his vehicle with gusto, and I didn't like the way he lingered over Clara. By the time he ushered us into the cell with Hank and had taken his own sweet time removing her cuffs, I'd had enough.

"Isn't it about time to call the state police?" I asked, a clear reminder of the tubby man's low position in the scheme of things.

He shoved me hard. Hands still cuffed behind me, I was headed for a face plant, but Hank steadied me. "Hey, man," he said to the constable. "Stop manhandling the customers. Being married to my partner doesn't give you that right!"

The constable was Iris's husband? I gave the little man a second look, thinking that was the marriage made in Mutt and Jeff land.

"If they hadn't fled the scene, they wouldn't be here. One of you people killed the tax man, and I'm going to find out who."

"Uncuff me," I said. "I want to call our lawyer."

With a huff, McMann freed my wrists. Beads of sweat appeared on his forehead even though the late day temperature was cool. He's in over his head, I thought, wondering why. He left the jail, leaving Roscoe to watch over us. Clara and I settled onto the hard benches. Hank apologized for our mistreatment, but I barely heard him. Some inconsistency buzzed around my mind.

Married to his partner. That was it.

I waited until Roscoe left the room for his nicotine fix, then asked Hank. "So Iris is McMann's wife?"

"Yes. In the past that's been an asset."

Un-huh. And now I asked Clara the question I'd been avoiding for fear of putting her in grave danger. "Honey, did you hear what the men were saying?"

She reflected before answering. "Not clearly, but the shooter wanted something and insisted it was hidden in the bathroom."

Suddenly the nonsensical events made sense.

"Hank," I said, "I think I know who killed your tax man, and why. We just need out of here to prove it."

"Hell, we can do that any time. It's Roscoe who's the problem."

"I can take care of Roscoe."

"He can," Clara interjected.

Hank leaned over and pulled a car-lock type clicker from inside his sock. A second later a particularly grotesque and large pixie flew through the window's bar and into Hank's outstretched hand. Keeping an eye out for Roscoe, Hank turned the mini-monster over, slid open its underbelly and pulled out a key. "I'm always losing keys," he explained. "This is a master key in case of emergencies. Next move is yours."

Roscoe walked back into the outer office and I gestured toward the door. When Hank unlocked it, Roscoe spun. "What the hell?"

But I was too fast. I pressed just the right nerve bundle in the base of his neck, then gently lowered an unconscious Roscoe, dragged him to the cell floor, then locked him in. Hank, Clara and I ran from the jail to the Toadstool.

A check confirmed that Iris was still in the gift shop and Hank quietly got us into the café, where we headed to the crime scene.

"The broom closet is a good start," I said the moment I spied it in the corner of the restroom. "We're probably looking for a ledger book or a computer disk."

I opened the closet door while Clara and Hank checked all the stalls. Pretty soon Clara was searching for secret doors. I had rearranged and torn apart everything in the broom closet, rapped on the walls, looked under shelves and still didn't uncover anything. This had to be about money, which meant there had to be records. Finding them would lead to the killer and my gut told me who that was. Or it had. I was beginning to waver. I'd been so sure this was where the tax man hid those records, but so far we'd found nothing. My doubts crept in unpleasantly.

Frustrated, I once again yanked out the mop, expecting the bucket it was in to follow. Instead, the bucket tipped over.

"Dammit," I said, hoping water wouldn't spill on my Bruno's.

A CD spilled on them instead. I swept the plastic case from the floor and read the label: INSURANCE POLICY.

"Evidence!" We all exclaimed simultaneously.

AFTER checking out the files on Hank's computer, we walked straight to the constable's car and, as he sputtered about us escaping, I demanded to know where his wife had been when the gunshot sounded. "Come to think of it," I said, "where is your wife now?"

"Look, Shriver," he said, jabbing a finger at my chest, "You're the crook and I'm the law around here." He gave a sideways glance at the deputy. "Roscoe, lock these folks back up."

"Sorry, sir, but I can't do that." Clara had already shown the deputy the documents that were saved on the CD and he'd been busy making calls. "The state police are coming."

In less than thirty minutes, they swarmed the place. Clara and I told them what we knew. Turned out they caught Iris at home, hastily packing bags for her and Morris. Soon, she and her husband were locked in the back of his constable wagon.

The police captain let Hank reopen the café since there was no place to eat, then joined us for dinner. The CD held the real company financials and proved that Iris had skimmed Faerie World profits ever since the park opened. She quickly confessed to murdering the tax man because he'd been blackmailing her and had threatened to expose her crime.

She'd only meant to scare the guy but when the gun went off, she knew she had to ditch it. It was her night to play the Horseman so she pulled on the costume and raced to the dell to dump the gun. When I caught up with her out there, she panicked.

There were still loose ends to tie up, but Iris was going away for a long time, and the constable wasn't getting off scot-free either. The captain ended our conversation by announcing that Faerie World could open again in the morning.

"We can get married!" Clara exclaimed with unabashed joy.

CLARA and Derek," the faerie queen proclaimed, "I now pronounce you man and wife."

Clara's glowing face filled my vision and I slowly lifted the veil.

"You may kiss the bride."

And did I ever. A swirling, world rocking, earth shaking kiss that marked the beginning of our life together. Finally, the hoots and hollers of our guests reminded us we weren't alone. Sheepishly we let go of each other and started down the steps from the altar.

When our feet hit the chapel floor, a flurry of pixies swept down to circle us, broadcasting a love song. Our guests laughed and clapped and for the first time I was glad to see the pixies. After I bought Faerie World I might even keep them. Right now, though, I had the love of my life on my arm and that would last a lifetime.

Clara smiled up at me and read my mind. "One amusement park is enough, darling."

Did I mention I love this woman?

CONNIE FLYNN has written ten romance novels for *Harlequin Enterprises* and for Penguin Publishing, and is most widely known for her award-winning, bestselling paranormal novels, which include *Shadow of the Moon* and *Shadow of the Wolf,* soon be back in print. Connie is co-founder of Bootcamp for Novelists Online and also teaches creative writing at Phoenix College. Visit her website at: ConnieFlynn.com.

TRAGEDY IN THE PINES
LORI HINES

THE twisting and clicking of the doorknob was unexpected—as if someone on the inside of the house desperately wanted to get out. Or be let in. Brandon Winn brushed his short, dark wavy bangs from his forehead as he stood on his wraparound porch. His piercing blue eyes peeked through the window of his vacation home in the tall pine forest near Flagstaff, Arizona. He saw no one.

Besides the crisp forest smell, he also detected smoke. Walking to both sides of the porch, he could see nothing but more pines and two deer, within twenty feet of the house, that stood eyeing him. He glanced skyward. The full moon and hundreds of stars peered down from between the trees.

But he didn't see smoke anywhere.

The doorknob continued to vibrate and rattle.

Brandon had moved into the two-story log house six months earlier and had experienced ghostly activity within the first few months. The next door neighbors, who lived a quarter mile away, had witnessed unusual phenomena on multiple occasions as they drove by—faux fires, sightings of children, and a mysterious red-haired woman had been seen from outside his vacation home.

He hesitated before touching the doorknob. As soon as he inserted the key and placed his right palm around the hardware, the knob turned of its own accord.

"Okay, Brandon," he said aloud. "Your house just opened its door for you. Now what?"

"Hello?" he yelled. He waited a few seconds. *Well what did you expect? The house to answer, "Yeah, I'm here. Welcome home buddy. Take a load off."*

He placed his laptop and luggage on the dark brown

leather couch and waited for his friend and fellow investigator to arrive. He wondered what he and Joseph might discover regarding the home's history. *Never thought I would have to investigate my own house.*

Though he wasn't easily spooked, Brandon felt unnerved. He walked out to his car to get his ghost hunting kit. When he returned, he saw a shadow rise from the hardwood floor and cross from the great room to the upstairs. The shape couldn't have been more than four feet tall.

Brandon was halfway up the stairs, intending to check out the mysterious figure when the floorboards in the living room creaked. He slowly turned.

"Hey," Joseph yelled from the front porch.

Brandon gasped and grabbed the railing. "You startled me," he said, as Joseph approached the stairs. "I just witnessed my first shadow in this place."

"Are you kidding?" the sandy haired, boyish looking, ex-football player asked.

"No. And the door opened for me by itself. I would say the knob was loose, but I saw the handle jiggle."

"Wow! How come you get to have all the fun? Hopefully we'll find some evidence as to what's going on. Maybe we'll spot some spirits. Where should I set up the night vision cameras?"

"Try one inside the entrance pointing in the direction of the stairs. We'll put another upstairs in the hallway."

"Did anyone die in the house? Or any tragic events?"

Brandon gazed at his upstairs hallway, watching for any sign of movement. "I wasn't able to get much history. It's been a year since this place was abandoned. I've talked with a few neighbors who have reported bizarre lights, shadows and screams emanating from inside the house. So far, all I've experienced are minor noises that I first attributed to the house settling—or my imagination. But last weekend, I was lying in bed and heard a conversation downstairs. I went to check it out and didn't see anyone."

"What were the voices saying?" Joseph asked.

"Hard to tell. It stopped when I came down. I heard a male and a female. No one seems to know what happened here."

"Sounds like there's some interesting history to this place. I'll start the baseline readings as a benchmark for our vigil tonight." Joseph removed the Trifield electromagnetic frequency detector, two other voice recorders, a handheld thermal imaging camera and motion detectors from Brandon's ghost kit.

Joseph checked the battery power on the voice recorders. "I almost forgot to tell you, I invited Lara to come and check out your place. It will be interesting to see what her psychic abilities pick up along with our equipment."

"Great idea. She's been in sync with the evidence we found in past investigations. Do you remember she solved an old murder at Vulture Mine with her medium skills? And the caretakers weren't even aware of that part of the mine's history."

"Of course I remember," Joseph said, replacing the batteries in one of the cameras. "I was in the assay office when she came running in saying she'd heard a gunshot. That was the same time we started smelling gunpowder."

When Brandon walked into the dining area to setup one of the cameras, he noticed his kitchen cabinets were wide open. And a ceramic black bowl, broken in four pieces, lay on the earthen-colored slate floor. The other three bowls were still stacked neatly inside the mahogany cupboard.

"Well, someone's having parties while I'm gone." Brandon snapped several pictures of the damage.

"What the heck?" Joseph walked into the dining area. "Has this happened before?"

Brandon shook his head. "Not like this—keys misplaced, objects missing—but I thought it was me being forgetful."

Joseph stared, mouth agape, into the living room.

Brandon followed his gaze and saw an opaque mist. Human in form at first, it transformed into an amoeba shape. Then in a split second, the vapor became a baseball-sized, pulsating light that glowed blue, green and white. Brandon and Joseph stared, mesmerized as it zipped in between them and paused, hanging in midair. The light hesitated as if checking them both out then vanished through the dining room wall.

Neither could speak for a moment.

"Oh man," Joseph finally said. "That was intense."

"Yeah, so intense, neither of us caught it on camera. The damn thing went behind the night vision camera, not in front of it. I'd say that thing had some intelligence."

"Ironic, isn't it?" Joseph's hands trembled as he placed fresh batteries in the thermal imaging camera. "The best investigation we've had, and it's at the home of the co-founder of our paranormal research team."

"I always thought it was exciting to pursue the paranormal," Brandon said. "But when it involves your own home, it changes your perspective. I have a new respect for homeowners and families going through this."

They finished setting up the rest of the equipment and completed the baseline readings. Then Brandon and Joseph sat down on the leather couch with their audio recorders going. Their flashlights scanned the living room for any sign of activity.

"Are we ready to try and communicate with the spirits?" Joseph asked.

"Let's do it." Brandon leaned forward, gripping tightly onto the recorder. "Who's with us? I saw a shadow earlier— were you the one who tried opening my door?"

They waited, giving whatever spirits might be with them a chance to respond. Thirty seconds later, a knock on the door made them both jump.

Joseph laughed. "Either that's Lara, or we might have an answer from beyond."

Brandon opened the door and welcomed Lara Lanier, psychic and medium. Long silky blond hair, five foot seven and fair skin, she took his breath away every time he saw her. Unfortunately, she belonged to Matt Keegan, pagan and a paranormal investigator on another team.

"Hi guys," she said, giving Joseph, then Brandon a hug. "Great to see you. I wish it was under better circumstances."

Brandon breathed in her sweet cherry vanilla scent and brushed his hand against her soft locks as he hugged her back.

"Good timing." Brandon turned away nervously. "We just started an EVP session in the living room. Maybe we can get a response from beyond. You missed one hell of a light show."

"Interesting. Well, I'll walk around downstairs for a few minutes to see what I can pick up." Lara stood between the great room and dining room, staring at the mess on the floor.

Joseph continued to question the spirits. "Is there a child here? Can you tell me your name?" He turned on his flashlight to detect any movement.

"Flash," Brandon said to prepare Joseph and Lara for the blinding light of the camera. Brandon slowly turned around, the hair on the back of his neck and his arms stood on end. Something waited right behind him.

Lara slowly turned her head and looked at Brandon.

She's staring past me. Brandon slowly glanced in the direction of her gaze.

Joseph picked up his camcorder and started filming Brandon and whatever else might be close to him.

A few seconds later, Lara said, "It's gone. But it was an angry presence. Not demonic, but not happy. I felt it brush by me and then it went behind Brandon."

"Makes sense," Joseph said. "There was an energy spike and the temperature dropped by five degrees near Brandon and me."

Half an hour of inactivity lapsed before Brandon said, "Let's head upstairs. Seems quiet down here for now. I'll leave my recorder on the kitchen counter."

Halfway up the stairs Lara abruptly stopped, grabbing the railing as she teetered to the side. "Something went right through me."

"Do you know if it was that same presence from the great room?" Joseph asked.

"No. I sensed a female. And she was frightened."

Brandon looked at his EMF meter to see how high the energy readings were. The 1.5 milligaus reading indicated there could have been something there.

A loud, repetitive screeching from upstairs startled the trio.

"Quick! The motion detector," Brandon said. They darted to the upstairs hallway where they'd placed the device. Brandon and Joseph reviewed images from the camera.

"Unfortunately, this didn't catch whatever set the alarm off," Joseph said.

The air became electrified with energy. Brandon noticed a drop on the temperature probe to sixty degrees—and still dropping.

"My God," Lara said. "Do you smell that?" She bent over, gagging repeatedly.

Brandon dashed to the guest bathroom and opened the door for her. She barely made it to the toilet.

A minute later, "I'm fine now," she said, dabbing her mouth with a tissue.

Brandon placed a reassuring hand on her shoulder. *It seems my private retreat is turning into a nightmare.*

Lara splashed water on her face, and Joseph handed her a towel. Patting her face, she turned toward the bathtub.

Brandon looked at the thermal imaging screen Joseph held. An obscure red figure stood behind the mahogany shower curtain. It seemed to be holding something.

SLOWLY pulling back the curtain, Lara saw a heavyset man, solid in form, wearing a navy blue shirt and worn blue jeans. His thick black hair was matted to his face and forehead.

The man's brown eyes widened, his breath coming in short spurts. Pressed against the cold shower tiles, he cradled a black cat with white paws. "It'll be okay," he whispered. "We'll get away."

Lara whipped around when she heard something drop behind her. Joseph's audio recorder lay on the tile floor.

"Holy crap!" he blurted.

When she looked back, the man was gone.

"Did you both hear what he said?" she asked.

Both men nodded.

"That was a man you saw right?" Joseph asked, picking the recorder up.

"Yeah," Lara said. "A very scared one."

They all continued to stare into the bathtub, as if the

entity would reappear.

"How about a vigil in the hallway?" Joseph asked. "That way we can catch whatever might be out there, or in the bathroom."

Lara didn't want to tell Brandon that his beautiful vacation home had more than a few spirits. She had picked up two Native American spirits, one of which was a Sinaguan woman—shorter inhabitants from 650 A.D. There was also extreme pain and suffering associated with the place.

Lara faced the bathroom where the phantom had appeared.

"Tell us about yourself," Joseph said to the spirit, still filming. "Lara saw you standing in the bathtub. What happened to you?"

Lara glanced into a room at the end of the hall. She felt drawn to its darkness.

"Lara, do you see something?" Joseph asked.

But she didn't answer. Entering a small room, she noticed piles of unpacked boxes stacked in the far corner. Obviously Brandon's workout room, it housed an elliptical machine, free weights, and a bench press with black and white Ansel Adams prints on the walls.

"Do you mind if I take a look in your closet?" she asked, while Brandon and Joseph waited just outside.

"Uh no, I guess not."

"She slid the door open to reveal some partially unopened boxes with miscellaneous computer parts. A photo album had fallen into one of Brandon's boxes, perched on top of a laptop. Lara knew Brandon was very organized, so she didn't think it was his. Removing the album from the box, she showed it to Brandon and Joseph.

"Where did you find that?" Brandon asked.

"On top of that computer," she pointed to the laptop.

Brandon gaped into the closet. "I was in there last week—in that very box. I didn't see it."

Lara and Joseph watched as Brandon flipped through the plastic-covered pages of pictures.

"Wait!" Lara said. "That's the guy I saw in the bathroom." She pointed to a photo of the dark-haired, chubby man standing next to a striking blond man, about six feet tall—both holding hard hats.

"Wonder who the other guy is?" Joseph asked. "Maybe they're business partners in construction—or work together. I can see a white truck with wording in the background."

They looked at the remainder of the pages.

"The cat!" Lara stopped Brandon from flipping another page. "That's the one I saw in the bathroom." All three investigators gazed at a picture of the black cat with white paws that a child held.

Lara looked at the picture she assumed was of the tall blond man's wife. She could have been a Celtic goddess with long curly red hair and fair skin. Teenage children stood beside the woman, a boy and a girl, who had the same features.

Lara suddenly sensed intense confusion. Then she sniffed the air. "I'm smelling smoke."

"That's funny," Brandon sniffed and glanced around the room and into the hallway. "I detected the same scent outside on the porch before you both arrived."

Joseph looked at the thermal imaging camera. "Wait a minute, this battery was full. Now it's dead."

"So is my recorder." Lara turned it off and then on. "Let's walk around and see if we can find where the smell is coming from."

"Lara, do you know who either of those men from the album are?" Brandon asked.

"Not yet," she said. "I'm thinking their family used to live here or at least on this property. I don't know why the man I saw in the bathtub would be involved."

"Maybe they left because of all of the activity." Brandon checked out the other rooms upstairs. "Maybe he was remodeling and it brought all of the spirits to the surface."

They both jumped when Brandon's phone rang. It was the realtor who sold Brandon the house.

"Oh, hey Sandy. Listen, I called to find out if you knew anything about the family who abandoned this place a year ago? There's some strange stuff going on."

"Hello?" Brandon said into his cell phone. "Hello?" He

shook his head in frustration. "I think she hung up on me."

"Man," Joseph said, wiping his forehead. "It is getting really hot in here. The temperature is eighty-four degrees and climbing. The baseline temp earlier was only seventy."

Soon, it felt like a sauna. Lara became faint with the overwhelming heat and nearly collapsed on the floor.

"Whoa," Brandon said, catching her from behind. "Let's get out of here." Joseph supported her other side as they moved downstairs.

On the stairs, Lara thought she heard crackling and popping. At the bottom, massive, orange-red flames suddenly popped up from the floor. They licked hungrily at the pine beams on the vaulted ceiling. Thick, swirling gray smoke engulfed them. And, screams of agony emanated from everywhere.

"Follow me," Brandon yelled, as he raced to the front door.

Dashing directly through the fire with Brandon and Joseph, Lara noticed she wasn't getting burned. *So this was one of the tragedies I picked up on. I can't believe the residual image is so vivid.*

Brandon quickly pulled his hand away just as the metal knob melted. Agonizing screams and uncontrollable coughs continued to come from behind them. In the midst of the smoke, Lara saw an unrecognizable human form melt away into a skeleton, then drop into a pile of ashes on the floor.

Then it all stopped. The smoke dissipated. The fire disappeared. The horrifying screams ceased. Quiet.

Gasping and shaking, Brandon and Joseph stood just outside the front door.

A black Buick pulled up in the circular driveway, and a petite woman jumped out of the vehicle.

"Are you all okay?" she asked excitedly. "I saw flames erupting from the house and started to contact the fire department. But then it stopped." She stared at Brandon's house.

"You saw more than that, didn't you?" Lara asked. The woman gazed at Lara as if she were nuts. But Lara was used to it—it came with the territory of being a psychic and a medium.

"Yeah," she responded, glancing from Lara to Brandon. "A tall blond guy. I couldn't see his features since he faced the house. He stood there watching while it burned."

She sighed, still staring at the house. "Well, since you're all okay, I need to get home to my kids."

"Wait," Brandon touched her arm. "What's your name?"

"Oh, sorry. My name is Celia Thompson. I live half a mile from here."

"I'm Brandon. And this is Lara and Joseph. I was wondering how long you've lived here?"

"Ten years. Why?"

"Could you describe the family who lived in this house last?" Brandon asked.

"The father was average height, bald, but nice looking. His wife was a little shorter and had short brown hair. Sad though—they had an eight year old son who was killed instantly when he found his father's gun and shot himself. It happened last summer."

"How awful," Lara said. "Thanks. You've been a big help."

After Celia left, Brandon said, "That might explain the smaller shadow I saw before you both arrived."

"Brandon, I'm getting something." Lara stood on the porch, her eyes closed in concentration. "There was another home here on your property twenty years ago. I'm seeing a slate blue ranch style house with white trim." She stared into the moonlit pines. "The man Celia saw standing in front of this house was actually standing in front of what used to be his home back then." Lara paused, looking back at Joseph and Brandon.

"This is the anniversary of two very tragic events that are crossing each other on your property. One was the death of that poor little boy."

"And the other was a fire from the past?" Joseph asked.

She nodded. "I need more time in your house. I'm starting to get more sensations and visions."

"Sure. Joseph and I will check on the equipment while you look around," Brandon said. "The downstairs camera had to have caught evidence of that fire. We should also play back the recorders to see if we got any audio that might provide a clue of what happened here."

They slowly opened the front door and peeked inside. "Seems pretty calm now," Brandon said.

While Brandon listened to portions of audio and checked the camera that had been placed downstairs, Lara walked back up to the second floor. He gazed up longingly, imagining her as a permanent fixture in his home.

Joseph cleared his throat. "I hate to interrupt your daydreams, but we did catch some bizarre flashing orange lights. I assume from that fire."

Brandon felt his face flush and he glanced down at the recorder he held. "That's not all we caught." Brandon stood transfixed, re-listening to a portion of audio. He rewound it and handed the device to Joseph.

"No other way out," a male voice whispered.

Brandon and Joseph glanced at each other.

"That didn't sound like the dark-haired man," Joseph said. "This person's voice wasn't as deep."

"It's not," Lara said.

Brandon turned around quickly to find her standing behind him.

Tears coursed down Lara's face. Her eyes were red and her face lined with streaks.

"It's the tall white-haired man that your neighbor saw in front of the house. His name is Brendon and he stabbed his family with a butcher knife then hunted down the dark-haired man, who was his business partner, before he burned his house."

"Oh my God!" Joseph said. "Brandon, buddy, your place has an overdose of history. Maybe there's something about this area that attracts tragedy."

"It gets even more peculiar," Lara said. "July twenty-fifth—I couldn't figure out why I kept seeing that date in my mind."

"What about it?" Brandon asked. "Is that the date of the fire?"

"Not just the fire. It's also the same day that little boy

accidentally killed himself a year ago. Your vacation home is caught between the history of the previously built home and the history of the last residents."

"That's a hell of a coincidence," Joseph said.

Lara pulled out the photo album from Brandon's workout room. "That's not the only coincidence." She flipped to the last page. "Think about the similarity of his first name to yours, and look at the names of the original occupants."

Brandon Winn stared at the words in a daze. *It can't be.* He suddenly realized why he was inexplicably drawn to the home in the woods. Why he had wakened one day and ended up here to see the FOR SALE sign. And why the album was in the home to begin with.

The inside back cover contained the following words:

PROPERTY OF B. WINN AND FAMILY

LORI HINES is a fulltime writer and editor, specializing in marketing-related content. She has completed her first novel titled, THE ANCIENT ONES, a paranormal mystery, and is in the process of finishing the second in the series. She has published three short stories and was awarded honorable mention for "A Glimpse Beyond" in the Desert Dweller Short Story Contest.

LOOSE END
DEBORAH J LEDFORD

THE phone rings. I jerk my body toward the handset on the kitchen counter, wondering if it's him again. The anonymous caller I've been hiding from since the day I saw him across the tight cove of water that separated us. He'd stood on the bank dressed in waders, long white hair waving in the wind, one hand clutching a fishing rod, binoculars hanging to his side in the other, mouth wide open in shock.

After four rings my recorded voice tells the caller to leave their number. I hold the breath caught in my lungs until they burn. Again, as the dozen times before, the voice says, "I know who you are. I saw what you did. Does he haunt your dreams?" Then the *click* and a *beep* announces: message received.

Mind scrambling in an effort to place the voice, I retrieve the only tangible memory from fifteen years ago. I've kept these pebbles for years. A coffee tin full at first, then whittled down to a plastic baggie, now a mesh covering tied with string.

I turn over the bag of multi-colored pebbles and examine them. Each one different, yet all the same in their smoothness. The memory, fresh as the day it was born snaps into my mind. The vision I cannot escape, hide from, or ignore any longer.

The stones scrape as they rub together, filling my mind with the remembered sounds of the pebbles crunching underfoot near the pier, in view of the two-story house that had been in my family for five generations. Where I had spent every vacation for the first twenty-five summers of my life. Tumbling these smooth rocks into the Café Bustelo coffee tin had been my last task before fleeing the summer cottage—never to return.

I squeeze my eyes shut and imagine the lull of gentle waves lapping the pier, the shriek of a hawk before it dives to pluck a sunfish from the shimmering lake. The mingled smells of algae, ancient driftwood, marsh grass damp from the morning's drizzle.

I'm back there again, feeling the burn on my left cheek. Falling in a heap onto the stones. Blood rushing to my already flushed face. Niko's top lip turned up in a sneer, yelled words I didn't hear. Time stood still. Then warmth stippled my face. Niko went down. A deafening *crack* reverberated across the water. My eyes dropped to my blouse spattered with red, to my crimson covered arm, to my blood stippled trembling hands. Niko's body splayed on the riverbank, water lapping his doeskin loafers, splotches speckling his usually pristine slacks and suit jacket. I fixated on the exposed rusty curls on his chest that I had run my fingers through the night before.

I blinked and raised my head, refusing to look at Niko's face, and instead focused across the lake for the stranger I had seen moments earlier. I scanned left to right again and again. This time my eyes found no one there. I turned and ran.

Saplings whipped against my chest as I scrambled deeper into the forest. Pine sap stung my nostrils, then the rich smell of loamy soil stirred a memory of working in the garden with my long dead grandmother. I invoke her spirit, to keep me safe, to stop my whirling mind, but no help emerged. Only a bird called out to me—a mournful, high-pitched call that pierced the air. I burst through yet another curtain of leaves, every step and breath labored. I stopped. Buzzing in my left ear alerted me of flies that had found the dried blood on my cheeks.

Unable to go farther I hid in the forest until hours after dark, whirling at every snapped twig, squeezing my eyes shut when a nearby cricket ceased its chirp. By the moon's half light I returned to the water's line. Niko was gone.

I scooped up two handfuls of pebbles at the edge of the water where his body had lain and shoved the stones into my jacket pockets. I sprinted into the cabin and in case he had survived, yelled his name over and over as I fumbled for my belongings in the dark. I stuffed the items into a duffel, then bolted to my Jaguar.

I've been running in my mind ever since.

I squint at the bag of pebbles in my hand, conjuring speckles of red painted by Niko's blood—impossible after so many years. Legs shaking, I rise from the couch and move to the answering machine. Listen to the stranger's words again. "Does he haunt your dreams?" Honestly, Niko rarely entered my thoughts, let alone my dreams. I don't know that I would even recognize him if I were to pass him on the street—as if that could be possible.

No, Niko doesn't haunt me.

This man does.

I can't report him to the police because he knows too much. Maybe he's exorcizing his demons, wants to come clean, merely speak to someone about what he witnessed. A white-haired man when the incident occurred, he's got to be eighty by now. Maybe he only wants to talk. I decide to pick up the phone next time. We'll meet, talk it all through. It'll be all right.

The phone rings again. Time has slipped away and I wonder how much has passed since his last call. With renewed confidence I click on.

Before he utters his third word, I say, "I need to see you."

I hear a low, long exhale, then, "Good. Good."

I slide open the kitchen drawer, take out my Sig Sauer handgun and ratchet a round into the chamber as quietly as possible. "Where?"

"You know where."

The vacation house. "When?"

"Tomorrow."

The anniversary of Niko's death.

NIKO is fresh in my mind now. Every man I see during the three hour drive reminds me of him. Shaken, disoriented, not knowing what to expect, my hands tremble as I attempt to unlock the front door to the cottage.

Could any place be more desolate? I wonder, settling down on the uneven plank floor of the vacation house no one has entered in fifteen years. I wait. The furniture and throw rugs have been removed or stolen, fixtures gone, interior doors detached from their hinges.

I sit there and think of all the mistakes that had led me to Niko. Twenty-five, invincible and fearless, playing and partying too hard, caring about nothing but my own needs. Niko had worked as a bouncer at one of my uncle's clubs. I pursued him mercilessly. I always got what I wanted—if not with money, with charm, or focused determination. Finally he agreed to accompany me on a three-day holiday.

The vacation began lovely as a honeymoon, sharing blackberries we had picked off the brambles up the road, lying before a blazing fireplace in the front room, sweet lovemaking throughout the night.

The next morning, crisp air blew our jackets as we walked along the lake in front of the cottage, the pebbles crunching underfoot. I learned of Niko's reason for agreeing to our vacation getaway. He had plans other than romance and wanted me to speak to my uncle about promoting him higher in the ranks. Niko was tired of being a bouncer. It was time to move up to the enforcing end of Uncle's business—where the real money could be made. I told him no, that I didn't get involved in my uncle's work. He snapped.

And, well, so did I.

The faint sound of a motor snaps me out of the memory. I raise my head to the whine and go to the cracked window to see a double bench powerboat coming from across the cove. A man about twenty-five years old steers the boat to the lake's edge, gets out, runs his hands through his hair and tucks in the tail of his plaid flannel shirt. Confused, I take a deep breath as I leave the cottage and make my way to him.

Neither of us speak until only a few yards separate us.

"Hello, Ms. Constance. You don't recognize me, do you?" he says, then smiles.

He stands with perfect posture, wide shoulders squared, legs slightly apart, hands clasped in front of him. Same as Niko. Crooked grin just like Niko. I close my eyes for a moment and refocus with blurry sight. *Niko?*

"I get that you're rattled. You were expectin' my grandfather. I'm Jacob." He lowers his head and his tone. "Granddaddy died last month." When he lifts his head again I see the glint of tears in his eyes. "Took your secret to his grave."

"And what will it take for you to do the same?" I ask, reassured by the feel of steel tucked into the waistband at the middle of my back.

"You think this is about money?"

"Isn't it always?" I mutter.

"I was a kid when it happened. Waited for you to come back every summer since. Been waitin' a long time. I used to watch you over here when I was a little boy. You and an older man would shoot cans off the pier. He taught you real good. You never missed."

He takes cautious steps toward me, steel gray eyes on mine. "Never seen you up close. Granddaddy and me would share the binoculars. He had 'em when…" He averts his gaze for a moment, then back to me, seeming to gain courage with each breath. "I knew you'd have blue eyes. Bluer than the sky. You're more beautiful than I even imagined. Prettier than mornin'." He closes his eyes and inhales. "Bet you smell like a field of clover after a spring rain, too."

The pit of my stomach stirs and I struggle to keep from reaching out to him. If only Niko had been so sweet…

"Granddaddy told me I couldn't tell anyone. That your family was powerful and rich and owned our cabin and every other place both sides of the lake. They'd find out it was us if we called the cops. Backwoods country folk like him and me would disappear and no one would know or care. I was only ten. It was just the two of us…Anyway, that little cabin's all we had, 'cept for each other. Where could we go?"

The words he speaks aren't a question, merely a statement. I wonder what I would do if put in the same position. I hadn't even told my uncle what had happened that summer day so many men ago.

"So we got in our little powerboat…" he points to the one moored on the pebbly shore. "Same one, matter of fact.

Then we crossed the lake. Thought Grandaddy was gonna have a heart attack he tugged at that body so hard. Damned near tipped over the boat." A chuckle escapes his mouth. He covers his lips with his hand and looks at me with wide eyes. "No disrespect, ma'am. We got out to the deep water and Granddaddy tied the anchor to that man's legs. Then we dropped him over the side."

I blink a few times, his flat emotionless expression reminding me of how my uncle would talk about doing a job correctly. How important it was to never leave a single loose end.

"We did the right thing, didn't we?" He takes a step closer and holds out pleading hands. "Ms. Constance, please tell me we did the right thing."

"We've been through a lot, Jacob. You can call me Connie. Yes you did the right thing. I only wish I'd have known. I would have thanked you years ago. And I would certainly have made your silence worthy of a reward."

A lazy grin lifts his lips. "It's not money I want. I've been thinkin' about you every night for fifteen years."

He seems to lose his train of thought, but I know where he's going until he says, "That man shouldn't have hit you. He deserved to get hisself killed." Sheepishly, he lowers his head, eyes on his boot toe digging in the pebbles. "This is where it happened, remember?"

My turn to go flat and emotionless. I stand there, waiting to hear the bribe.

"Nobody lives around here anymore. Grandaddy quit payin' rent ages ago. No one ever came to kick us out, so he figured your family must've forgot about this place."

"No one stayed?"

"Not to live. Get some fishin' boats sometimes. Hear hunters come turkey season. That's about it."

"What do you do for a living?"

A proud smile lights up his face. "I build cane rockin' chairs. Deliver them to Atlanta when I get a big enough order. Got back a couple days ago, so I don't need your money. Not that I'd ask."

"Would you do something for me, Jacob?" I ask the last

remaining witness to my deed.

"'Course. Anything."

I motion toward the still water. "Take me to where you and your grandfather dropped him in the lake."

"You sure?"

"Yes. I need to say goodbye." I place my hand on his solid bicep and give a little squeeze. "You understand, don't you?"

"Sure. Gotta let the demons out, Grandaddy always used to say."

I offer him the most seductive smile I can conjure. "Thank you, Jacob."

He extends his hand and steadies the rim of the boat. His grip, callused and firm, holds mine as I step into the swaying craft. My eyes drop to the anchor tucked under the rear bench. He gets in beside me and yanks the motor to life.

DEBORAH J LEDFORD is the award-winning author of the Inola Walela and Steven Hawk suspense series. Three-time nominee for the Pushcart Prize, her short stories appear in the print publications *Arizona Literary Magazine*, *Forge Journal* literary magazine, *Twisted Dreams Magazine*, *AnthologyBuilder*, and other Sisters in Crime anthologies to name a few. Deborah invites you to visit her website for a complete listing of credits: DeborahJLedford.com.

DESERT GETAWAYS

THE PLACE I WAS BEFORE
Suzanne Flaig

I wouldn't be in this mess if I had walked out after our one-night stand.

I'm thirsty, she said, brushing a scarlet streak onto a long fingernail, then blowing gently.

Last night, in the throes of passion, or whatever, this trip had seemed like a good idea. Romantic, even. Never been out of Arizona, she said. Wanted to see the ocean.

At the time, it had sounded like a fun vacation.

In the light of day, in the August glare of the California desert, it was less than romantic. Stupid, even. Sure. I'll take her to the ocean. Leave her there.

I slapped the steering wheel in frustration. The last sign of civilization was about twenty miles back.

How long to the next place?

An hour and a half, at least, I said.

We drove on in sullen silence.

Look! A shiny red fingernail pointed off in the distance.

I didn't see a thing. I'd been down this road too many times to count, and there was nothing but sand and rocks for at least a hundred miles.

The heat must be getting to me, I thought as I squinted off into the distance and noticed a tiny speck on the horizon.

But the speck kept getting bigger, until we were bearing down on what looked like a set from an old west movie. A brightly painted sign read COLD DRINKS.

Stop! she demanded.

What the hell. I was thirsty, too.

The building looked deserted. No other cars in the lot. But she acted like she owned the place as she barged right in the door under the sign GENERAL STORE AND SALOON.

The dark, cool room felt refreshing after the long, hot drive. A haunting melody played quietly in the background, soothing my frayed nerves.

We sat at the bar, a scarred wooden expanse, and drank draft beer from frosted mugs with bases chipped from years of banging against the oak countertop.

She smiled at the bartender and winked. You've got a great place here, cowboy.

She roamed around, browsing through Southwest cookbooks and checking out high-priced souvenirs. She came back and tugged on my arm. You should see what's back there. I shrugged at the bartender and put five bucks on the bar as she pulled me toward the rear of the store.

Next to a shelf filled with canned goods stood a screen door that let in the bright desert sun and a view of another row of buildings. Gift shops, it looked like. Tourist traps, although how the hell they attracted tourists along this godforsaken stretch of road was beyond me. The music was louder now, a siren's song luring me on.

Come on, she urged, pushing on the screen door until it screeched in distress. Curiosity and her mysterious allure drew me outside with her.

We wandered the length of the dusty road, reading rusted metal signs hung from chains. The shops reminded me of a bygone era...Silversmith...Sundries...Taxidermy...

Let's get going, I said, looking for the screen door that led back into the store.

I saw rows of storefronts on both sides of the dirt road. None was marked GENERAL STORE AND SALOON. At either end, high adobe walls closed off the old town from any view of the highway.

Where's the door we came through? I asked.

She didn't answer, just gave me a strange enigmatic smile.

I dragged her into the nearest shop.

The old man's brown and crinkled face looked like it was made from the same leather as the old worn saddle on the swaybacked horse tied outside the taxidermy shop.

Do you have another door, one that leads to the highway?

Ain't no other door, sonny. Ain't no highway neither.

Sure there is. We just drove in from Phoenix. *Crazy old geezer.*

Ain't no other door, he repeated.

I just want to get back to the place I was before.

The old man's face creased into a monkey's grin. And where might that be?

I'm parked in front of the saloon.

Ain't no saloon in these parts. This here's a dry town, son.

The music swelled to a crescendo. She hooked her arm into mine and laughed.

SUZANNE FLAIG, writer, editor and publisher, is the author of numerous short stories, including "The Twelve Days of Christmas" in the 2009 Desert Sleuths anthology, *How Not to Survive the Holidays*. She has completed two mystery novels featuring piano teacher/amateur sleuth Missy Jenkins and is seeking an agent while working on the third book in the series.

THE OLD MINER
HOWARD B. CARRON

"I'VE always had a hankerin' to visit a genuine ghost town, Sally," George threw out as he strolled to his favorite chair on the patio.

"A hankerin'! You've been watching too many old Westerns, George."

"Really, Hon, we could drive up to Gammons Gulch then over to Tombstone and Fort Bowie, stay overnight and then head for Swansea. We have a three day weekend coming up and Swansea is a real ghost town, a 1920s, copper mining camp out in the desert northeast of Parker. There are over a dozen buildings still standing, including the store, train depot, a whole row of miners' cabins and lots of foundations and ruins from the smelter."

"Okay, okay, you've obviously done some research and it does sound interesting."

WE were on the road the following weekend, headed toward the High Desert of Cochise County. About 161 miles from Phoenix, Gammons Gulch is an Old Western Mining Town with an authentic mine, hotel, large saloon, church/schoolhouse, a miners cabin and mercantile. There is also a working assay and blacksmith shop, and an authentic jail. A mix of the 1880s to the 1930s, with a collection of antiques, old cars that are still running and movie memorabilia.

The closer we got to Benson the more ominous the weather became. A fine mist of suspended dust and sand started to gently cover the hood and windshield of the car. When the mist cleared, the heavy particles moved like a thick carpet over the desert. We were experiencing the beginnings of a sandstorm. Of course Cochise County was no stranger to storms, flash floods and even some tornadoes. The idea of a sandstorm was disconcerting as well as exciting.

We finally arrived at the Gammons Gulch Museum and promptly forgot about the storm. Because of the weather there was only one other couple in the museum and soon we were left alone. The lady running the ticket sales said she was going to lunch and we could wander around at our leisure. After a short time we were greeted by an "old miner". He introduced himself as Gene Harris and offered to serve as our guide.

After forty-five minutes of pleasurable, albeit knowledge-able, rambling supplied by our guide I happened to pass by a window. The few trees I could see leaned into the wind and the carpet of sand that had suddenly blown to block the doorway was about eighteen inches high, now. The streets were deserted. I turned to Gene and somewhat tremulously informed him of the change in weather.

"Well, folks, we could be in for a four minute, or four day storm, so we might as well make ourselves comfortable," the old miner said. "I'll be right back."

He left the room leaving Sally and I looking at each other and quickly returned with some frosty bottles of Birch Beer. Gene told us about himself from the time he left school at fourteen and started punching cows to his days driving the last of the stagecoaches in the area. We sat, quietly sipping our Birch Beer, wondering exactly how old he was when he asked if we wanted to hear about another sandstorm he'd remembered. Considering our present circumstances and being naturally curious, we agreed. Taking off his hat and scratching his shiny bald head he settled into his chair.

"Imagine the scene out in the desert after a storm had passed through. Remember those two lava rocks as you folks came into town? Well, gray sands had piled up against the hill…"

BESIDE one rock the hind legs of a horse stuck up out of the sand. They were stiff and flayed of flesh nearly to the bone. Between the horse and the rock on the right the sands began to move. For half a minute the sands shook violently.

Finally the head and shoulders of a man emerged. After a time he laboriously pulled himself out and sat on a rock.

He took a long pull from his canteen, and struck a match to examine his arm in the failing light. He carefully ripped off the arm of his shirt to reveal a mangled, useless mess. The shoulder was dislocated, the elbow split open to the bone, the wrist seriously sprained—result of his horse's last desperate fight against the storm.

To the left of the dead horse the head of another man slowly arose. Holding his arm carefully as he stood up, Blackburn saw the muzzle of a gun aimed at his head as the other man's eyes raked Blackburn's hip.

"Too bad you din't have sense enough to carry extra cartridges, 'eh Morgan?"

"What happened to your iron? Sand crawl away with it?" Morgan replied.

"Yep." Blackburn looked into the red rimmed eyes of this bandit, thinking of the night before when he and his boys had caught Morgan rustling at the river. They had shot it out, Morgan's crowd hightailing it into the desert. Then the storm broke. It seemed as if the whole desert picked itself up and wrapped itself around the punchers and rustlers alike.

"Lucky thing for me I ducked behind these rocks. The rest of the boys are probably buried beneath the sand," Blackburn said.

Morgan sat down on a rock twirling the empty cylinders of his pistol. He cursed and sent the gun hurtling into space, sat down and rolled a cigarette, and lit it. His eyes glowed red and brutal in the flare.

Blackburn glanced over at Morgan. With each puff of the cigarette Blackburn could see the murder in Morgan's eyes. He watched Morgan, a gigantic silhouette against the angry dawn, with a hatred just as cold as the outlaw's—animal and hot. Morgan was spoiling for his blood, and the fact filled him with grim satisfaction. But right now he'd have to handle him as best he could. He needed him. Blackburn smiled. He thought it was damned funny that two men who meant to kill each other would have to save each other now.

"You Blackburns was always uppity about yer

eddication," Morgan growled abruptly. "Let's see yer damned book learnin' get us out of here."

"Maybe it will," Blackburn said in a flat, emotionless voice. "Come here and spring my shoulder back in place."

Morgan looked over at him, his eyes narrowing. "You got a knife?"

"Yeah, an Opinel with a lock and five-inch blade," Blackburn agreed. "I aim to get out alive, Morgan."

"Then fix yer arm yerself!" Morgan said maliciously. He sat watching Blackburn struggle with his arm. It finally snapped into place with an agonizing jerk. Blackburn winced and frowned with pain.

Morgan chuckled. "That don't rightly hurt yet, wait 'till the sun's been on it a spell."

"That'll be bad for you Morgan," Blackburn gasped. "It'll take two of us to get out of here."

After a while Morgan said, "We ain't gonna get outta here, not afoot, with no trail and every landmark changed! We ain't gonna do nothin' but make special buzzard bait."

"They'll sure get poisoned on you," Blackburn offered.

"That'll be after they finish you. I'm tough, and I ain't got that arm. I aim to sit me down and watch the buzzards peck out yer yellow guts while you're still crawlin'."

Blackburn's face was gaunt and grim. Unless he got Morgan in hand, the outlaw was likely to be right. Morgan was viciously enjoying himself now, his eyes fired with fiendish mirth at each pain-wracked twitch of Blackburn's arm. It would be different after thirst and the heartbreaking march afoot and the fierce heat had inflamed the sullen murder in him.

Morgan stood up and stretched his powerful body against the sky. Suddenly he turned and jumped to the sand between them. Blackburn jammed his hand into his pocket and pulled out his knife. Morgan glared at him but he had respect for a knife. He had seen Blackburn slice up Jack Davis, no bad hand himself.

"We need to work together to figure out how we can get out of here. Empty yer pockets, Blackburn ordered.

Startled into action by the tone in Blackburn's voice,

Morgan squatted on his haunches and began emptying his pockets. There was a pile of American folding money, some Mex gold, a nearly empty tobacco pouch, some cigarette papers, three or four matches and a lucky charm. The last item was a shiny metal piece the size of a silver dollar and bright as a mirror. Morgan flipped the coin a few times and then drew back his arm to throw it into the desert.

"Wait! We can use that," said Blackburn

"What for? To powder yer nose in?"

"I want it," Blackburn repeated in a steady voice.

"What you got to give?" demanded Morgan.

Blackburn laid out the contents of his pockets: a full sack of tobacco, a book of cigarette papers, a metal container of matches, a horseshoe nail, a piece of rawhide, the broken end of a small running brand and a watch.

"I'll swap ya. Yer makings and the matches."

"Half," countered Blackburn.

Morgan shrugged and slowly drew back his arm. "It's worth more to see you go diggin' for it."

"Your pot," Blackburn growled. He shoved out the papers and tobacco with trembling fingers.

"Matches," Morgan said with a cunning look.

Blackburn looked at him with a hard, level gaze. He didn't say a word. Morgan snorted and tossed over the disc. Blackburn threw the matches to him.

He put the disc on his knee and began carefully to quarter lines across it with his knife until he made twelve lines, evenly spaced, marking the hours of the day. Scraping the horseshoe nail clean, straight and thin he notched it carefully. Then he made a small notch at the edge of the disc and fitted the nail on at an angle. Blackburn placed the broken running brand as flat as possible in the sand and poured one single drop of water on the solid middle. It began to move. His fingers juggled with the brand until the drop came back to center and stayed still. He placed the disc atop this and pointed it carefully at the sun. He looked up abruptly at the outlaw.

"This is a compass of sorts, Morgan. But it only works while I'm alive."

A look of malevolence mixed with fear crept over the

outlaw's face. Blackburn dug down in the sand next to his horse and came up with a lariat. He slung it over his shoulder and started trudging in the direction of the mesa rim where he knew the stage would pass.

The sun came out, strong and hot. Blackburn tried to keep his arm in the shade of his body, but an occasional moan escaped him.

Morgan grinned and said, "Ain't never walked with cooking meat before."

Blackburn made several more calculations with his makeshift compass. Each time he used another drop of water. The sun rose to the top of the sky, white and blazing. The sand in front of Blackburn started to dance as the pain in his arm sapped his strength.

As the afternoon wore on, not a word passed between the two men. Blackburn's arm began to fester and smell. About five in the afternoon he called a halt.

Morgan sat down on a rock and rolled a cigarette. The aroma of the tobacco drifted across to Blackburn. He began to think that if he killed Morgan, he could have a smoke. The last time he had a cigarette was before the storm and he felt a great need, a hypnotic desire. He had to shake his head a few times before this notion took possession of his brain. Without Morgan, he could forget about getting out of the desert alive.

"How about giving me a smoke, Morgan?"

Morgan's face shaped a cruel smile. "What'll you trade me for one, Blackburn? Yer pants?"

The temptation of a smoke was too much for Blackburn. He stripped off his pants, standing there, a ridiculous figure in his long underwear, shirt, and vest. The sun hit him with all its force and he felt as if he were on fire. He inhaled deeply, letting the smoke filter slowly through his nose.

As night crept in on them, Blackburn headed for a group of rocks. The evening breeze was like balm on his arm. His mind cleared enough to work through directions in his mind. If the moon rose before the sun set, the illuminated side would be the west. If the moon rises after midnight, the illuminated side would be the east. This obvious discovery would provide him with a rough east-west reference during the night.

Knowing he couldn't trust Morgan, Blackburn took his knife from his shirt pocket, sprung the blade and lashed it to his wrist with the rawhide thong. He tried to get some sleep, but the pain in his arm permitted him no more than a few winks at a time. Each time he awoke, he saw Morgan sitting on a rock near him, smoking a cigarette, watching him.

The heat of the morning sun awakened him with a start. He looked around for Morgan, but he was nowhere in sight. Picking up his lariat and canteen, he shot the sun with his makeshift compass and started off in the direction of the mesa rim. After a while Morgan came panting up to him with a kind of scared look on his face.

"Afraid you'd die our there alone, Morgan?"

"Aw, shut up, Blackburn. I ain't scared o' nothin'. I'll still watch the buzzards pick yer bones."

The pain in Blackburn's arm increased a dozen fold, accompanied by the rays of the sun slicing through the thin covering of his underwear like a knife.

At about noon, when the sun reached its highest point, Blackburn called a halt to take another reading. From the way the canteen was tilted, Blackburn estimated that it was just shy of being half full. Morgan reached for the canteen, almost getting his hand on it when Blackburn's knife slashed down between his hand and the canteen.

With an enraged oath, he lunged for the knife; but Blackburn snapped it back with the thong he had tied to it. Blackburn could see that in a little while even the threat of a belly full of knife would have no effect on him. He also knew he was running out of strength. Blackburn knew that he couldn't last more than three or four hours more. He knew that Morgan knew that fact also.

He turned around and said, "You'll have to tow me on the end of the rope, Morgan.

A cruel grin split Morgan's face. "It'll cost you yer shirt and vest, Blackburn."

"When I want to get someone, Morgan, I don't shoot him in the back." Stripping off his shirt and vest, he stood there in his long underwear. The sun him with tremendous impact.

Taking his lariat, Blackburn tied it around his waist so that Morgan couldn't pull him down by jerking the rope. Measuring off about ten feet, he ordered Morgan to start marching due east.

"We're gonna end up in one of them finger deserts, smack up against those shifting dunes Blackburn, where no one will ever find us. You don't know where yer goin'."

"What's the matter, Morgan? Turning yellow already?"

Calling a halt, Blackburn took another reading. "We're more'n five miles from that stage road on the mesa rim, Morgan. Ought to make it before sundown. Straight ahead is the—"

Jerking the rope suddenly, Morgan pulled Blackburn down and grabbed the canteen. Drinking off half the water, he slung it over his shoulder and started off straight ahead.

Blackburn started to throw his knife but dropped it as the full impact of Morgan's deadly act dawned on him. A grim smile played about his lips.

As the afternoon went on, he made a few more readings without the use of water for his final direction.

Blackburn's calculations weren't perfect, but they served the purpose. His vision started to dim, each step agony, until finally he felt that all he had to do was to lie down and sleep and everything would be all right.

COOL water flowed over his face, snapping Blackburn back from the emptiness he floated in. He opened his eyes and stared into the face of the stage driver, Baldy Harris. Baldy said impatiently. "G'wan, you was tellin' me Morgan had taken your canteen."

Smiling through his parched and split lips, Blackburn said, "All that folderol with the makeshift compass was just meant to keep Morgan from jumpin' me. I had no idea what I was doin'. The moon gave me a rough east-west direction, tha's all. It was more of a sundial. Too bad Morgan didn't wait until I finished talking before he made his play. I started to tellin' him that straight ahead was probably the finger desert!"

GENE stood up slowly, removed his hat and rubbed his bald pate. "All that story tellin' has given me a powerful thirst. I think I'll mosey on back and get us some more Birch Beer."

Sally and I both nodded absentmindedly, still dwelling on the story we had just heard.

Suddenly the door to the museum opened noisily and the ticket lady walked in.

"You folks okay? Couldn't get back sooner 'cause of the storm but it's moved on. I hope you weren't too bothered by it."

Sally smiled, "Not at all. Gene, the old miner gentleman, kept us enthralled with a great story. Does he entertain all your visitors?"

This seemed to fluster the lady. "We don't have any guides here and certainly not any old miners." With that she turned and went into the back of the Museum.

Sally and I looked at each other, unspoken words floating between us. As we started to leave I noticed a grouping of pictures on the wall near an old stagecoach wheel. There, big as life was a picture of Gene. Sally pointed to the note below it.

GENE (BALDY) HARRIS
LAST OF THE BUTTERFIELD OVERLAND
STAGECOACH DRIVERS (1861)

HOWARD "DOC" CARRON, born Brooklyn, NY. PhD, photographer, musician, teacher, ceramist, silversmith, sculptor, wood block artist, writer, editor-in-chief and writer *for Cigar Lovers Magazine*, librarian and chef. Taught in Japan, Okinawa, Korea, Azores, Philippines and Germany. Currently Supervisor of Adult Services at Queen Creek Library. Credits: "The Happy Cooker" series MCLD magazine *Fishline*, "The Last Habano" 2005 in *Medley of Murder*, "A Favor for the Mayor" 2008 in *Medium of Murder*, and "Christmas Came Late" 2009 *How Not to Survive the Holidays*.

THE ROUGH EDGE OF SPRING
Robin Merrill

Cruising along the Sultan Sea near Niland, California, my eyelids weighed heavy and tension twisted an iron fist in the muscles of my upper back and neck. I'd spent long, tense days driving my RV from my frigid home outside Milwaukee, leaving the depressing record-breaking snow, cold and unemployment behind in search of something to thaw my soul and ease the relentless stress—something like a few months wallowing in the hot sand and free spirit of Slab City, the no-frills boondocking haven near Niland.

Ever since I'd turned off I-10 at Indio, the temperatures had risen and time stepped backwards as little towns and roadside stops seemed locked in a vignette of yesteryear. I pulled over at a sixties-era gas station/café and changed into shorts and tank top. I'd already shucked the parka for a jacket this morning before leaving Amarillo, but the cold wind blowing across the Texas plains hadn't encouraged bare skin. I needed bare skin. Skin stripped of excess clothes and despair and all the ugly things that hung on me after months of winter storms and bitter court battles.

Niland proved to be another time-frozen town, buffeted by winds off the more-sand-than-water expanse of lake a few miles away. Some homes boasted small pockets of greenery, flowers and trees emerging into colorful blossoms, leaves unfurling along stark branches. Funny. Two days ago I kicked snow off my boots before entering my RV. Now sand mired my flip-flops as I stepped outside the general store in search of directions. Not that I was lost. I just couldn't find the right road. Besides, I needed to stock up on cold drinks and sunscreen.

Redirected, a cock's tail of dust rose behind my car as I traveled into a desolate land, an ocean of sand broken by gullies and washes with few signs of living anything, including people. Then the road shifted and I saw Salvation Mountain. The painted façade encompassed an entire cliff face, the gigantic rendering of religious fervor and celebration, one man's lifetime dedication to his symbolic stream of consciousness repainted and rebuilt into an ever-growing hillside of colorful folk art. I knew I had arrived.

My smile grew as the oddities continued. I'd heard stories about the Slabs, pale images of its reality. Delight soon overpowered exhaustion and escaped into fits of giggles and outright hoots of laughter. A virtual forest of scrub trees thinly populated the area, crisscrossed with potholed and sand-blown streets. Multi-slide couches with satellite dishes and solar panels mingled with hippie-style hand-painted buses.

Some campers were lined up like storefronts, with fences and even the trucks and utility trailers parked alongside decorated with every kind of discarded debris imaginable— tools, cans, toys, shells, rocks, figurines—glued to their surfaces. Bizarre and yet amazing. I had clearly entered another dimension in the expression of art.

Promising to come back later for a closer look at a few exceptional displays, I spotted a hand-lettered piece of plywood stuck alongside the road touting breakfast specials and social events at the Oasis Club, and thought I'd start my search for my friend and fellow RVer, Maggie, there. I hadn't figured out exactly how, or if, I could find her once I arrived. I didn't have her phone number, and I knew there was no office, no check-in process or fees. No crowds, either, jammed awning to awning, yet perhaps I'd misjudged the difficulty of finding her among the surprisingly large number of RVs haphazardly spread throughout the huge camp area. I'd thought to merely ask someone—after all, she'd been coming here every winter for over thirty years—but now I might end up driving by each rig, looking in vain.

No cars graced the Oasis Club's parking lot. A lone man played horseshoes in the sand next to a gray, concrete slab patio with three old trailers lining the edges. A short breakfast menu hung above a counter outside one of the trailers. Assorted tables clustered in the open area. Overhead tarps formed a sun barrier, snapping and humming in the steady wind. No one else appeared.

After I'd leaned on the counter a few minutes, the man wandered over. "The Club's not open until morning, but is there anything I can help you with?"

"Do you know Maggie Kellen?" At his puzzled look, I lost a little more confidence, readily seeing a door-to-door search in my future, so I prodded his memory. "She's been coming here thirty-some years…has a Class C?" Every time I'd seen Maggie in the Wisconsin Dells on her leisurely fall migration from upstate New York to Slab City, she'd been the only one in a little cab-over-the-driver motor home.

"Oh, that Maggie. She's parked right over there, the rig in the middle." He pointed to the nearest group of RVs, located beyond the parking lot and across a sandy field.

There she was; a pea between two pomegranates. Well, her 42 foot long neighbors didn't overshadow quite that much, but how she lived fulltime in a 28 ft rig including the cab I couldn't fathom. I had a 34 ft Class A with a living room/kitchen slide and went stir crazy after two-week vacations at the Dells. If I hadn't been so desperate for a break I wouldn't consider spending several months in an 8-foot tube with a fat midsection.

I knocked and waited, bubbling with anticipation and unexpected relief that I'd found her. Her shocked surprise was worth every moment of anxiety. "Hey, Maggie. Told you I'd see you at the Slabs sometime."

"Rebecca!" Squeals, hugs and a cup of tea later we caught up on our news. She looked as stylish and elegant as ever, her gray hair neat and curly, subtle makeup softening the faded look of lines and age. She'd told me once she was in her mid-seventies. I could only hope to be as spry and excited by life if I ever reached a similar age.

The first night I parked near Maggie, then spent several days exploring the Slabs. Early walks—before the midday heat discouraged activity—discovering huge sand pits, cracked foundations and potholed dirt roads that crisscrossed the skeletal remains of the Naval training base, Camp Dunlap. Abandoned since WWII, the camp seemed haunted now by glitzy RV escapees and derelicts beyond those left behind. Social extremes looking for similar holes in the tall brush and hot sand somewhere, content to hibernate in solitude.

I found my hole with a spectacular view of evening colors over the Chocolate Mountains in the distance. Maggie brushed aside my apology for moving away. "Pshaw, Rebecca, everyone picks out the right stop after a while. You need your space to heal. Besides, it gives me an excuse to ride my motorcycle."

Like she needed an excuse. She spent more time tooling around the roads on her putt-putt motorcycle than she did walking. Still, I appreciated her support. I'd witnessed the murder of a client's boyfriend, and gone through months of stressful anxiety until the killer—the ex-husband—was finally convicted shortly before I left Milwaukee. Now the poisons of the last eighteen months slowly seeped out, a melancholy process that seemed a fitting counterpoint to the nightly yips and yikes of the coyotes living on the gifts of our human spawned trash cans and left-out food. That included Fritz, the neighbors' poodle left outside one night as the silent gray predators ghosted through the camp.

Two weeks later, while I enjoyed summer-like temper-atures, the rest of the country broke out into record rainstorms and floods, with a crop of tornadoes thrown in for variety. That rough edge of spring seemed far away from my refuge where flower boxes outside the RVs flourished in bright array. I flourished, too, drifting into a peace I hadn't felt in…well, never. Maybe boondocking fulltime suited me more than I'd thought.

The Travelin' Pals, one of RVers social groups Maggie belonged to, were giving a Spring Festival at their clubhouse, with events scheduled throughout the day and a party that night. The first event after the breakfast buffet was a Treasure Hunt using our handheld GPS units. I'd geocached around Milwaukee, finding hidden notes and tokens with my GPS from clues posted on the web. This should be a piece of cake, and get me out on a longer desert walk than usual, too.

Eight a.m. sharp I bee-lined to the Treasure Hunt table, manned by George, a Slab year-rounder. A long, gray scraggly braid lashed his hair back from a receding hairline; one of his own line of Slab City tie-dyed T-shirts encased his oversized belly. I waited behind several other eager hunters.

"You have a plan, don't you?" Brad, another Treasure Hunt volunteer, asked, grinning as he came over. I'd heard that he and George spent days planning the route and planting clues, which made the challenge more interesting.

"I do," I assured him. "I'm going to head for them thar hills and find gold."

Brad laughed. The sound somehow grated on my nerves. He was near my age, attractive, single. I'd met him at my first Travelin' Pals' meeting. He'd arrived at the Slabs eight years before, camped under a tree for ten days—no tent, no gear, nothing—then headed home, sold everything he could, bought an RV, and has spent every winter here ever since. I found his story fascinating, but the man less so.

"Well, I see you've at least put on shoes," he said. "Don't forget a hat and plenty of water. You're going out with a partner, right?"

"Does my cell phone count?" I moved up a couple spaces.

He frowned. "No. Well, it's required, but seriously, you shouldn't go out into the desert alone."

I appreciated his concern, but I'd been solo for a long time. "Not to worry. I've got my super duper Bushnell ONIX GPS tracker and the decoder ring, too. Besides, I never get lost."

He didn't look reassured. I took my clue sheet and waved as I headed out. My belt already sported dual water containers, but I grabbed an extra bottle for my fanny pack. Energy bars, a sandwich and apple, sun screen, a bandana and snake bite kit filled the rest of the bulging pack.

Floppy hat firmly on my head, I programmed the first set of coordinates. The most interesting early stop was the Pet Cemetery, where rocks and things outlined memorials in tribute of family pets left behind as their people journeyed on. I located the clue attached to the plastic flowers dedicated to Josie, a Cocker Spaniel who died ten years ago, and jotted the coordinates down on the sheet. From there, I headed into the open desert, meandering over rocky ground and weaving through swaying boughs of shrubs taller than my head.

Unfortunately, I got...off course. I wasn't lost. I'd entered a coordinate wrong, and hiked for an hour before I corrected it and headed back on track. Hungry, I perched on a large rock and ate a snack bar with the second bottle of water. Sweat soaked my T-shirt, beaded my brow and slid down the back of my neck before I mopped it up with the bandana. Two clues remained. I pushed off with considerably less enthusiasm then I'd had at the club house.

I had no warning whatsoever. I merely walked between two scrubs and into a scene from hell. The coyotes registered first. Four or five, maybe more, shied restlessly as I entered the sandy clearing. My attention fixed on the alpha male. He faced me unmoving, slightly crouched, eyes staring in challenge, his lips raised in a low-throated snarl that sent a shaft of instinctive terror through my body. Blood marked his snout. My God, what had I stumbled upon? Had they taken down a deer or a...A checked shirt lay at the coyote's feet. No, not a shirt, a man, a body sprawled there, half-hidden by a curve in the rolling surface.

Breath hitching in panicky gulps, I caught the movement of the pack out of the corner of my eye and glanced over about twenty or thirty feet. A pair of boots stuck up from another sandy hump. Another body. No, no, no, no. The bitter taste of bile scored my throat. For one horrible moment my mind replayed the image of Matt, my client's boyfriend, falling in a spray of blood.

Another growl that ended in a yipping cough warned me away from their kill. The ones near the alpha tensed, fangs gleaming white. Anger burned stronger than terror, or even common sense. I let out yell and charged, baring my own blunted fangs. "Come on, you bastards! Let's see you face someone alive. Come on!"

The coyotes broke as I took a few menacing steps toward them, scattering into the brush. For a moment, I thought it had worked, but they didn't go far. I could hear them, feel them, lingering around the clearing. I stood still, trying to gather my flagging courage. Funny how facing down a pack of wild beasts seemed easier than facing the human remains lying motionless before me.

Please, God, hadn't I seen enough death? I fought the nightmare image of Matt's murder and concentrated on the first body. The animals had gotten to the exposed flesh, but a bullet hole drilled the chest dead center. No gun lay near him. I pressed my hands against my mouth, my stomach, as if I could keep down the snack I'd eaten. Then I studied the other man. I felt the blood drain from my face. A chill raced down my spine, terror fisted around my throat. He appeared to have dragged himself ten or fifteen feet, bleeding all the way. I couldn't see a gun around him, either, but that didn't mean anything. It could be under him or buried nearby. Coyote tracks added to the scuffed sand around him, as if he'd flailed around, perhaps keeping them at bay. His sightless eyes and torn flesh indicated he'd lost that battle some time ago. How long? To my horror, I realized they looked awfully fresh, given the heat.

Once I rinsed my mouth out after tossing my cookies, I struggled to clear my mind. What now? I couldn't leave the...bodies there alone. I just couldn't. Not with the flickers of coyotes moving in the brush beyond the clearing. Fumbling in my fanny pack, I pulled out my cell phone and checked for a signal. Thank God, I had bars! I felt a little more confident, until the call to 911 dropped...and dropped again. Panicking, I brought my recent call list and called the last number in the queue, praying somehow it would ring through.

"Maggie?" My voice quivered as soon as I heard her sweet hello. Tears breeched my eyes. "I...I—"

"Rebecca? What's wrong, dear?"

"There's been a...an accident out here in the desert. No, not me, a couple of guys I never saw before. They, ah, didn't make it, Maggie." Reassuring her again that I was okay calmed me. I asked her to call 911 for me, fumbled a moment with my Bushnell and then gave her my GPS coordinates to pass along. The eminent threat of coyote occupied my eyes. I licked my lips. "Is George or Brad there?"

After a terse explanation to Brad, I gave him the same

coordinates and waited for reinforcements. I kept the animals at bay, snarling my own threats and waving my arms, pitching a few rocks as they crept out into the clearing. Hit one of them, too. Soon, the sound of a dune buggy broke the silence. A trek that had taken me over three hours took them only thirty minutes. Hugs never felt so welcome, sweaty shirt, teary face and all.

Brad brought George and another fellow from the club with him. Mindful of the crime scene, I'd waved him off as he'd approached the clearing. George tried to approach the bodies, pooh-poohing my warnings.

"Damn it, George," I finally threatened, "you watch TV! You're going to have the cops on your ass if you disturb the evidence."

"I was just going to look! Are you sure they're dead?"

An image of torn flesh and bloody trails arose and I shook it off. "Yes, I'm sure. You can look from back here, okay?"

Now we waited for the police to arrive from Calipatria, about ten miles from Niland. The noise had chased away the coyotes. Too bad I didn't have something to chase away my latest nightmare. As selfish as it seemed, I thought more about being in court again on the wrong side of the bench than about the men lying a few feet away. Their battles were over. Mine could just be beginning. Or maybe, just maybe, my old one had followed me here.

"You should go on back to camp," Brad urged for the fifth time. "I'll wait here with George. We'll stay back, I promise. Oh, and beat off the wild animals, if they come back."

I snorted at his attempt of humor. Bet he didn't believe me about the coyotes hanging around. Hysterical woman, right? Jerk. Still, I rethought my decision as the sun beat down and I sweltered in the musty old buggy with a fringed canvas top. What was taking so long, anyway?

"Let's give it another half hour," I said, lifting the hair off my neck. We'd already debated every theory we could think of, except the one I kept to myself, and had nothing more to say. Fortunately, the cops arrived before I melted and a

Detective Longmore took our preliminary statements. He said they'd already blocked off the access road and had officers going through the long process of checking camper to camper. I gave him directions on how to find my RV, and he told me to stay there and stay silent. Yeah, I knew the drill.

I'd hydrated, showered, and eaten dinner by the time Longmore came around. "Would you like something cold or hot?" I offered, waving him to the kitchen table. "I brewed a fresh pot of coffee, if you're interested."

"Coffee, please, Ms. Aimsworth." He waited until I'd settled across from him with my own cup before starting his questions. Step by step, we went over the events again. He seemed easily satisfied. Too easily.

"Do you know who those men were, or what happened?" I asked.

"No, ma'am, we're pursuing all possible leads at this time."

Yeah, but would he really want the one I had to offer? Did I want to tell him, or would it needlessly complicate my part in the investigation? Or worse, would it deflect the police from the real culprits? No, that wasn't the worst. The worst would be having them focus on me as the culprit. I sighed. I'd long since lost faith in the justice system. Then again, he'd find out during his background checks. Guess it'd be better coming from me.

"There is one other thing. Probably doesn't have any bearing on what happened out there, but…"

He raised an eyebrow.

"I'm an attorney. About eighteen months ago, I witnessed a murder in Milwaukee. I was leaving work late, trying to juggle my briefcase and purse and lunch box and keys, and my cell phone fell out, slid under the edge of the car. I should have cursed. Would have saved me a lot of grief, although probably wouldn't have saved Matt. Matt Michaels. He was the new boyfriend of my client, Sharon Thompson. Their relationship had a…a special spark about it, an effervescent joy. He was on top of the world, and she'd started to bloom again, a flower finding the sun. Her ex-husband objected. He'd objected to many things during the divorce. Hell, almost a year later, he was still filing motions against a settlement that took over six months to work out!"

I paused, dreading the next part. Longmore simply watched, impassive: a quiet witness to the maelstrom whirling around me. "I heard some men talking by the elevators while I fished out the phone. I waited a moment, embarrassed. What if they caught me on my knees, ass up between two cars in a parking garage? That time of evening, lots of people used the garage for downtown events and such. Only when I stood up, I knew them. Matt and Larry Thompson, Sharon's ex. For a second, I thought I'd forgotten an appointment, but where was Sharon? Then their voices became angry. Vicious. I'd heard some scuttlebutt about Thompson's harsh business reputation, but nothing violent and Sharon had refused to discuss any grounds based on domestic violence. I sensed, no, I knew she'd been knocked around some, but an attorney can only push so far.

"Thompson already had his gun out when I saw them. He shot Matt, two bullets right though the chest. I—I just stood there. Frozen. The ramp partly obscured the view, but I saw Thomson step closer. He bent down, and fired again. I ducked low, eased the door open, and got the hell out of there."

Longmore gave me a moment to calm down. I had never spoken about the incident in such detail, except officially. Stories such as these make good fiction, not friends. The horror stays locked inside, forever a barrier between me and everyone else.

Then he asked the key question. "Is Thompson a threat to you?"

Pushing back the inevitable panic attack that crawled up my throat whenever I thought too much about those days, I tried to be objective. "I'm not sure. He'd killed Sharon earlier that same night, before luring Matt to my office. He made threats. He's a very wealthy man, with unsavory connections." I shrugged. "The police took him seriously enough to provide protection once my name came out, and during the trial. He's in prison now doing life, but…the coincidence…"

"I understand, Ms. Aimsworth. We'll look into it." A smile, more a grimace, glanced off his lips.

I nodded, but doubted he placed any credence to my concerns. Thompson had served his revenge hot, twice, but surely it'd grown cold. At least Longmore couldn't confront me about the case later.

By late evening, the police had completed their door-to-door and left. The camp returned to normal, abuzz with the grand excitement. Brad followed me around the clubhouse as volunteers finished the clean up from the festivities. "They kept asking me about dune buggies and ATVs. What did they ask you?"

"Nothing much."

"Aw, come on, Rebecca. What'd they want? Did you see anything, you know, earlier?"

Finally, I'd had enough. "Earlier? Look, Brad, I told them the same thing I told you guys out there, I didn't see anything but dead bodies, earlier or otherwise!"

I stormed out and walked back to my rig. George approached from the other direction, slowly pedaling toward me on his relic of a bicycle, balloon tires and upright handlebars with a big squeeze bulb horn. His bald head glistened above the long braid, Pooh Bear on a bike. I grinned and exchanged pleasantries as he passed, humor restored.

THE following morning, Brad was supervising the installation of my new solar panels when the police arrived. Not that he had any business supervising, I'd bought them from a retailer here, one of the permanent Slab City residents, and Hank was installing them himself. Brad just couldn't help himself. "You need to move it to the left, Hank. A little more…little more. Keep going."

The detective's arrival distracted us and probably saved Hank from making some snarky remark. Naturally, Brad tagged along when I went to meet Longmore and his partner. Why were they here? Cops didn't make social calls, but sometimes…they did deliver news. Bad news, usually. After a week of hearing nothing, I'd had more than enough of churning tension and disturbing nightmares. I'd take anything, if it ended this ordeal. "Good afternoon, gentlemen. Can I help you with something?"

"No, ma'am. Actually, we're here to speak to Mr. Prichart."

Prichart? Who was that? He headed toward Brad. Oh.

"Mr. Prichart, you're under arrest for the murder of Henry Moore and Frank Edwards. You have the right…"

As he began to Mirandize Brad, my mind fell into broken bits. Brad? Amiable jerk Brad? Tag along schmoozer Brad? God! I turned slightly and watched in stunned disbelief as Longmore, a cuff clasped in his hand, reached for Brad. Face twisted with rage and perhaps desperation, Brad dodged in my direction and before I could move he wrapped an arm around my throat and dragged me backwards. A hard shape pressed against my head. "Stay back, or I'll shoot!"

I fought against the instant flashback. That voice, vicious and ugly, deeper than I'd ever heard from Brad, froze me in place. Longmore's hand stilled. I could see the butt of his weapon gripped in his fist beneath his lightweight jacket. Beside him, his partner paused, hand at his lower back. Locked in place, they radiated immanent action.

My nails bit into the arm throttling me. "Brad," I croaked, wishing I could yell.

"Shut up, it's your fault they were found, anyway! I told you to take someone. But no, you never get lost, you said. Bitch! You even had a fancy freaking GPS!" He dragged me farther back. "Throw your guns down, now!" The barrel dug into my scalp. "Now!"

As soon as the guns plopped into the sand, he switched his aim toward the cops, and mercifully the choking eased. Air rushed into starved lungs. I realized where he was dragging me, toward his SUV parked around the edge of my rig. Voices from a self-defense class echoed through my head: Never allow yourself to be taken to a secondary location without a fight. I knew I'd be dead if I didn't stop him from taking me with him. I picked my legs up off the ground, my weight loosening his hold. Desperate, I struggled to jerk away. Away from his grasping hands. His gun. Then what felt like a ton of bricks fell from the sky.

For a long moment, I sprawled on a hard ground, pain obscuring all thought, all vision, all awareness. Gritty hot sand burned my cheek, my arm. A voice registered. "Are you all right, Ms. Aimsworth?"

Longmore. The world made sense again. Sort of. "I—I think so. What happened?"

I slitted my eyes against the fierce pain in my head and back, moved just enough to peer behind me. A body lay there, silent, unmoving, the solar panel that had smashed into us wedged on its side, edges smeared with blood. Maybe even mine. From the trail of oozing wounds about his head and chest, Brad had borne the brunt of impact. Moving gingerly, I looked up.

Hank crouched at the edge of my roof, stricken face staring at the havoc he'd wrought. "Is he dead?"

"Good question," I said, turning to Longmore as he lifted the panel aside to examine the still body. We waited, and in a crazy moment I wondered if Brad would be happy now that Hank had moved the panel far enough to the left.

"He's alive."

Thank goodness. I didn't want Hank to bear that burden. Heroes rest better untainted.

I put my head back down, and let the haze pull me away from the pain.

THEY kept me in the hospital for two days before releasing me. Since then, Maggie and George almost took up residence, a couple of fluttering but much appreciated chatterboxes.

"I can't believe it," George lamented for about the tenth time. "Brad, conducting over-the-border business with the cartels."

"You think he's been doing it all the years he's come here?" Maggie had brought her knitting. Needles flashed in and out of the growing yarn whatever-it-was with only an occasional glance to check her pattern.

"I don't know, Maggie." He sighed. "People used to come here for the adventure, the excitement of boondocking without a bunch of rules and the next guy's awning in your face. Now…how could a drug-running murderer be one of us?"

The needles paused. Our eyes slid from one to another. No one had an answer.

"What went wrong, did Longmore ever say anything?" Maggie asked, her needles flying once more.

I nodded. "He came to see me yesterday at the hospital. Brad struck a deal. Seems a cartel rep demanded a meeting that morning. He met them early on, away from the Treasure Hunt area, never suspecting it'd turn violent. Said they tried to blackmail him, and he knew their demands would never end. He didn't have time to dispose of the bodies before he had to be at the club, just hid their ATV and waited until all the Treasure Hunters came back in. Longmore said he'd seemed very concerned about leaving the club in a lurch, like it meant something to him to finish his job."

"Yeah, an alibi," snapped George. Then he looked sheepish.

Maybe Brad did have reasons other than needing a cover story. I don't claim to understand human complexities. I'd seen it all during more than twenty-five years handling Family Law. Much of it tore my heart out. Nothing is simple once people's emotions get involved.

I do know one thing. I needed a vacation from my vacation. Now that spring has settled into a softer edge, maybe I'll head back north and dance with a few tornadoes.

ROBIN MERRILL lived more than half her life in Alaska. She has also lived in California, Phoenix, and Chicago. Now she spends time with her grandbabies in Chicago and writes the winters away in Phoenix, working on, among other things, her autobiography about her life as an early Alaskan homesteader. Her works include mystery short stories "Coffee Break", *Map for Murder*, "Fast Pace," *Medley of Murder*, and her latest romantic suspense novel *Some Like It Red Hot*, available through most bookstores and online booksellers.

THE HAUNTED HOGAN
Nancy Nielson Redd

The Arizona Chronicle, August 1, 2006

> *After a day of high winds, Lake Powell Park Rangers found a luxury boat, the Sweet Dreams, adrift in debris at the head of Navajo Canyon, thudding relentlessly against the rock cliff. The key in the ignition, still turned on, gave evidence that the boat had stopped after it had run out of gas. They found the rope-tangled body of Samuel Phillips, 56, at the stern, legs mangled by the slashing of the propellers. Though not immediately apparent, they also found a gunshot wound in his neck, so placed that it could not have been self-inflicted.*

THE call came as Valerie sank back into her pillows, ready for sleep. A dreadful, sinking sensation swept over her when she heard Alysha's whisper. Her breath caught.

Did they actually go through with it? She wondered. *Yeah, we joked about it, but none of us took the death threats seriously. I know I didn't.*

Tired as she was, Valerie's apprehension destroyed any possibility of sleep. She remembered Sam, healthy and handsome, turning on his charm, radiating fun-loving humor, exuberance, and generosity. The problem was, he could and would turn his charm off just as quickly.

Sam had always enjoyed his inherited wealth. His family owned a business on the Navajo Reservation, and he, taking the path of least resistance, gravitated to it, though he played more than he worked. A party animal, he liked to drink, have affairs, fly his plane and drive his boat from one spontaneous event to another.

Sam loved women. In return, women responded to him. Early on, Sam led a charmed life, but after a few car accidents, one plane crash, many drugs to heal his injuries, and years of alcoholism, his fun-loving ways became addictions. Then the other side of Sam surfaced; he became surly and demanding, resorting to verbal abuse when his demands were not met.

Valerie mentally ran through the list of his wives, all beautiful, capable, decent women, all swept off their feet when Sam chose them over others. Each one wanted to love him and share life with him. But he, often under the influence of alcohol or high on drugs, didn't recognize the generosity or the fragility of their love. He tossed them aside like soiled socks.

Sam liked to be married, but he didn't want marriage to cramp his style. Each of his first four wives, for her own reasons, had reached a moment when she'd had it with Sam. Valerie shook her head. Such a waste.

AT the end of July, all of Sam's wives gathered at Wahweap Marina on Lake Powell for a vacation, organized by Valerie, ex-wife number three. Valerie invited his other exes, Sarah, Barbara, and Mary, as well as his current wife, Alysha, who would be an ex-wife if only she could afford it.

When she set up the trip, Valerie laughingly advised them of her one rule: "This vacation is all about us. It's a retreat from Sam. No talk about him. Forget him. We're going to wipe him right out of our minds."

Initially, Alysha had turned her down. "Sam's not going to like it. He tells me I shouldn't hang out with you, you'll poison my mind against him."

"Fat chance," Valerie told her. "He doesn't need my help. He can do that all by himself." In the end, Alysha joined the others at the lake, because even though she, a beautiful, young Navajo woman, still clung to many of her Native American traditions—in her tribe, women rule.

VALERIE had rented a houseboat, which came filled with gas. She bought the groceries and packed them in. Tied to the back was the old speedboat she'd bought from Sam when he upgraded. Sarah and her husband owned a speed boat as well.

Valerie suggested Sarah bring it along so they could ski more. Mary would ride with Sarah. They could all sleep on the houseboat, but Valerie planned to camp on a quiet beach, build a fire, and then cool off in the water after the heat of the day. The others could do their own thing.

"I've got my gun with me, girls, so I can protect us if I need to," Mary said.

"Protect us from what?" Valerie asked.

"Whatever—snakes or coyotes, anything slinking, slithering, or walking. You never know."

They relaxed, laughed, snapped pictures, and talked a lot about everything but Sam, who, after all, was the focal point of their connection.

On the third evening of their retreat, while cooking hamburgers on the beach, who should motor up to their campsite but Sam. Typical Sam. He always thought everything was all about him. Alysha cringed when she saw him.

Sam obviously wanted to be invited to eat with them. All eyes swiveled toward Valerie. She raised her eyebrows in a questioning glance back at them. Each one shook her head.

"Sorry, Sam. This little vacation is all about us. You'll have to go somewhere else to eat."

He rolled his eyes and drove his boat to another beach, several hundred yards away. It had been peaceful, not even thinking about Sam. Now, like a hippo on the houseboat, he dominated the conversation.

"Damn Sam. I could strangle him," first wife Sarah exploded.

"Strangle him? You'd have to get too close. Why not poison him?" Barbara, who liked to cook, asked.

"Or shoot him," Mary, number four, offered. "He could be considered a snake in the grass."

Valerie spiced up the plan. "Let's drown him. He spends all his time on the lake anyway."

In their joking mood, they all laughed.

Valerie, clinging to her idea, said, "I'm telling you girls, the most natural way would involve his boat."

"You're right," said Mary. "He's always on it and he's

always drinking. Remember last year when the Park Rangers found him hanging onto a rope being pulled through the water while the boat chugged up-channel? He had fallen in and would have drowned then if the rope hadn't been handy. I don't think anyone would question another 'accident' since they've saved him from his own carelessness more than once."

"Yeah," Valerie said. "The trick would be making it look accidental."

"It would take two boats." Barbara, seriously planning, thought out loud. "If a couple of us took Sarah's speed-boat…"

Alysha, seeming not to have heard Barbara said, "You know, something really weird happened when we were in Phoenix last week. Sam always has me do the driving. He has what he thinks is a smart little scam figured out. We went to several doctors he knows who gave him prescriptions for Percoset. Then we went around to different pharmacies to have the prescriptions filled.

"About ten o'clock that night, I drove him down Central Avenue south of the freeway. I'm not really even sure where we were. I stopped when he told me to. Sam got out and talked to three odd-looking guys. One of them was super tall. Another one was short and almost square, and the third was kind of average, but chunky. While I watched, I thought that I might not recognize their faces, but if I ever saw them all together again, I'd recognize their shapes. In my mind, I named them 'The Three Bears.' Then Sam got in the car carrying a package about the size of a shoe box. He told me, 'Come on. Let's get out of here.' It was pretty scary."

"He did stuff like that when I was with him, too," Mary said. "I don't know why he hasn't overdosed long before now. Or been knifed in South Phoenix."

Bringing the conversation back to their macabre game, Sarah said, "We could always do an overdose, but I like the poetic justice of the boat."

The conversation suddenly seemed too serious. Valerie concluded the fantasy by yawning and heading for her tent. "Okay. Sam's always good for a joke, but enough about him.

Dream about him if you must, but I'm doing just fine with him alive, as long as he's not with me. He's not worth the hassle."

"It's just a game, Val, we'd never actually do it." Barbara looked at the group of women. "Would we?"

Yawning, Sarah said, "You know what? It's so peaceful out here, I can probably do without my sleeping pill tonight."

"Hmm. I didn't know you had trouble sleeping," Mary said.

"Oh, yeah. Insomnia is my middle name," Sarah laughed. "I practically need a tranquilizer dart to put me to sleep."

IN the morning, Sam steered his boat by their beach, carelessly trailing a long wake that splashed up onto their campsite. With an arrogant grin, he flipped a casual salute. Valerie and Mary, loading an ice chest, grabbed the sides of their rocking boat.

"Look at him, flaunting his beautiful boat," Mary said. "He thinks money entitles him to treat us with contempt." She flipped a finger to his retreating back.

After another day exploring the canyons and soaking up the sun, they camped on Padre Bay, the best place for skiing. That night, to their dismay, Sam arrived again.

"How are we going to wipe him out of our minds if he keeps showing up?" Mary grumbled.

"We don't want to get Alysha in too much trouble with Sam or he won't let her come with us again. If she weren't with us, I'd tell him to get lost," Valerie murmured.

Grudgingly, they invited Sam to stay for supper. After he had shared their food, and cluttered up their thoughts, they cleaned up the camp. Sam insisted that Alysha leave the retreat and go with him, but they all protested so loudly that he gave up. They all watched as the *Sweet Dreams* chugged out of sight.

The ex-wives took a last, lazy splash in the smooth-as-glass water. Valerie sighed with pleasure at the sight of their faces, soft and beautiful in the peachy, watercolor afterglow of sunset.

Later, dry and warm around the fire, the conversation

ebbed and flowed under a clear night sky. They roasted marshmallows and watched the moon's reflected path glistening across the lake. So mellow, and yet...

Valerie knew the anger and frustration Sam had aroused in his wives the moment he had intruded on their peaceful vacation.

Sarah, Sam's first wife, had fallen in love with him when he was young and sober. While still a toddler, Sophie, their daughter, had been brain-damaged in a fall, an avoidable accident caused by Sam. Sarah had lived with the heartbreak of Sophie's handicap for more than twenty years now, and would continue till her last breath.

When Sam couldn't talk Sarah into staying with him, he married Barbara, a young woman tired of waitressing in Flagstaff. They stayed together until she caught him at home with another woman.

Valerie, his third wife, met him when he commissioned a painting from her. With the proceeds, she opened her gallery, where he'd pop in, scattering compliments like confetti. Valerie developed a grateful affection for him, then married him, becoming part of his "collection."

Mary left him when, drinking from his vodka-filled water bottle, he stumbled into her while they were on the escalator at Scottsdale Fashion Square. She fell, broke her ankle, and had a miscarriage. He blamed her for being clumsy. She was never able to conceive another child.

They liked to retell their experiences as one of Sam Phillips' wives, laughing till they cried, and sometimes crying till they laughed. Valerie cringed when asked to tell her break-up moment, because her experiences with him didn't come close to the hurt and humiliation the others had suffered, especially Sarah and Mary.

They all knew her story and urged her to tell it. Just before she divorced him, he introduced her to a state senator as "Wife number three, Ms. ABC—Artsy Bitsy Craftsy," mocking her successful business as a trivial pursuit.

In the telling, with hands on her hips, Valerie assumed a haughty pose. "I looked at him, raised my eyebrow, and said to the senator, 'Sam is my husband number one. 'A' number one. Stands for Ass…terisk.'" The ex-wives loved the story because in that one sentence, Valerie had managed to diminish Sam to a footnote in her life.

Alysha, just twenty-four years old to his fifty-five, married him for his money. She didn't tell him that, but Valerie and the other women all knew it.

ABOUT ten o'clock on the fifth morning, the wind kicked up, so Valerie decided to head for the marina. Sarah wanted to wait the wind out in one of the canyons because fighting the waves made her nervous. Mary stayed with Sarah.

In the high winds, the water whipped back and forth between narrow canyon walls, the waves surging bigger and bigger. Out of the canyons in the open waters, the ungainly houseboat towing the speed boat pitched with frightening intensity, forcing Valerie to concentrate all her energy on controlling the craft

By the time she'd driven the boat into its docking slip, unloaded and cleaned it with the help of Barbara and Alysha, and then driven to Page, she was exhausted.

"Thanks, Val. I've loved this week, except for Sam butting in. This retreat was just what we all needed," Alysha said when Valerie dropped her off at her house.

When they arrived at Valerie's house, Barbara said, "You have the first shower. I'll put things away."

The next day, after taking Barbara to the airport to catch her plane, Valerie went to the gallery to check things out. She found that one of her favorite portraits had sold, so she started painting another. Immersed in business, another day flew by. Another day that she ended feeling tired to the bone. At home again, she checked her messages and was relieved to hear Sarah say that she and Mary were home safe.

She'd just sunk back into her pillows and turned on the TV when the phone rang.

"Sam is dead," Alysha whispered, her voice shaking.

Her quivering voice unleashed waves of emotion. Valerie gasped.

"It's just like we talked about, and the police are questioning me," Alysha said. "But I didn't do it…you know

I didn't do it, Val."

"Alysha, what happened?"

"The police will question you and Sarah, too, Val, and they told me that Mary and Barbara will have to come back for questioning."

"How did he die?" Valerie asked.

"He was shot." Alysha struggled to control her voice. "Maybe strangled…maybe drowned…poisoned…and for sure overdosed. They think the gunshot killed him, but they're not sure yet. They do know we were all out on the lake last week."

The reality was so eerily close to the scenario the ex-wives had joked about, it gave Valerie chills. Of course, the beauty of their plot had been that a fatal accident could so easily happen, given Sam's unhealthy lifestyle.

WHEN the police interviewed Valerie, she simply told them she didn't know who had murdered Sam. They had no reason to doubt her, but after he finished his questions, the officer in charge said, "Please don't leave town. We'll want to talk to you and the others again."

SATURDAY afternoon, Valerie sat with Sarah and Sophie, Barbara, and Mary at the stately funeral of their supposedly filthy rich, but dead, ex-husband. Alysha, wiping away tears, sat in the front row. Alysha's brother, Tony, an elite Native American tracker, sat next to her. Alysha had told Valerie more than once that Tony was her protector, that he'd looked out for her since they were kids. "He worries about me more than ever since I married Sam," she'd explained.

Valerie watched as Sarah cried. Sophie cried, probably because her mother did, but Alysha cried the most. Valerie supposed that Sarah cried for the memories of sweet but shattered dreams. And she was sure that Alysha cried because she realized that there was nothing but debts left for her to inherit.

The expressions on Barbara's and Mary's faces showed only the usual serious contemplation of mortality. Valerie kept her face as unemotional as she could. She looked around at the assembled crowd. She knew some of them and wondered who others were.

Two good-looking Anglo guys she didn't know sat in the row ahead of her. She thought they looked governmental, definitely not mourners, because of the way they continually scanned the group.

Valerie also felt concern about two other unknowns seated a couple rows ahead on her left. She pegged them as slick and shady, like guys Sam might have met on the back streets of South Phoenix. One of them was markedly tall and the other was short and wide.

She noted, too, several Navajo men in the back, watchful eyes inspecting those who had come to pay their last respects to Sam Phillips.

After the services, the family filed out first. As Alysha passed Valerie, she reached out to her for a hug. She whispered, "Those guys, the tall one and the short one, are two of the guys Sam got the package from in South Phoenix."

VALERIE, who had volunteered to host the after-funeral gathering at her house, breathed a sigh of relief when the last guest left. Sarah had returned to her house with Mary, who was again staying with her. Barbara and Alysha sat at the table discussing Sam.

She heard the front door slam and footsteps in the hall. Surprised, she looked up expectantly, thinking someone had forgotten something.

The unmistakably tall guy and the noticeably short guy from the funeral burst into the kitchen. The short one held a gun and the other held a baseball bat nonchalantly over his shoulder.

"All right, ladies. Let's talk," the short, square one said.

Valerie stared, open-mouthed in alarm, too surprised to speak. Alysha put her hand to her heart and gasped. Barbara sat wide-eyed and silent.

"Sam owed us big time. We're here to collect."

Her stomach clenched in fear, Valerie staggered back to support herself against the sink, wishing Mary, holding her

9mm pistol would come through the door.

"How much does 'big time' mean?" Alysha asked, in a wobbly voice.

"Sam owned us fifty-nine thousand bucks. We're willing to set up a payment schedule. With interest, of course."

"Why did you let Sam's debt get so big?"

"Because we thought he had tons of money. Now, we find out he went bankrupt. So it's your debt."

"You've got to be kidding…" Valerie blustered.

"You think we're kidding? You wanna end up like Sam, floatin' at the back end of a boat?"

The other man, tall and thin, spoke for the first time in a smooth, purring tone. "I think these ladies need some time to think about it, Alex. Let's take 'em to a good, quiet place. You know that place we found out on the rez. We don't wanna stay here, where the neighbors could come in at any time." The menace in his voice sent chills up Valerie's spine.

When the men said, "Come on, let's go," they went. Valerie's mind raced, searching for any ideas to help them break away, but escape seemed hopeless. In desperation, she wondered, *Where's Tony? Alysha needs him, and so do I.*

The vehicle they were led to, a big, black Hummer, sat in Valerie's driveway, the third man in the driver's seat. Valerie and Barbara got in the back, squeezed between the two who'd entered the house. They ordered Alysha to sit in front with the driver.

"Okay, ladies. Hand over your cell phones. We'll give you until morning to figure out how to pay Sam's debts. None of you is gonna get hurt as long as we get our money. You can find a way, so think it over and come up with a plan. We're just talkin' smart financial plannin' here."

They rode in silence past the Salt River Power Plant, out toward Kaibeto. Not far from the trading post, the driver turned onto an unpaved, rutted road. They jolted over that road for fifteen minutes and stopped at what appeared to be a deserted hogan, surrounded by sagebrush and scrub cedars.

"My uncle died in this hogan. Nobody will come anywhere near here," Alysha said. "Spirits…" Her voice trailed off, and, shivering, she started to cry. "Will you let me stay outside? Please."

Ignoring her pleas, Short Square pushed her into the abandoned hogan. Tall Skinny, ominously silent, herded Valerie and Barbara behind them. The driver stayed in the Hummer.

An old, frayed blanket covered the door opening. Once inside, Short Square said, "Don't try to run. There's nothin' out there but snakes and coyotes and us. This ain't no game, ladies."

They had nowhere to sit but on the dirt floor. Before leaving them, Tall Skinny said, "We'll be outside waiting."

In a grim flash of humor, Valerie pictured this deserted, earth-packed hogan with a huge Hummer parked outside. She wondered why Phoenix drug lords would bring their victims to the reservation. She also wondered if they would really let them go, or if they were soon-to-be dead women.

HOURS later, settled on the hard-packed dirt floor in the middle of the darkening room, and after listening to endless rustlings and scurryings and howlings, Valerie's common sense kicked in. She knew the men didn't want dead bodies to dispose of, they wanted money. To get it they'd have to take the women back to town, because none of them had checkbooks or credit cards or cell phones with them. Valerie concluded that these guys actually seemed stupid. Bringing them out here was a terrorism tactic without teeth.

"WHAT do you think?" Valerie asked. "I haven't got fifty-nine thousand dollars."

Barbara spoke through tears. "It took the last of my savings to fly back here, but I can't stay here with field mice and rattlesnakes…and maybe even the spirit of Alysha's dead uncle." Alysha gasped but Barbara went on, "I'll pay whatever I can just to get out of here. Maybe I can borrow from my parents."

"I guess I could sell my boat and mortgage my business and go into debt up to my eyeballs," Valerie said.

Alysha trembled violently. Valerie put her arms around her and spoke out of the darkness.

"I wonder where your brother Tony is? Do you think he saw them take us?"

"I know he's out there," Alysha answered. "He asked me about these men at the funeral, and my other brothers watched them from the back."

"Do you think we can raise all that money? Are they right? Was Sam bankrupt?" Barbara asked.

"I didn't tell you this before, but Sam declared bankruptcy a couple of weeks ago. He was going to lose the boat. He said he was on his last trip." Alysha whispered.

"He didn't know how right he was." Thinking out loud, Valerie continued, "You know, I wonder if these guys really did kill Sam. They want money more than anything. How did they know where to find him? How did they get out there?"

Barbara agreed. "I've been wondering how they thought he could give them money if they killed him?"

"Right," Alysha said. "It doesn't make sense, does it?"

"It seems to me that a simple shot to the head would have been enough," Valerie continued. "All the extra details struck me as overkill."

She waited a couple minutes, then said, "Do either of you have to pee as bad as I do?" The other women nodded in vehement agreement. "Let's all go together, then." They'd just about worked up the courage to leave the hogan when the sound of throbbing drums broke the silence.

The drums grew louder and they saw flickerings of light beyond the tattered door covering. Voices began a rhythmical chant. Alysha shrieked and ran to the hogan's opening, pulling back the blanket. Valerie and Barbara followed her.

The vivid scene of burning torches, warriors wearing war paint, and riders on horses brandishing weapons greeted them. With wild yips and yelps, Indian youths were rocking the Hummer side to side. Tall Skinny and Short Square sat inside wide-eyed and terror-stricken, mouths agape. Arms reached in to pull the men out. The driver stood outside the vehicle with his arms raised, looking ridiculous, wires from earbuds snaking across his face. One of the painted dancers held the man hostage with what Valerie supposed was Short Square's gun.

Alysha, her terror cast off, joined the warriors with a natural abandon; Valerie and Barbara just stood transfixed and watched while their three tough captors were stripped to their underwear and tied together, back to back, faces twisted with abject fear.

Finally the raucous war party began to wind down. The drums stopped and the chanting subsided. Valerie hadn't recognized the faces of any of the dancers under their war paint, but now with Alysha standing next to him, she realized that Tony had led this brilliantly conceived rescue.

One of the warriors called out, "Tony, the honey holes are ready."

Tall Skinny, the one with the perilously soft voice, bellowed in a panicky howl, "Honey holes? What are honey holes?"

"Simple. We bury you up to your necks in an ant hill. Then we pour honey on your head," Tony grinned.

The howls and yips and yelps began again, this time from the captives, pleading for mercy.

Equally horrified, Valerie whispered to Alysha, "Will they really do that?"

"I don't know," she whispered back. "First I've heard of it. Imagine ants crawling in your ears and eyes, and you couldn't brush them away." She shuddered again, but this time with a laugh and a comic expression.

Six Navajo men grasped the three kidnappers under the arms and started dragging them away from the fire. The three resisted with all their strength, wailing and thrashing in terror. Their bare knees scraped across the rocky, cactus-strewn ground.

That moment, a Navajo Tribal Police truck pulled in sight. The truck was followed by a van with a logo Valerie couldn't read in the dark, and a Page city police car. Bringing up the rear was Sarah's lime green Volkswagen.

The plainclothes officers they'd seen at the funeral emerged from the van, accompanied by a seriously fierce-looking dog growling and lunging on a leash. The three humiliated gangsters were handcuffed and loaded into the van, their clothes thrown in after them. An officer locked the doors leaving the dog in the front seat, fangs bared, watching every move.

Sarah parked her Volkswagen behind all the official vehicles. She and Mary jumped out and raced toward the milling crowd.

"What? How did you...?" Valerie stammered in confusion.

"We were driving up to your house and watched a guy with a gun and another one with a bat force you into that Hummer, so we called nine-one-one," Sarah said. "The city police said the Drug Enforcement Agency was in the area conducting a drug operation."

Mary picked up the story. "We said we were going to follow the Hummer and they told us to stay out of their way. We told them we'd go anyway, so in the end, they gave in and let us follow them, when they were ready to go. Waiting for hours almost drove us crazy, but here we are."

The five women hugged and laughed. "Thank you, thank you, thank you, thank you. If we'd known you were watching, we might not have felt so abandoned," Barbara said.

With a big, tension-relieving whoosh, Valerie said, "I've never been so scared in my life, and never so glad to be encircled by a war party. But dang, girls," she continued, hands on her hips. "You missed all the fun."

"I can't wait to hear all about it," Mary said. "I'm almost sorry I wasn't kidnapped. I feel like I missed all the excitement."

"Trust me, you don't want to be kidnapped for any amount of excitement," Barbara answered her.

Valerie sought out Tony and asked, "How did you manage to sneak up on them without being shot?"

Tony grinned. "Surprise attack. Two of them were asleep, and the other one was kicked back listening to music or something on his earphones. The windows were down, and the gun was on the console."

"Yeah," Another warrior joined in. "They were way too overconfident. I just sneaked up and after I got the driver in a chokehold, the war party surrounded them. They never heard a thing until it was too late."

"You guys are awesome," Alysha said, enfolding Tony in a hug. "We were so scared."

"No kidding. You wouldn't catch me inside that hogan," Tony said, with an overemphasized shiver.

The officers conferred, and the warriors laughed and jostled, letting off steam. In the confusion, Valerie pulled Sarah aside and asked in a low tone, "Which canyon did you go into to wait out the storm?"

"Navajo Canyon," Sarah replied.

"Did you and Mary have anything to do with…uh, you know…Sam's murder?"

A strange expression crossed Sarah's face. She hesitated. Then a mischievous smile lit her features. She raised her eyebrows and said, "Wouldn't you like to know?"

NANCY NIELSON REDD lives in Gilbert, Arizona with her husband, Bob. They owned and operated several successful businesses including a convenience store, a trading post, and an RV park. Her nonfiction credits include special interest articles for the Page, *Arizona Chronicle*, and other newspapers, as well as articles in Blue Mountain Shadows, an historical quarterly. In fiction, her short story "Still Life, With Snow" was included in *Map of Murder* (Red Coyote Press, 2007) and short story, "The Last Resort" in *How NOT to Survive the Holidays* (DS Publishing, 2009).

SHE'S MAKING YOU CRAZY

Margaret Morse

"DON'T answer it."

Jake charged across the motel room and lunged at the ringing phone on the night stand.

I'd been reading in bed. He'd moved so fast I'd barely reached for the receiver.

He turned his back to me and listened. "No one here by that name."

Returning to the desk, he picked up *Peak Experiences: Hiking the Sangre de Cristo Mountains.* Before the phone call, he'd been staring at it without turning the pages.

I put aside the brochure from the Santa Fe Opera. "Tell me what's wrong. Don't make me guess."

Jake closed the book. "I saw Lisa Duering today."

Seated at the desk fifteen feet away, he had his profile to me. I needed to study his face up close. He'd just told me that he'd seen a dead woman.

I got up, half sat on the desk and touched his shoulder. "Look at me."

He lifted his face. His blue eyes focused on mine. He had his brown hair pulled back in a ponytail. Wearing a T-shirt that featured a dancing moose, he appeared to be a guy all set for a fun getaway in Santa Fe.

Brushing back strands of his hair, I asked, "You mean, you saw someone who looks like Lisa?"

The corner of his mouth twitched. "I saw Lisa at the Georgia O'Keefe Museum. You were explaining to the guard why the flower paintings are obscene. Then, all at once, I saw Lisa coming out of the next gallery. I tried to follow, but a tour group blocked the hall."

"That's why you walked away. I thought I was embarrassing you with my art critique."

Whenever I heard Lisa's name my body tensed with anger. Just before she killed herself by overdosing, she'd left Jake—her therapist—the last message of her life. Sent the voicemail in the middle of the night, knowing he'd get it too late. I remembered him walking stiff-legged into the kitchen that morning, his eyes unfocused as a blind man's. *Lisa killed herself last night,* " he'd said, and thrown the cell phone on the floor. It cracked apart on the ceramic tile.

I continued, "I understand you thinking about Lisa. She only died two months ago. Her mom called last week and asked you to write something for her web memorial."

I pulled together the counseling lingo I'd learned from living with him for two years. "You're transferring your obsessive thoughts about Lisa to the real world. So when you see a woman with straight black hair and jutting eyebrows, you assume it's Lisa. That's it."

Feeling hyped up, like I do when I explain a puzzling fact to the judge, I moved away from the desk and opened the curtains. Our second floor room faced six lanes of traffic zooming up and down Cerillos Road. Across the street, a strip mall with an adobe facade housed a Circle K, the My Thai Café, and Chili Garza's Taco Shop. The view did include a sight of real New Mexico, azure sky over jagged mountains.

"There's more, Anne."

Jake stood next to me. He tapped keys on his cell phone and held it between us. A woman with a deep voice spoke, spacing the words out, "Lisa is coming for you."

"Do you recognize the voice?" I asked.

"I'm pretty sure it's Lisa's significant other, Edith. She and Lisa had couple's counseling twice."

Edith, a pale blonde with hot black eyes, had appeared at Lisa's funeral. Right after they lowered the casket, Edith marched up to Jake and yelled, *This is your fault!*" Then she bolted.

"She is the obvious suspect. How many times has she called?"

"Twice a day for the last week."

I recalled his lunge for the motel phone. He must have

dreaded checking messages. Why hadn't he confided in me? I needed to be a mind reader who knew just when to ask what was wrong. "Did you try calling the number?"

"I never get anything but voicemail."

The sun had lowered enough to shine directly in our eyes. I closed the curtains and said, "No wonder you've been jittery lately. All day, I felt like you were looking for something. Anything else you need to tell me?"

"She also showed up when we were having lunch. She was in a car, a red convertible."

Today, we'd had lunch on the patio of a terrific restaurant. They had the best chiles rellenos ever. That was when I still thought we were having a fun vacation. "Is that what made you choke on your margarita?"

"I would've chased her but when I stopped coughing, the car was gone."

"You're too close to this problem. Let me work on it."

Five times, I traced out a path between the queen-sized bed, the desk, and the one comfortable chair. I had to step over our carry-on bags, flung down when we'd arrived last night from Phoenix. Jake sat on the bed with his laptop, probably checking e-mail. Ever since Lisa's death, he'd been fanatic about checking all messages.

I sat on the bed. "Here's my take. Lisa's suicide haunts Edith and makes her crazy. Edith blames you, because she needs a focus for her anger. She broods until she snaps and starts leaving you spooky voicemails. That way, you're haunted by Lisa like she is. When we come to Santa Fe, somehow that sets Edith off, and she takes it up a notch. She hides her blonde hair with a black wig and pencils in some dark eyebrows. Transformed into Lisa, she stalks you."

He closed the laptop. "How did she know I was here in Santa Fe?"

I flipped open my phone. "I've got some ideas. I'm going to run them by Keegan."

Keegan did investigations for my law firm. I knew he wouldn't mind me calling on a Saturday. Ever since last year, when I successfully defended him on a murder charge, he's been eager to show his gratitude.

While I left a message, Jake leaned back on the propped-up pillows. Looking up at the rough textured ceiling, with its years of grime-darkened crevices, he said, "Anne, I thought I was going crazy when I saw Lisa."

"You didn't see Lisa. Your mind played tricks on you. I know I'm a lawyer, not a therapist, but I'm pretty sure you're not crazy."

Jake's index finger had been circling and swirling on the lid of his laptop. He stopped his mystery writing, reached for my hand and kissed it. "What would I do without you?"

I went into my pep talk. "We're a team. I'm on the case now. I'll help you accumulate proof of her stalking activities. If she shows up again, I'll take pictures. I'll find out who has the phone number of the anonymous caller. As soon as we have proof it's her, I'll file an Order of Protection and sue her for harassment."

"If it's Edith, she really needs help."

"She needs to stop stalking you. You did everything you could for Lisa. You can't make someone want to live."

Jake's lips twisted down. "Yeah, I did everything just fine."

He stayed on the bed and played online Scrabble with a guy from Liverpool. Going for long runs and playing online word games calmed him down. Fine with me. I didn't want him riled up. When Lisa committed suicide, he didn't stop functioning. He kept on seeing clients. The problems came out at night. He suffered from insomnia and terrible dreams when he did sleep. He got a psychiatrist friend to prescribe an anti-depressant and Valium. The nights got better. Jake said he wasn't going to take drugs forever.

I called Keegan. We decided he'd check Jake's car and office and then our condo for bugs. I had Jake give me the number of the woman who'd been calling him so Keegan could trace it. To keep busy, I did a web search on civil harassment lawsuits.

When Keegan called forty minutes later, I turned on the speakerphone and gestured for Jake to join me.

"I got some answers for you," Keegan said in his husky voice. "Found two bugs on your car."

"Where?" Jake asked.

"A GPS taped on the right rear fender and a mini voice-activated tape recorder in the glove compartment—under a pile of papers and junk."

Jake winced. "I always lock my car."

"I bet she used a Slim Jim like me. Question—if this Edith retrieved the tape from the recorder anytime this past week, would she have learned about your travel plans?"

I jerked back in my chair as the intrusion into our lives hit me. "Last Friday, on the way to dinner, I told Jake about the opera tickets and hotel reservations my friend couldn't use."

"One more thing," Keegan said. "I researched the number of Jake's anonymous caller. It belongs to someone named Edith Lisa Duering."

"How freaky is that, taking over her lover's name," I said. "And not too bright. Thanks, Keegan, you helped us out."

"Right. I'm leaving the bugs in place and setting up a surveillance camera to catch anyone messing with the car. Jake can make a police report when he returns. Sorry this ruined your weekend." He disconnected.

Jake looked like he had a bad taste in his mouth. "Last week, I called Lisa's mother when I was driving. I agreed with her about not including Edith in the memorial." He closed his eyes. "I have to make a list of all the calls I made to clients in the car."

Reaching for the pad printed with MOUNTAINAIRE INN on the top, he wrote five names, stopped, then added three more. He tapped keys on his cell phone, frowning at the screen. When he wrote down ten more names, I assumed he'd checked his phone log.

Jake tossed down the pen. Then he slammed himself inside the bathroom. The running of the shower drowned out all sound. I hated it when he went off without saying anything. I worried that the rushing water covered up something, like throwing up or crying or opening pill bottles. Over my time with him, I'd learned that therapists aren't their own best patients, just as lawyers mess up when they represent themselves.

I knew what was driving him crazy. He had a hands-free

cell phone holder, so both sides of his car conversations would've been recorded. He zealously protected his clients' confidences. Someone had stolen that from him.

I spent my life representing clients who broke the law. I fought for them. This crazy woman threatened the man I loved. I was going to take her out.

I went to my suitcase to unpack dress-up clothes for the opera. When I lifted the lid, I saw a white card with black lettering:

Enjoy the opera.

My red bra and panties lay in shreds on top of a turquoise blouse.

Hands trembling, I checked Jake's clothes. Nothing destroyed. Edith had probably bribed or tricked a maid to get into our room. I shuddered, picturing her wearing that black wig, pawing through my underwear.

Using my phone, I punched in the number of Jake's anonymous caller.

"This is Anne Rakowitz. I'm Jacob Herz's lawyer. This is to give you notice that as soon as we return to Phoenix, I'll be serving an Order of Protection on you. You'll be talking to law enforcement the next time you harass Mr. Herz."

Jake stood at the open bathroom door wearing only a towel. He had the lean firm body of a runner. "I like your non-confrontational style."

Certain Edith had to be the stalker, I told him, "Look at my suitcase. Edith's getting more hands-on."

When he reached for the card, I said, "No, don't touch it. I'm going to make a police report. It'll be part of the paper trail about the harassment."

After calling the cops, I told him, "They won't be here for a while. They don't consider it an emergency since we're not in immediate danger."

He studied the shredded lingerie. "Maybe we'll have to miss the opera."

"No way. We have a deal. You go with me to the opera tonight. Tomorrow I go hiking with you. And you might even like *Don Giovanni*. If the cop doesn't come in time, I'll leave a note on the door."

Jake rummaged in his suitcase and pulled out navy dress pants and his dancing moose T-shirt. Even though he'd showered, he just had to put his favorite back on. Brushing it off, he said, "Edith is escalating exponentially. She needs intervention."

"She needs stopping."

My phone rang. I recognized the number of the woman who'd been calling Jake.

"What do you—?"

She whispered, "You won't be going to court if you're dead," then disconnected.

AT 6:30, I told Jake, "Time to leave for the opera."

He didn't put down his laptop. "You said it didn't start until eight-thirty."

"It takes a while to drive there and park. We need time for a few drinks at the bar. It's fatal to attend the opera sober."

He hung up the moose T-shirt in the closet. After shaking out a short-sleeved dress shirt, which had been under his hiking boots, he pulled it over his head without unbuttoning it. I'd already changed into black dress pants and a silky turquoise blouse.

I checked out the window to make sure the stalker wasn't lurking outside the door. Perched just above the mountains, the sun sent out long slanting rays. The cement walkway was clear, but in the strip mall across the street, I spotted a woman with straight black hair sitting in the driver's seat of a red convertible.

"Jake, we've got a problem. Come here and see if that's her."

As we looked out, the woman raised something to her eyes, possibly binoculars. We jerked back.

"Yeah, that's her."

"You call the cops this time," I said. "You're actually the victim. I'll take a picture while you phone in case she leaves before the cops get here."

I grabbed the camera out of the suitcase and headed for the door.

Jake blocked me. "If she sees you with a camera, that might set her off."

"We can use the photo when we get back to Phoenix and go to court."

I moved left. Jake did a fast sidestep to stay in front, cupping his hands on my shoulders. "Anne." He waited until I looked at him. "You need to stay inside. This woman is very unstable. Anything, even pointing a camera at her, might make her escalate."

I tried to stare him down. He was three inches taller, so I actually had to look up into his sky blue eyes, flecked with silver. He massaged my shoulders.

"Oh, all right." I twisted away.

He pressed three buttons on his cell. "My name is Jake Herz. I'm a therapist from Phoenix, staying at the Mountainaire Inn, Room two twenty-three. I need help with an unbalanced woman who's stalking me." He listened. "Right now, she's parked across the street."

Seated on the bed, fists on my knees, I gave a start as Jake's tone sharpened.

"Look, I'm saying we're in immediate danger and you need to get some officers here right away. She just made a death threat against my girlfriend."

He kept talking, giving them background about Edith and Lisa and about my earlier phone call to the police. I stopped listening while I clenched and unclenched my fists. This woman had tried to drive Jake crazy. She'd violated my privacy. I wished I owned a gun. I wanted to go out there and get in her face, that unbalanced woman in a wig, living out her anger.

He sat next to me and covered the mouthpiece with one hand. "She says a patrol car is only a block away. They'll stop and talk to Edith or whoever it is."

"Mr. Herz?" came through the earpiece.

Jake listened and went back to the window. "Yeah, they're just pulling in. One of the officers is approaching her." He listened for a moment. "Thanks for your help. We'll wait and talk to the officers." He let out a deep breath as he pocketed the phone. "This might take care of the problem."

I picked up the camera from the bed. I needed to do something. "Or make it worse. In case she reappears in Phoenix, I'm taking a picture. She and the cops will be too busy to notice."

Stepping to the railing, I lifted the camera and froze with my finger on the shutter. The woman talking to the cop held a dark-haired wig in her hand. She had fiery copper hair. Not blonde-haired Edith.

I turned to tell Jake. The door of the room next to ours swung open so hard it banged on the inner wall. A woman hurled herself out, her blonde hair flying around her face. Knife clasped in her hand, she charged at me, baring her teeth. I threw my camera at her. She stopped to bat it aside. Her blow sent my Nikon crashing into the cinder block wall.

With a tremendous leap, Jake flew across the walkway and tackled her by the legs. She crashed sideways against the railing, the knife blade clanging on the wrought iron.

She'd landed on her butt, yet kept her death grip on the knife. She twisted out of Jake's hold and used the railing to pull herself upright. As she lurched forward, she stabbed the knife at me. I stepped back and flung out my hands. Jake lunged and clutched at her shirt, dragging her backward.

Snarling, she swiveled toward him. I grabbed hunks of coarse blonde hair in both hands. I yanked with so much force she lost her balance and fell against me. Wrenching herself away, she whirled and slashed out. I jumped back and felt the blade slice the air within inches of my breast.

Jake came at her from behind and clamped his hands on the arm that held the knife. Grunting, she kicked his legs out, knocking him down. He kept his grip on her knife hand and she fell with him. She continued struggling, the blade jerking back and forth. They rolled and Jake ended up on top.

I kicked her in the face. Her nose made a crunching sound as my foot struck. She let go of the knife, which flew out and thudded against our door. Blood spouted from her nostrils. Kneeling on her stomach, Jake held down her arms.

A cop came running down the walkway, a gun held in both hands.

I pointed at the knife. "We got it away from her."

Holstering his gun, the cop took one of her arms as Jake held the other. They managed to get her face down on the ground. Arms cuffed behind her back, she thrashed her legs and squirmed, screaming random indecipherable words.

She had her head turned, facing the door of our room. Blood pooled under her nose. I thought I recognized Edith through her contorted features. Jake was red-faced. He got up and leaned on the railing, breathing heavily. In her struggles, she inched herself closer to the knife.

The cop kneeled on her lower legs. Edith stopped thrashing. She howled in harmony with approaching sirens. The combined wailing filled my head.

With my toe, I slid the knife away from her. She screamed, "I'm going to kill you and him!"

The knife had a shiny black handle. My fingers curled as if they grasped it. My arm tensed, ready to take the blade and slash out. Leaning forward, I reached for the weapon.

"Hey," cried the cop.

"Anne," Jake warned, as he kicked the knife away and clasped his hand around my elbow.

Yanking free, I backed away as if he were attacking me. I bumped into our door and flailed my hands at him. Edith's blood splotched the front of his shirt.

In the parking lot below, another patrol car jerked to a stop. Its siren and flashing lights jolted me. I dropped my hands and leaned back on the door for support. The siren shut off as car doors slammed and footsteps pounded up the steps.

Edith's howls, reaching a crescendo with "Kill me now," changed into grunts and moans of garbled words.

The back-up cops shackled her feet.

Released from kneeling on her legs, the first cop said, "Maybe she'll calm down if you folks step into your room."

She stopped her noise the second we closed ourselves in.

I went straight for the bathroom. The adrenalin rush I'd felt outside had vanished. I shook all over and my stomach quivered. Jake filled a glass with water and handed it to me. I drank it in slow gulps, wiping off the drops that dribbled down my chin with the back of my hand. Jake took off the bloody shirt and tossed it in the trash.

"I've never kicked anybody in the face before."

Jake looked as if he couldn't see or hear me. He went to his suitcase and pulled out the dancing moose T-shirt.

I joined him and stood close. "I wanted to grab the knife and cut her. I went crazy for a minute."

Not a word from Jake. Picking me up, he sat me on the bed and wrapped us in the blue and mauve bedspread until I stopped shaking. We stayed there holding each other until the officer who'd arrived first on the scene, Sergeant Garcia, knocked on the door.

Garcia questioned us separately outside the room. He kept the interview short, letting me tell the story in my own words. He was a nice guy, didn't get impatient when my eyes kept straying to a motel maintenance man who scrubbed at Edith's blood that had begun to stain the concrete. Disinfectant filled my nostrils.

When he finished our interview, Garcia followed me into the room and gave us a stack of pamphlets about victim's rights.

I sat on the bed next to Jake. "What about the woman in the wig?"

"She was an actress hired by Edith," Garcia explained. "Claims she thought it was a practical joke. I'm not recommending that any charges be filed. That okay with you folks?"

We said "Yes" at the same time.

Jake patted me on the back. "Too bad we're missing the opera."

"It's only eight forty-five," Garcia said, "No traffic this time of night. They seat late arrivals during scene shifts. You can still get some of your money's worth."

I jumped up. "Let's go."

"You've been traumatized. You need to process what happened."

"The opera will help me with that."

After we shook hands with Garcia, I tugged Jake from the room.

In the car, he smoothed out wrinkles in the moose T-shirt caused by the seat belt. "When's the soonest Edith can get out of jail?"

"As soon as she arranges bail. If they get her to night court right away, she could be out by dawn."

Stopped at a traffic light, Jake rolled down the window. From the car next to us, a song in Spanish blared out, wailing words set to a quick beat. "You came in handy during the fight."

I pictured the night court judge issuing futile orders to Edith: *"Don't leave the state. Have no contact with the victims."*

I opened the window and felt a chill from the wind coming down the mountain.

Tomorrow, I will buy a gun.

MARGARET MORSE lives with her husband Duane and nine rescued dogs in South Phoenix. After working as an attorney for twenty-five years at the Maricopa County Public Defender's Office, she retired and began a second career as a writer. Her current project is a fantasy murder mystery. She has had two short stories published in the *Arizona Attorney* journal.

Praise For Sisters in Crime Desert Sleuths Chapter Anthologies from DS Publishing

SO WEST: SO DEADLY

† 2016 International Book Awards Finalist - Best Anthology

"The Wild (South)West has never been so much wicked fun. This exceptional collection showcases new and exciting talent, while exploring the Southwest in all of its magnificence...and malfeasance."

> ~ HILARY DAVIDSON, Award-Winning author of
> *Blood Always Tells*

"What a constellation of talent there is amongst The Desert Sleuths! There are echoes of short story greats in this anthology—Stephen King, Lee Child, Laura Lippman—but with unique shadings that come deep from Arizona's dry, hot heart. There is something for everyone in this not-to-be-missed collection."

> ~ JENNY MILCHMAN, Mary Higgins Clark Award-Winning author of *Cover of Snow* and *Ruin Falls*

SOWEST: CRIME TIME

"Suspenseful, surprising and sometimes even hilarious! This twisty and entertaining collection of revenge, retaliation, and diabolical deeds not only showcases the gorgeous and unique southwest—but also the skill and originality of these incredibly talented sisters in crime. Loved it!"

> ~ HANK PHILLIPPI RYAN, Agatha, Anthony, Macavity, Mary Higgins Clark Award-Winning author

"From the desert to the mountains, from the grungiest cabin to the swankiest mansion, from the oldest native traditions to streets in Scottsdale where the stucco isn't dry—these stories bring the southwest to exuberant life. Heart swelling hero(in)es, dastardly villains, and a glorious rabblesome chorus of authentic folks jump off the pages. What a box of delights!"

> ~ CATRIONA McPHERSON, Anthony, Agatha, Macavity, Bruce Alexander Award-Winning author

Praise For Sisters in Crime Desert Sleuths Chapter Anthologies from DS Publishing

SOWEST: DESERT JUSTICE

† *Suspense Magazine*'s Best Anthology of 2012 Finalist
† New Mexico-Arizona Book Awards Finalist –
Best Anthology 2012

"Arizonans and all who love their mountains and deserts spiced with danger are in for a treat. The Sisters in Crime Desert Sleuths have put together another anthology of stories that powerfully evoke all the beautiful (and deadly) aspects of their state: white water rivers, hidden caves, steep mountain trails, blast-furnace deserts and yes, diamondback rattlers. Visit at your own risk!"
~ MARGARET MARON, Award-Winning author of
Three-Day Town and *The Buzzard Table*

"Reading SoWest: Desert Justice is like smacking open a piñata and having 20 engaging, enticing and enthralling stories rain down in their brilliant jewel-toned wrappers for a reader to snatch up and savor.
~ JENN MCKINLAY, *New York Times* bestselling author

SOWEST, SO WILD

† *Suspense Magazine*'s Best Anthology of 2011 Finalist

"Arizona proves hot, dry, and deadly in this anthology. There's something for everyone to enjoy here, in tales of murder ranging from the humorous to the macabre."
~MEG GARDINER, Edgar Award-Winning, *New York Times* bestselling author of *The Nightmare Thief*

"An old time sheriff only had six bullets loaded into his gun to take care of the bad guys—with *SoWest So Wild*, twenty different authors take aim and each one hits the bulls-eye. You'll never look at the Wild West the same way again."
~ TONI L.P. KELNER, co-editor of the *New York Times* bestselling anthology *Death's Excellent Vacation*

www.ingramcontent.com/pod-product-compliance
Lightning Source LLC
Chambersburg PA
CBHW051458170626
46811CB00002B/538